New
TOEIC
第1次就考好
聽力

Contents 目錄

工廠 / 經營 / 人事管理
Factory Management and Personnel

生活 / 娛樂
Life and Entertainment

法律 / 理財
Law and Finance

CHAPTER 01
辦公室篇

教學重點	多益實戰
⊙辦公室重點單字	⊙Part 1 照片描述
⊙易混淆字：paper / pepper	⊙Part 2 應答問題
⊙[æ]、[ɛ]、[ʌ] 的發音	⊙Part 3 簡短對話
⊙連音技巧：字尾子音＋字首母音	⊙Part 4 獨白對話

主題字彙與發音

MP3-001

聽聽看這些單字的正確發音,並比較英美腔調的不同。

file cabinet (n.) 檔案櫃
[ˋfaɪl ˋkæbənɪt]

ceiling (n.) 天花板
[ˋsilɪŋ]

monitor (n.) 顯示器
[ˋmɑnɪtɚ]

negotiate (v.) 協商
[nɪˋgoʃɪˏet]

cubicle (n.)(辦公室)隔間
[ˋkjubɪkəl]

staff (n.) 全體職員
[stæf]

carpet (n.) 地毯
[ˋkarpɪt]

folder (n.) 資料夾
[ˋfoldɚ]

wastepaper basket (n.) 廢紙桶
[ˋwestˏpepɚ ˋbæskɪt]

cabinet (n.) 櫃子
[ˋkæbənɪt]

screen (n.) 銀幕
[skrin]

keyboard (n.) 鍵盤
[ˋkiˏbɔrd]

plants (n.) 植物
[plænts]

laptop (n.) 筆記型電腦
[ˋlæpˏtɑp]

discuss (v.) 討論
[dɪˋskʌs]

blazer (n.) 西裝外套
[ˋblezɚ]

shelf (n.) 書架
[ʃɛlf]

lighting (n.) 燈光
[ˋlaɪtɪŋ]

colleague (n.) 同事
[ˋkɑlig]

paper clip (n.) 迴紋針
[ˋpepɚ klɪp]

主題易混淆字

聽力上也常會遇到的一個問題，就是有些字的發音非常相近，
在聽的時候，如果沒有整合前後文內容，很容易就聽錯。
以下我們整理了幾組容易弄錯的單字，請聽光碟朗讀，選出句中出現的字。

字音

1. folder / holder

2. desk / deck

3. file / fire

4. lightning / lighting

5. staff / stuff

6. paper / pepper

字義

7. keyboard 鍵盤 / 電子琴

8. tape 膠帶 / 錄音帶

9. receiver 接收器 / 話筒

10. cabinet 櫃子 / 內閣

解答

1. Did you delete all the documents in the **folder**?（資料夾）
2. I like to sit on the **deck** when the weather is good.（甲板）
3. Which cabinet should I put this **file** in?（檔案）
4. Poor **lighting** is bad for your eyes.（燈光）
5. There's too much **stuff** in the office.（東西）
6. The **paper** is kept in the storage room.（紙張）
7. Who taught you how to play the **keyboard**?（電子琴）
8. If you erase the **tape**, you can use it again.（錄音帶）
9. Did you forget to hang up the **receiver**?（話筒）
10. How many members are there in the **cabinet**?（內閣）

單字聽讀力 | 聽懂 [æ]、[ɛ]、[ʌ] 的發音

MP3-003

教學說明：

主題單字中，「plants」、「shelf」，你知道如何正確發音嗎？在美語中，[æ]、[ɛ]、[ʌ] 是非常容易混淆的幾個發音。如果不知道怎麼念對，就容易聽不懂。

現在就讓我們來聽聽正確的發音，並且跟著大聲念出來吧。

[æ] cat	ban	mad	rat	fan
[ɛ] bed	pen	set	red	men
[ʌ] but	fuss	cut	run	ton

辨音測驗：

MP3-004

經過了剛才的發音練習，現在讓我們做個辨音小測驗，看看是不是聽懂更多了呢？請聽光碟播放，圈出跟題目發音相同的字。

1. 圈出有 [ɛ] 的字：
Don't let the cat sleep on the bed.

2. 圈出有 [æ] 的字：
Where did you get that hat?

3. 圈出有 [ɛ] 的字：
I need to get a hair cut.

4. 圈出有 [ʌ] 的字：
How much money do you have?

5. 圈出有 [æ] 的字：
Allan fed the dog at seven.

解答

1. Don't (let) the cat sleep on the (bed).
2. Where did you get (that)(hat)?
3. I need to (get) a (hair) cut.
4. How (much)(money) do you have?
5. (Allan) fed the dog at seven.

句子聽讀力 | 連音技巧：「字尾子音＋字首母音」

MP3-005

教學說明：

通常我們寫句子的時候，字與字之間會有分隔，但是講話的時候，卻不是如此。英文也是一樣，我們不會把每個單字一個個切開來讀，於是就會有的音黏在一起，要是說得快一點，就容易聽不懂，聽得一頭霧水了。

這就是這一課我們要學的句子**連音技巧**中的「字尾子音＋字首母音」。

聽聽看／念念看：

聽聽看下面的句子，並試著練習連音技巧。

1. What are you doing this afternoon?

2. I have a class at half past eight.

3. It isn't easy to speak in front of a crowd.

聽力小測驗：

MP3-006

聽懂了嗎？現在讓我們做個小測驗，將下列某人聽音打字輸入錯誤的句子改正一下吧。

1. They say ~~known uses~~ good news.

_____

2. ~~Wind Jew~~ get back from vacation?

_____

3. I've never ~~her July~~ before.

_____

4. We ~~stop choosing~~ the radio when we got a TV.

_____

5. The police follow ~~dim~~ to the station.

_____

解答

1. They say **no news is** good news.
2. **When'd you** get back from vacation?
3. I've never **heard you lie** before.
4. We **stopped using** the radio when we got a TV.
5. The police **followed him** to the station.

多益聽力實戰

PART 01 照片描述
PHOTOGRAPHS

請看圖片並聽光碟朗讀圖 1～4 的四段敘述，選出與圖片最相符的敘述。

1. _____

2. _____

3. _____

4. _____

PART 02 應答問題
QUESTION-RESPONSE

請聽光碟朗讀，並選出最適合的答案填在空格中。

1. _____ **2.** _____ **3.** _____ **4.** _____ **5.** _____

PART 03 CONVERSATION 簡短對話

請聽光碟朗讀從選項 A、B、C、D 中選出正確的答案。

_____ 1. Why does the woman go to see the man?
A. To give him a report that she promised him
B. To ask him to have lunch with her
C. To see if he has time to review some figures
D. To put some final touches on the report

_____ 2. When does this conversation probably take place?
A. After work
B. In the morning
C. During lunch hour
D. In the evening

_____ 3. What does the man agree to in the end?
A. To have a romantic mean with the woman
B. To review the quarterly figures after lunch
C. To pick up foreign clients at the airport
D. To go over the sales figures over lunch

PART 04 SHORT TALK 簡短獨白

請聽光碟朗讀，並根據內容回答以下題目。

_____ 1. Who is probably listening to this talk?
A. A customer
B. The speaker's manager
C. A senior employee
D. A new employee

_____ 2. What is the listener's likely job title?
A. Librarian
B. Accountant
C. IT manager
D. Office manager

_____ 3. What will the listener probably do next?
A. Make coffee
B. Go to the bathroom
C. Start working
D. Talk to Kathy

解答與解析

PART 01 照片描述 PHOTOGRAPHS

1. **C** A. There's a chair in front of the deck.
甲板前有張椅子。
B. The lights are on in the office.
辦公室燈開著。
C. There's nobody working at the desk.
沒有人在辦公桌前工作。
D. The office has good lighting.
辦公室有很好的燈光。

2. **D** A. Everyone is hard at work.
每個人都很努力工作。
B. The workers are on their lunch break.
員工正在午休。
C. The man is playing the keyboard.
這男人在彈電子琴。
D. The man is typing on his keyboard.
這男人在鍵盤上打字。

3. **C** A. The man is wearing a blazer.
男人穿著西裝外套。
B. The man is talking to his colleague.
男人正在跟他的同事講話。
C. The office is divided into cubicles.
辦公室分成許多小隔間。
D. The man is using a laptop.
男人正在使用筆記型電腦。

4. **C** A. The man is sitting at the desk.
男人坐在辦公桌前。
B. The woman is sitting on the desk.
女人坐在辦公桌上。
C. The colleagues are discussing a report.
兩個同事正在討論一份報告。
D. The couple is making plans for the weekend.
這對夫妻正在作週末的計畫。

PART 02 應答問題 QUESTION-RESPONSE

1. **B** Q: Can I borrow some paper clips?
　　　可以借我一些迴紋針嗎？
A. I think so.
　　我想是這樣的。
B. Sure, help yourself.
　　好，請自便。
C. What kind of paper do you need?
　　你要哪種紙？

2. **A** Q: Can I get a refund if I'm not satisfied?
　　　如果我不滿意的話，可以退錢嗎？
A. Yes, if you keep your receipt.
　　可以，如果你有保留收據的話。
B. Actually, I'm quite satisfied.
　　其實，我還挺滿意的。
C. Yes, I received a refund.
　　是的，我收到退款了。

3. **B** Q: Can I speak to your supervisor?
　　　我能跟你上司說話嗎？
A. Yes, you're the supervisor.
　　可以，你就是上司。
B. I'm afraid he's not in now.
　　他現在恐怕不在。
C. Sure, I can speak with him.
　　好，我能跟他講話。

4. **C** Q: Are there any discounts available?
　　　有沒有折扣呢？
A. Sorry, we're all out.
　　抱歉，我們全賣完了。
B. She's busy at the moment.
　　她現在正在忙。
C. Only if you buy in quantity.
　　除非你買到一定的數量才有。

5. **C** Q: Would you like to place an order?
　　　請問你要訂貨嗎？
A. I'm not sure where I placed it.
　　我不確定我把它放在哪裡了。
B. Yes, that's an order.
　　對，那是命令。
C. Yes, I'd like a dozen roses.
　　對，我要一打玫瑰花。

PART 03 簡短對話 CONVERSATION

M: Hey, you must be here to give me that report you promised me.
嘿，妳一定是來給我妳答應要交的報告。

W: Actually, I'm still putting some final touches on it. I was just wondering if you've got time after lunch to go over this quarter's sales figures with me.
其實，我還在做最後的修飾。不知道你午餐後有沒有空跟我一起看看這季的銷售數字？

M: Well, I guess I can squeeze it in. But we'll have to make it quick—I'm going to the airport to pick up some clients from Japan at four, and you know how they hate to wait.
這個嘛，我猜我可以挪出時間看看，但是我們得動作快點 - 我四點要去機場接些日本來的客戶，妳瞭解他們有多討厭等人的。

W: In that case, why don't we do it over lunch?
這樣的話，我們何不在午餐時討論呢？

M: It's a date!
那就說定時間了！

1. C   Q: 為什麼女人要見這個男人？
A. 交一篇她答應要交的報告
B. 邀請他跟她一起吃午餐
C. 問他有沒有時間審查一些數字
D. 在報告上做些最後的修飾

2. B   Q: 這段對話大概是何時發生的？
A. 下班後
B. 早上
C. 午餐用餐時間
D. 傍晚

3. D   Q: 男人最後答應做什麼事？
A. 跟女人去約會
B. 午餐後審視一下季報數字
C. 去機場接國外客戶
D. 午餐時看完銷售數據

PART 04 簡短獨白 SHORT TALK

Hi, I'm Steve, the assistant department manager. This is your cubicle over here. Your computer is all set up and ready to use. All you need to do is choose a password. All of the accounting software you'll need has been installed already. If you need any other software, just let someone in IT know. For office supplies, just ask the office manager and she'll bring them from the supply room for you. Kathy will come by later to explain the books to you. If you have any related questions, be sure to ask her right away, because tomorrow will be her last day. There's a lounge down the hall with coffee and snacks, and the bathrooms are across from that. Well, I guess that's it. I'll let you get busy now.

嗨，我是史提夫，副部門經理。你的隔間在這邊。你的電腦已經都設定好可以使用了，你只要設定密碼就行了。所有你會需要用到的會計軟體已經安裝好了。如果還需要其他軟體，只要告訴 IT 部門就可以了。至於辦公用品，就問總務，她會幫你把這些東西從儲藏室拿給你。凱西晚一點會過來跟你解釋帳目。如果你還有相關問題，記得馬上問她，因為明天就是她上班的最後一天。走廊那邊有個休息室，有咖啡及點心，洗手間就在那對面。嗯，我想就差不多是這樣了。現在趕緊去忙吧。

1. **D** Q: 聽到這段對話的人可能是誰？
A. 一個顧客
B. 說話者的經理
C. 一位資深員工
D. 一位新進員工

2. **B** Q: 這位聽者最可能的職稱是什麼？
A. 圖書館員
B. 會計
C. 資訊經理
D. 總務

3. **C** Q: 此聽者接下來最可能去做什麼？
A. 泡咖啡
B. 去洗手間
C. 開始工作
D. 跟凱西說話

CHAPTER 02
辦公室科技篇

教學重點

- ⊙ 辦公室科技重點單字
- ⊙ 易混淆字：stock / stack
- ⊙ [ə]、[ɪ] 的發音
- ⊙ 輕音字：冠詞、連接詞、介系詞

多益實戰

- ⊙ Part 1 照片描述
- ⊙ Part 2 應答問題
- ⊙ Part 3 簡短對話
- ⊙ Part 4 獨白對話

主題字彙與發音

MP3-011

聽聽看這些單字的正確發音，並比較英美腔調的不同。

video conference (n.) 視訊會議
[`vɪdɪˌo `kɑnfərəns]

fax (n./v.) 傳真
[fæks]

pointer (n.) 雷射筆
[`pɔɪntɚ]

stapler (n.) 釘書機
[`steplɚ]

projector (n.) 投影機
[prə`dʒɛktɚ]

communicate (v.) 溝通
[kə`munɪˌket]

intranet (n.) 內部網路
[`ɪntranɛt]

minutes (n.) 會議記錄
[`mɪnɪts]

scan (v.) 掃瞄
[skæn]

stock (n./v.) 庫存；補充
[stɑk]

capacity (n.) 容量
[kə`pæsəti]

durable (a.) 持久耐用的
[`dʊrəbəl]

process (n./v.) 步驟，程序；處理
[`prɑsɛs]

initiative (n.) 第一步
[ɪ`nɪʃətɪv]

stack (n.)（一）疊
[stæk]

attend (v.) 參加（會議）
[ə`tɛnd]

technically (adv.) 技術上的
[`tɛknɪkəlli]

slide (n.) 投影片
[slaɪd]

printer (n.) 印表機
[`prɪntɚ]

copy machine (n.) 影印機
[`kɑpi mə`ʃin]

主題易混淆字

聽力上也常會遇到的一個問題，就是有些字的發音非常相近，
在聽的時候，如果沒有整合前後文內容，很容易就聽錯。
以下我們整理了幾組容易弄錯的單字，請聽光碟朗讀，選出句中出現的字。

字音

1. stock / stack

2. Internet / intranet

3. scan / scam

4. protector / projector

5. fax / facts

6. computer / commuter

字義

7. screen 螢幕 / 隔板

8. button 按鈕 / 鈕扣

9. speaker
   演說者 / 喇叭（揚聲器）

10. capacity 容量 / 能力

解答

1. When you load the printer, make sure the **stack** of paper is straight.（疊）
2. Our company is thinking of switching **Internet** providers.（網路）
3. I'll **scan** the documents and send them to you in an e-mail.（掃瞄）
4. How many slides does the **projector** hold?（投影機）
5. Did you receive the **fax** I sent you yesterday?（傳真）
6. How many **commuters** are there at your office?（通勤者）
7. Someone from the IT department is coming to fix my **screen**.（螢幕）
8. The manual explains what each **button** is for.（按鈕）
9. Have you set up the **speakers** for the presentation yet?（喇叭）
10. How can I find out the **capacity** of the hard drive?（容量）

單字聽讀力　聽懂 [ə]、[ɪ] 的發音

MP3-013

教學說明：

主題單字中，「pointer」、「video conference」，你知道如何正確發音嗎？在美語中，[ə]、[ɪ] 是非常容易混淆的幾個發音。如果不知道怎麼念對，就容易聽不懂。

現在就讓我們來聽聽正確的發音，並且跟著大聲念出來吧。

[ə]	banana	garden	correct	support	woman
[ɪ]	cabbage	begin	music	minute	women

辨音測驗：

MP3-014

經過了剛才的發音練習，現在讓我們做個辨音小測驗，看看是不是聽懂更多了呢？請聽光碟朗讀，並將下列標示套色母音的單字按照 [ə] 和 [ɪ] 分類。

orange, carrot, support, police, talking, regret, lettuce, away, tolerate, surprise

[ə]：

[ɪ]：

解答

[ə] carrot, support, police, away tolerate, surprise

[ɪ] orange talking, regret, lettuce

句子聽讀力 | 輕音字：冠詞、連接詞、介系詞

教學說明：

一般來説，冠詞、連接詞、介系詞在句中都屬輕音，只有在特別強調，或是凸顯對比時，才會使用重音。

冠詞 a 用於子音前，an 用於母音前。要注意的是，母音字母開頭的字不一定發母音，如 u 發音為 [ju]（例如 university、useless trash）的時候，冠詞要用 a。

冠詞	重音發音	輕音發音
a	[e]	[ə]
an	[æn]	[ən]

連接詞亦只在特別強調，或是凸顯對比時，才會使用重音。

連接詞	重音發音	輕音發音
and	[ænd]	[n] 或 [ən]
but	[bʌt]	[bət]
or	[ɔr]	[ɚ] 或 [ər]

介系詞 for 後接母音時，要保留 [r] 的音，發 [fɚ]；to 後接母音時，要發 [tu]。

介系詞	重音發音	輕音發音
at	[æt]	[ət]
for	[fɔr]	[fɚ]
from	[frʌm]	[frəm]
of	[ʌv]	[əv]
to	[tu]	[tə] 或 [tʊ]

聽力小測驗：
請圈出下列套色字處需念重音的單字。

MP3-016

1. A: Would you like some coffee or orange juice?
B: Actually, I'll have coffee and orange juice.

2. A: What are your hours?
B: We're open from nine to six.

3. A: Who is this present from? Is it from you?
B: It's not from me, it's for me.

4. A: Is this the train to Berlin or from Berlin.
B: Actually, it's going to Munich.

5. A: Chicken or beef, sir?
B: I'd like chicken and beef.
A: Sorry. You can only have chicken or beef—you can't have both.

解答

1. A: Would you like some coffee or orange juice?
B: Actually, I'll have coffee (and) orange juice.
2. A: What are your hours?
B: We're open from nine to six.
3. A: Who is this present (from)? Is it from you?
B: It's not (from) me, it's (for) me.
4. A: Is this the train (to) Berlin or (from) Berlin.
B: Actually, it's going to Munich.
5. A: Chicken or beef, sir?
B: I'd like chicken (and) beef.
A: Sorry. You can only have chicken (or) beef—you can't have both.

多益聽力實戰

PART 01 PHOTOGRAPHS 照片描述

請看圖片並聽光碟朗讀圖 1～4 的四段敘述，選出與圖片最相符的敘述。

1. _____

2. _____

3. _____

4. _____

PART 02 QUESTION-RESPONSE 應答問題

請聽光碟朗讀，並選出最適合的答案填在空格中。

1. _____ **2.** _____ **3.** _____ **4.** _____ **5.** _____

PART 03 簡短對話
CONVERSATION

MP3-019

請聽光碟朗讀從選項 A、B、C、D 中選出正確的答案。

_____ 1. What is the woman's problem?
A. The printer is broken.
B. She's late to her meeting.
C. She can't make copies.
D. Her report isn't finished.

_____ 2. Why isn't the printer working?
A. It's out of paper.
B. It's out of toner.
C. There's a paper jam.
D. It's not turned on.

_____ 3. What does the man tell the woman to do?
A. Call a repairman
B. Go to the storage room
C. Fix the paper tray
D. Check the paper tray

PART 04 簡短獨白
SHORT TALK

MP3-020

請聽光碟朗讀，並根據內容回答以下題目。

_____ 1. Where would this message be heard?
A. At a bank
B. At an office
C. At home
D. At a meeting

_____ 2. What can we assume about Rachael?
A. She is Bob's friend.
B. She is Bob's client.
C. She is Bob's co-worker.
D. She is Bob's wife.

_____ 3. Which of the following wasn't turned off yesterday?
A. The air conditioner
B. The lights
C. The photocopy
D. The copy machine

PART 01 照片描述 PHOTOGRAPHS

1. **C**   A. The woman is copying a document.
那位女士正在影印一份文件。
B. The woman is inputting facts.
那位女士正在輸入資料。
C. The woman is sending a fax.
那位女士正在傳真一份文件。
D. The woman is making a phone call.
那位女士正在打一通電話。

2. **D**   A. The woman is typing on her desktop computer.
那位女士正在用桌上型電腦打字。
B. The screen gives the woman privacy while she types.
隔板讓那位女士打字時保有隱私。
C. The woman is surfing the Internet on her computer.
那位女士正在用電腦上網。
D. The woman is looking at her laptop screen and typing.
那位女士正看她的筆記型電腦螢幕打字。

3. **A**   A. The people are holding a conference call.
那些人在進行視訊會議。
B. The students are taking notes in class.
那些學生在課堂上作筆記。
C. The employees are watching TV in the lounge.
那些員工在休息室裡看電視。
D. Everybody is attending the meeting in person.
每個人都親自到場參加會議。

4. **C**   A. The people are smiling for the camera.
那些人對照相機擺出微笑。
B. The audience is enjoying the movie.
那些觀眾看電影看得很高興。
C. The people are watching a slide show.
那些人在看投影片。
D. The critics are reviewing the play.
評家們在檢討這齣戲。

PART 02 應答問題 QUESTION-RESPONSE

1. B　Q: Where can I plug in my laptop?
　　　　我可以把筆記型電腦插到什麼地方充電？
　　　A. There's a plug on the wall over there.
　　　　那邊的牆壁上有插頭。
　　　B. There's a power strip under the desk.
　　　　辦公桌下有電源延長線。
　　　C. Sure, you can plug it in anywhere.
　　　　好，你可以把它插到任何地方。

2. A　Q: Could you enter these figures into the database for me?
　　　　替我把這些數據輸入資料庫中好嗎？
　　　A. Sure. What file should I save them to?
　　　　沒問題，我應該把他們存到哪個檔案裡面？
　　　B. Yes. I'll put them in the file cabinet.
　　　　可以，我會把它們放到檔案櫃中。
　　　C. Sure. I'll calculate them for you right away.
　　　　沒問題，我馬上幫你計算。

3. C　Q: Do you commute to work every day?
　　　　你每天都通勤上班嗎？
　　　A. Yes. I work with computers every day.
　　　　對，我每天都用電腦工作。
　　　B. No. I drive to work from the suburbs.
　　　　不是。我每天都從郊區開車來。
　　　C. Yes. I take the commuter train.
　　　　對，我都搭通勤火車。

4. C　Q: Have you set up the projector yet?
　　　　你架設好投影機了嗎？
　　　A. Yes. The protector is ready to use.
　　　　對，保護器已經準備好了。
　　　B. Yes. It's in the storage room.
　　　　對，它放在儲藏室。
　　　C. Yes. It's all ready for the presentation.
　　　　對，已經為簡報準備好了。

5. A　Q: Will you hook up the speakers for me?
　　　　你能幫我接上喇叭嗎？
　　　A. Sure. Where are the jacks?
　　　　可以，喇叭孔在哪裡？
　　　B. Yeah. I'll call them right now.
　　　　好，我立刻打電話給他們。
　　　C. Yes. Where are the hooks?
　　　　好，鉤子在哪裡？

PART 03 簡短對話 CONVERSATION

W: Oh, no! The printer isn't working.
噢，糟了！印表機沒有反應。

M: Is it turned on, Sarah?
它的電源打開了嗎，莎拉？

W: That's the first thing I checked, Paul.
我第一個就是檢查這個，保羅。

M: OK, let's see. It could be a paper jam. Or it could be out of toner.
那好，我想想。卡紙有可能造成機器無法運作，也可能是碳粉用完了。

W: What if it's broken? I have a meeting in five minutes, and I need to make copies of this report!
如果是壞了怎麼辦？我五分鐘後有個會要開，必須列印這份報告。

M: Relax, the paper tray is empty—no need for a repairman. There's paper in the storage room. Hurry up or you'll be late!
別緊張，紙匣是空的，不需要找修理人員了。儲藏室裡有紙，快點，不然妳就要遲到了！

1. **C**　Q: 那個女士有什麼麻煩？
   A. 印表機壞了。
   B. 她開會遲到。
   C. 她沒辦法列印。
   D. 她的報告還沒有寫完。

2. **A**　Q: 為什麼印表機無法運作？
   A. 紙用完了。
   B. 碳粉用完了。
   C. 卡紙了。
   D. 電源沒有開。

3. **B**　Q: 那位男士叫那位女士做什麼？
   A. 打電話叫修理人員
   B. 去儲藏室
   C. 修理紙匣
   D. 檢查紙匣

PART 04 簡短獨白 SHORT TALK

Hi, Bob. This is Rachael. I guess you're not back from the bank yet. I hope you get this message before you go home. I just wanted to give you a reminder. Before you leave for the day, could you please remember to turn off the air conditioning and the lights? Oh, and also please turn off the photocopier next to the receptionist's desk too. Somebody left it on again last night. We all need to do our best to save energy around here. Thanks a lot, and I'll see you tomorrow.

嗨，鮑伯，我是瑞秋。我想你應該還沒從銀行回來，希望你回家前會聽到這段留言。我只是要提醒你，在你今天離開前，請記得要關掉冷氣和電燈好嗎？噢，還有總機座位旁的影印機也請關掉，昨晚又有人沒關。我們所有人都必須盡其所能節約能源。非常謝謝，明天見。

1. **B** Q: 這則留言會在哪裡聽到？
A. 在銀行
B. 在辦公室
C. 在家裡
D. 在會議中

2. **C** Q: 我們可以推測出瑞秋是誰？
A. 她是鮑伯的朋友。
B. 她是鮑伯的客戶。
C. 她是鮑伯的同事。
D. 她是鮑伯的太太。

3. **D** Q: 哪樣東西昨天沒關掉？
A. 冷氣
B. 電燈
C. 影印的文件
D. 影印機

CHAPTER 03
會議篇

教學重點

⊙ 會議重點單字

⊙ 易混淆字：proceed / precede

⊙ [ε]、[e]、[æ] 的發音

⊙ 子音的連音

多益實戰

⊙ Part 1 照片描述

⊙ Part 2 應答問題

⊙ Part 3 簡短對話

⊙ Part 4 獨白對話

主題字彙與發音

MP3-021

聽聽看這些單字的正確發音,並比較英美腔調的不同。

---

stage (n.) 舞台
[stedʒ]

address (v.) 致詞,發表演說
[ə`drɛs]

session (n.) 會議,集會
[`sɛʃən]

audience (n.) 聽眾,觀眾
[`ɔdiəns]

convention (n.) 大型會議
[kən`vɛnʃən]

proceed (v.) 繼續進行
[prə`sid]

handout (n.) 講義
[`hænd‚aut]

chart (n.) 圖表
[tʃart]

podium (n.) 講台
[`podiəm]

panel (n.) 專題討論小組
[`pænəl]

refreshment (n.) 茶點點心
[rɪ`frɛʃmənt]

marker (n.)
馬克筆;用作註記的物品
[`markɚ]

aisle (n.) 走道,走廊
[aɪl]

facilitate (v.) 促進
[fə`sɪlə‚tet]

diagram (n.) 曲線圖,圖表
[`daɪə‚græm]

chairman (n.) 主席
[`tʃɛrmən]

attendee (n.) 出席者,與會者
[ətɛn`di]

postpone (v.) 延遲,延期
[post`pon]

trainer (n.) 訓練者
[`trenɚ]

seminar (n.) 專題研討會
[`sɛmɪ‚nar]

主題易混淆字

聽力上也常會遇到的一個問題，就是有些字的發音非常相近，
在聽的時候，如果沒有整合前後文內容，很容易就聽錯。
以下我們整理了幾組容易弄錯的單字，請聽光碟朗讀，選出句中出現的字。

字音

1. sit / seat

2. hall / hole

3. read / lead

4. proceed / precede

5. session / section

字義

6. minutes 分鐘 / 會議記錄

7. capacity
   （最大）容量 / 能力 / 身分

8. panel 壁板 / 木板 / 專題小組

9. address 致詞 / 地址

10. chair 主席 / 椅子

解答

1. Do you mind if I **sit** here?（坐）
2. How many people can fit in the **hall**?（大廳，會堂）
3. Where did you learn how to **read**?（閱讀）
4. We decided to **proceed** with the plan.（繼續進行）
5. Do you plan on attending the afternoon **session**?（會議）
6. The meeting will only take a few **minutes**.（分鐘）
7. Are you here in a professional **capacity**?（身分）
8. A **panel** of experts will be available to answer questions.（專題小組）
9. Did you listen to the CEO's **address**?（致詞）
10. The **chair** will sit at the head of the table.（主席）

單字聽讀力 | 聽懂 [ε]、[e]、[æ] 的發音

MP3-023

教學說明：
主題單字中，「seminar」、「stage」、「panel」，你知道如何正確發音嗎？在美語中，[ε]、[e]、[æ] 是非常容易混淆的幾個發音。如果不知道怎麼念對，就容易聽不懂。
現在就讓我們來聽聽正確的發音，並且跟著大聲念出來吧。

[ε]	head	set	check	leg	test
[e]	mate	came	wait	bay	age
[æ]	ham	cash	back	sang	dance

辨音測驗：

MP3-024

經過了剛才的發音練習，現在讓我們做個辨音小測驗，看看是不是聽懂更多了呢？請聽光碟播放，圈出每題中唯一一個母音發音不同的字。

1. plane blame play plan

2. break great head weight

3. dead carry match pack

4. hair they their pair

5. blabber pepper grabber catcher

解答

1. plane blame play (plan)
2. break great (head) weight
3. (dead) carry match pack
4. hair (they) their pair
5. blabber (pepper) grabber catcher

句子聽讀力 | 子音的連音

教學說明：

當字尾是子音，而下一個字首也是子音的時後，前面字尾子音會變成悶音，以順利連接下一個字首的子音，有時候聽起來會像在講另一個字，譬如 They shot bears. 的 shot 會聽成 shop。請聽下列連音並試著跟讀：

1. a bad cold（bad 像 bag）

2. ever tried Belgian beer?（tried 像 tribe）

3. taught classes this morning（taught 像 talk）

當字尾的子音和下一個字首的子音同音時，拉長第一個字尾子音，把兩個聲音連起來，有時候聽起來會變成只有一個字，譬如把 half full 聽成 hafull，還以為是個自己不懂的單字，但其實並沒有 hafull 這個字。

聽聽看 / 念念看：

請聽下列連音並試著跟讀：

1. Want some milk?

2. class struggle

3. Can you spell "lettuce"?

聽力小測驗：

聽懂了嗎？現在讓我們做個小測驗。請聽光碟朗讀句子，圈出正確的單字。

1. lock / lot

2. play / played

3. trick / trip

4. planned / plan

5. right / ride

解答

1. The downtown area is a ⟨lot⟩ safer now.

2. We ⟨played⟩ tag at the park last Saturday.

3. Dan tried to ⟨trick⟩ Mark into giving him money.

4. I ⟨plan⟩ to go to college next year.

5. We took a ⟨right⟩ turn and crossed a bridge.

多益聽力實戰

PART 01 PHOTOGRAPHS 照片描述

🇺🇸🇬🇧 **MP3-027**

請看圖片並聽光碟朗讀圖 1 ～ 4 的四段敘述，選出與圖片最相符的敘述。

1. _____

2. _____

3. _____

4. _____

PART 02 QUESTION-RESPONSE 應答問題

🇺🇸🇬🇧 **MP3-028**

請聽光碟朗讀，並選出最適合的答案填在空格中。

1. _____ **2.** _____ **3.** _____ **4.** _____ **5.** _____

PART 03 CONVERSATION 簡短對話

請聽光碟朗讀從選項 A、B、C、D 中選出正確的答案。

____ **1.** **What are the man and woman discussing?**
   A. An award ceremony
   B. A marketing seminar
   C. A sales seminar
   D. A sports conference

____ **2.** **Why has the activity been postponed?**
   A. The room isn't ready yet.
   B. The decorations aren't ready yet.
   C. The trainer has other plans.
   D. The location has been changed.

____ **3.** **What was the problem with the original location?**
   A. It wasn't available.
   B. It wasn't big enough.
   C. It didn't have the right equipment.
   D. It wasn't decorated.

PART 04 SHORT TALK 簡短獨白

請聽光碟朗讀，並根據內容回答以下題目。

____ **1.** **Who is the audience of this speech?**
   A. History students
   B. Staff trainers
   C. New employees
   D. Convention attendees

____ **2.** **What will Ms. Rogers do?**
   A. Hand out the employee handbook
   B. Introduce the training program
   C. Meet with the trainers
   D. Answer policy questions

____ **3.** **When will the film be shown?**
   A. This afternoon
   B. This morning
   C. At lunch time
   D. Tomorrow afternoon

解答與解析

PART 01 照片描述 PHOTOGRAPHS

1. **B**   A. The people are discussing business over lunch.
人們正邊吃午餐邊討論公事。
B. Two people have their laptops open.
有兩個人的筆電是打開的。
C. All the men at the meeting are wearing ties.
所有會議中的男士都打著領帶。
D. The mood of the meeting is very serious.
會議的氣氛非常嚴肅。

2. **D**   A. The audience is enjoying the performance.
觀眾正在欣賞表演。
B. All the seats are full.
所有的座位都滿了。
C. The lights are on in the movie theater.
電影院的燈是開著的。
D. A speaker is standing at the podium.
有位演講者正站在演講台上。

3. **C**   A. The experts are discussing panels.
專家正在討論壁板。
B. The audience is enjoying the concert.
聽眾正享受這音樂會。
C. The panel is sitting in front of the audience.
專題小組坐在聽眾前面。
D. The panels are talking to the audience.
壁板正與聽眾對談。

4. **B**   A. Everyone is sitting in chairs.
每個人都坐在椅子上。
B. The chair is addressing the audience.
主席正在對聽眾演講。
C. The speaker is wearing glasses.
演講者戴眼鏡。
D. The women are listening to the speaker.
這些女士正聆聽演說者演說。

PART 02 應答問題 QUESTION-RESPONSE

1. **C** Q: Did you get a handout?
      你有拿到講義嗎？
      A. Sure, I could use a hand.
         好啊，有人幫我忙也不錯。
      B. I don't need any help.
         我不需要幫助。
      C. No, they're all out.
         沒有，全都發完了。

2. **B** Q: Is the meeting still in session?
      會議還在進行嗎？
      A. Yes, it's over.
         是的，已經結束了。
      B. It just ended.
         剛剛才結束。
      C. No, I'm not going.
         不，我不去了。

3. **A** Q: Can I speak to Mr. Carlson, please?
      可以幫我轉接卡爾森先生嗎？
      A. Sorry, he's in a meeting.
         抱歉，他在開會。
      B. When are you meeting him?
         你什麼時候與他有約？
      C. I've never met him.
         我從沒見過他。

4. **A** Q: Excuse me, I didn't catch that.
      抱歉，我沒聽清楚你剛剛說什麼。
      A. I said I support the proposal.
         我說我支持這個提議。
      B. I'll throw another one.
         我再丟一個。
      C. You can come next time.
         你可以下次再來。

5. **C** Q: Do you have the minutes from our last meeting?
      你有我們上次會議的紀錄嗎？
      A. I think it was over an hour.
         好像進行一個多小時了。
      B. I'm not sure how long it was.
         我不確定進行了多久。
      C. Yes, I have them right here.
         有，在我這邊。

PART 03 簡短對話 CONVERSATION

M: Sandy, do you know what time the sales seminar is supposed to start? I thought it was supposed to start at 1:00, but there was nobody there.

珊蒂，你知道業務研討會預計幾點開始嗎？我以為一點開始，結果沒人在那邊。

W: Oh, didn't you know? The seminar's been postponed till 2:00 because they're taking down the decorations in the auditorium left over from the award ceremony.

喔，你不知道嗎？研討會延到兩點開始，因為他們要把頒獎典禮留下的裝飾拆除。

M: But I thought the seminar was being held in the conference room in the marketing department.

但我以為研討會舉行的地點是行銷部的會議室。

W: That was the original plan, but the trainer said he needed more space.

那是原訂的計畫，但訓練師說他需要更大的空間。

1. **C** Q: 這位男人與女人在討論什麼？
A. 一個頒獎典禮
B. 一個行銷研討會
C. 一場業務研討會
D. 一個運動會議

2. **A** Q: 為什麼活動延遲了？
A. 房間還沒準備好。
B. 裝飾還沒準備好。
C. 訓練師有其他計畫。
D. 地點變更了。

3. **B** Q: 原先的地點有什麼問題？
A. 無法使用。
B. 不夠大。
C. 沒有所需的設備。
D. 沒有裝飾好。

PART 04 簡短獨白 SHORT TALK

Good morning everybody. My name is Robert Lang, and I'd like to welcome you to our new staff orientation. To start off, I'll spend about half an hour talking about the training program you'll be attending this week. After a short coffee break at 9:30, Barbara Rogers from Personnel will go over the employee handbook with you and answer any questions you may have about company policy. After a lunch break from noon to one, we'll watch a short film about the history of the company. Then, at two, we'll separate into groups by department so you can learn more about the operations of the department you'll be working in and meet your trainers.

大家早安，我是羅伯朗，我想要歡迎你們來到我們新進人員員工訓練。首先，我會花半小時左右講解你們這星期將會參加的訓練課程。九點半中場休息之後，人事部的芭芭拉羅傑斯會帶你們看一遍員工手冊，並回答各位對公司政策可能有疑問之處。中午到一點的午餐休息之後，我們將會看一段公司沿革的影片。然後，兩點時，我們會依部門分組，讓你對即將到職部門的運作有更多瞭解，並認識你們的訓練員。

1. **C** Q: 這段演說的聽眾是誰？
A. 歷史課學生
B. 員工訓練員
C. 新進員工
D. 參與會議者

2. **D** Q: 羅傑斯小姐將會做什麼？
A. 發放員工手冊
B. 介紹訓練課程
C. 和訓練員會面
D. 回答政策相關問題

3. **A** Q: 短片將在何時播放？
A. 今天下午
B. 今天早上
C. 午餐時間
D. 明天中午

CHAPTER **04**
職業烹飪篇

教學重點

- ⊙ 職業烹飪重點單字
- ⊙ 易混淆字：frame / flame
- ⊙ 子音 [s]、[z]、[ʃ]、[tʃ]、[θ]
- ⊙ 省略音節

多益實戰

- ⊙ Part 1 照片描述
- ⊙ Part 2 應答問題
- ⊙ Part 3 簡短對話
- ⊙ Part 4 獨白對話

主題字彙與發音

MP3-031

聽聽看這些單字的正確發音,並比較英美腔調的不同。

chef (n.) 主廚
[ʃɛf]

apprentice (n.) 學徒,徒弟
[ə`prɛntɪs]

grill (n.) 烤肉架
[grɪl]

profession (n.) 專業
[prə`fɛʃən]

mitt (n.) 手套
[mɪt]

culinary (a.) 烹飪的,廚房的
[`kʌlə͵nɛri]

flame (n.) 火焰
[flem]

microwave (n.) 微波爐
[`maɪkrə͵wev]

roast (n./v.) 烤肉;烤
[rost]

ingredient (n.) 原料
[ɪn`gridiənt]

boil (v.) 煮沸
[bɔɪl]

cuisine (n.) 料理,菜餚
[kwɪ`zin]

bowl (n.) 碗
[bol]

fry (v.) 炒,煎,炸
[fraɪ]

dish (n.) 菜餚;盤子
[dɪʃ]

steam (v.) 蒸
[stim]

slice (n./v.) 薄片;切片
[slaɪs]

apron (n.) 圍裙
[`eprən]

season (v.) 調味
[`sizən]

range (n.) 爐子
[rendʒ]

主題易混淆字

聽力上也常會遇到的一個問題，就是有些字的發音非常相近，
在聽的時候，如果沒有整合前後文內容，很容易就聽錯。
以下我們整理了幾組容易弄錯的單字，請聽光碟朗讀，選出句中出現的字。

字音

1. chief / chef

2. grill / girl

3. mitt / meat

4. frame / flame

5. roast / rust

6. boil / bowl

字義

7. dish 菜餚 / 盤子

8. slice 薄片 / 切

9. season 季節 / 調味 / 養鍋

10. range 範圍 / 爐灶

解答

1. The restaurant just hired a new **chef**.（主廚）
2. Is the **grill** good for cooking steaks?（烤肉架）
3. Can you recommend a good oven **mitt**?（手套）
4. The chicken should be cooked on a low **flame**.（火焰）
5. Did you remove the **roast** from the oven?（烤肉）
6. Bring the broth to a **boil** and then add the noodles.（煮沸）
7. Did you do the **dishes** last night?（碗盤）
8. The recipe calls for a **slice** of lemon.（切片）
9. Is this the right **season** for crabs?（季節；產季）
10. The **range** has four burners and an oven.（爐子）

單字聽讀力 | 聽懂子音 [s]、[z]、[ʃ]、[tʃ]、[θ]

教學說明：

主題單字中，「season」、「chef」，你知道如何正確發音嗎？[s]、[z]、[ʃ]、[tʃ]、[θ] 這幾個子音是非常容易混淆的。如果不知道怎麼念對，就容易聽不懂。

現在就讓我們來聽聽正確的發音，並且跟著大聲念出來吧。

[s]	summer	lesson	pronounce	quartz	celebrate
[z]	husband	cousin	scissors	dizzy	frozen
[ʃ]	fashion	chef	delicious	passion	cautious
[tʃ]	chocolate	future	kitchen	cello	temperature
[θ]	theater	month	thumb	everything	sixth

辨音測驗：

經過了剛才的發音練習，現在讓我們做個辨音小測驗，看看是不是聽懂更多了呢？請聽光碟朗讀圈出正確單字。

1. mouse / mouth

2. chairs / shares

3. plays / place

4. sign / shine

5. seats / sheets

6. thought / taught

7. sick / thick

解答

1. It's important to keep your (mouse) clean.

2. I didn't have any luck selling the (shares).

3. Tell me about your favorite (place).

4. Did you get him to (sign) your shoes?

5. Could you wash the (sheets) for me?

6. You should have asked him what he (taught).

7. Robert is a little (sick) in the head.

句子聽讀力 | 聽懂「省略音節」

教學說明：

雙音節以上的某些字，輕母音有時會被省略。雖然，這不是必要的，不過省略這些輕音節母音會使句子說得更自然、流暢。被省略母音經常落在 [r]、[l] 或 [n] 之前，如此會讓字聽起來少一個音節。這就是這一課我們要學的省略音節。

1. average

4. similar

2. accidentally

5. personal

3. directory

6. aspirin

有些字省略的是開頭第一個音節，甚字連書寫的時後也會被省略。

We should get there about seven thirty.（about 也可寫成 'bout）

Everyone except Daniel passed the test.（except 也可寫成 'cept）

I woke up late because my alarm didn't go off.（because 也可寫成 'cause）

聽力小測驗：

請仔細聆聽慢速單字朗讀，在第一個空格寫下你所聽到的音節數量，接著再聽單字例句，若單字音節數量不變，則在句子後面的空格寫 S (same)，數量不同則寫 D (different)。

1. __ temperature/ Did the doctor take your temperature? ____

2. __ machinery / The machinery needs to be maintained regularly. ____

3. __ cavity / The dentist said I didn't have any cavities. ____

4. __ desperate / The couple is desperate for news of their missing child. ____

5. __ traveling / My father used to be a traveling salesman. ____

解答

1. [4] temperature / Did the doctor take your **temperature**? [D]

2. [4] machinery / The **machinery** needs to be maintained regularly. [D]

3. [3] cavity / The dentist said I didn't have any **cavities**. [S]

4. [3] desperate / The couple is **desperate** for news of their missing child. [D]

5. [3] traveling / My father used to be a **traveling** salesman. [D]

多益聽力實戰

PART 01 照片描述
PHOTOGRAPHS

MP3-037

請看圖片並聽光碟朗讀圖 1 ～ 4 的四段敘述，選出與圖片最相符的敘述。

1. _____

© Evelyn Proimos / flickr.com

2. _____

© Faraways / Shutterstock.com

3. _____

4. _____

PART 02 應答問題
QUESTION-RESPONSE

MP3-038

請聽光碟朗讀，並選出最適合的答案填在空格中。

1. _____　　2. _____　　3. _____　　4. _____　　5. _____

PART 03 簡短對話
CONVERSATION

請聽光碟朗讀從選項 A、B、C、D 中選出正確的答案。

____ **1.** **What type of food is the man making?**
A. bread
B. cake
C. chicken
D. cookies

____ **2.** **How will the food be cooked?**
A. It will be grilled
B. It will be microwaved.
C. It will be fried.
D. It will be baked.

____ **3.** **When will the food finish cooking?**
A. In 15 minutes
B. In 30 minutes
C. In 35 minutes
D. In 40 minutes

PART 04 簡短獨白
SHORT TALK

請聽光碟朗讀，並根據內容回答以下題目。

____ **1.** **Where would this talk be heard?**
A. On TV
B. On the radio
C. At a cooking class
D. In a restaurant

____ **2.** **How is the onion prepared?**
A. It is chopped finely.
B. It is cut into slices.
C. It is peeled and diced.
D. It is cut in half.

____ **3.** **What happens after the spices are added?**
A. Water and olive oil are added.
B. The ingredients are boiled.
C. The ingredients are mixed in a bowl.
D. The flame is turned down.

解答與解析

PART 01 照片描述 PHOTOGRAPHS

1. **D** A. The girl is cooking a sausage.
   那位女生在烤香腸。
   B. The customer is waiting for his order.
   那位顧客在等待他的餐點。
   C. The restaurant is open for business.
   那家餐廳正開門營業中。
   D. A sausage is cooking on the grill.
   香腸在烤肉架上烤。

2. **B** A. The chef is wearing a white apron.
   那位廚師穿著白色的圍裙。
   B. The man is making a sandwich with roast meat.
   那位男人在製作夾烤肉的三明治。
   C. The cook is cleaning rust off the stove.
   那位廚師在清除爐子上的鐵鏽。
   D. The man is slicing the meat with a knife.
   那位男人在用刀子切肉。

3. **C** A. A man is cooking on the range.
   有位男人在爐子上煮菜。
   B. The waitress is bringing a customer's order.
   女服務生送上顧客的餐點。
   C. The woman is holding a tray of pastries.
   那位女人拿著一盤糕點。
   D. The woman is taking the pastries to the oven.
   那位女人把糕點拿到烤箱裡。

4. **B** A. The woman is seasoning the pot.
   那位女人在養鍋。（編註：養鍋是用油塗抹鑄鐵鍋以防生鏽）
   B. The woman is seasoning the dish.
   那位女人在為菜餚調味。
   C. The woman is cooking food in the oven.
   那位女人在烤箱裡烤食物。
   D. The woman is stirring the pot.
   那位女人在攪拌鍋子。

PART 02 應答問題 QUESTION-RESPONSE

1. **C**   Q: Do you have an electric range?
你有電子爐嗎？
A. We offer a full range of electronics.
我們提供各式各樣的電子產品。
B. I'm not sure about the temperature range.
我不太確定溫度的範圍。
C. No. Ours is gas.
沒有。我們的是瓦斯爐。

2. **B**   Q: Do I need to preheat the oven?
烤箱要預熱嗎？
A. No. It's already turned off.
不用，它已經關掉了。
B. Yes. Set it to 350.
要，設定 350 度。
C. Yes. Just turn it on and put in the roast.
要。直接啟動烤箱再把肉放進去烤就好。

3. **C**   Q: Would you like a bowl of noodles?
你要來一碗麵嗎？
A. I like them better fried.
我比較喜歡用炒的。
B. Sure. I can boil some for you.
好啊。我可以煮一些給你。
C. Yes—but just a small one.
好，但只要小碗的。

4. **A**   Q: How should I season the tuna?
這個鮪魚應該怎麼調味？
A. How about using rosemary?
用迷迭香怎麼樣？
B. Yes, Tuna is in season.
對。鮪魚現在正當令。
C. Tuna season is in the summer.
鮪魚的產季在夏天。

5. **B**   Q: Can you toss the salad for me?
你可以幫我拌這沙拉嗎？
A. Why do you want to throw it away?
你為什麼想把它丟掉？
B. Sure. Where's the dressing?
好啊。沙拉醬汁在哪裡？
C. OK. Be careful not to drop it.
好。小心別掉了。

PART 03 簡短對話 CONVERSATION

M: OK, all the prep work is done. I just have to pour the batter into the pan. It'll be ready for the oven in five minutes.

好了，所有的準備工作都完成了。我只要把麵糊倒進平底鍋裡，五分鐘後就可以進烤箱了。

W: Did you preheat the oven?

烤箱有先預熱嗎？

M: Yeah. I turned it on ten minutes ago.

有。我十分鐘前就啟動烤箱了。

W: How long will it take to cook?

大概要烤多久？

M: Half an hour. That'll give me plenty of time to make the frosting.

半個鐘頭。所以我有充份的時間可以來做糖霜。

1. **B** Q: 那位男人的在製作什麼樣的食物？
A. 麵包
B. 蛋糕
C. 雞肉
D. 餅乾

2. **D** Q: 食物會以什麼方式烹調？
A. 用燒烤的。
B. 用微波的。
C. 用煎的。
D. 用烘烤的。

3. **C** Q: 食物幾分鐘後會烹煮完成？
A. 十五分鐘後
B. 三十分鐘後
C. 三十五分鐘後
D. 四十分鐘後

PART 04 簡短獨白 SHORT TALK

For all you listeners at home, the following recipe is for a basic tomato sauce that's perfect for serving over spaghetti or other pasta. First, brown a pound of ground beef lightly in a skillet and set aside. In a large pot, combine two cans of peeled tomatoes and one can of tomato paste. Peel a large onion, slice in half, and add to the pot. Next, add a cup of water, three tablespoons of olive oil, and season with two teaspoons each of basil and oregano. Bring the ingredients to a boil, stirring frequently, until everything is thoroughly mixed. Then reduce to a low flame, add the meat and simmer for one hour. When the sauce is ready, remove the onion and serve over cooked pasta, preferably homemade.

各位在家收聽的聽眾，以下食譜製作的基本番茄醬汁非常適合淋在各式義大利麵上。首先，將一磅牛絞肉放在炒菜鍋中煎到稍微變色，放到一旁備用。在大鍋子裡，倒入兩罐去皮番茄、一罐番茄醬拌勻。將一顆大洋蔥去皮切半，再加進鍋中。接下來，加入一杯水、三湯匙的橄欖油，並用各兩茶匙的羅勒及奧勒岡香料調味。將這些食材煮到沸騰，經常攪拌，直到所有東西都完全融合，然後轉小火，把肉加進去，以小火慢慢煮一個鐘頭。等到醬汁煮好，將洋蔥撈出，再把醬淋到煮好的義大利麵上，自製麵條為佳。

1. B   Q: 這段話會在哪裡聽到？
      A. 電視上
      B. 收音機上
      C. 烹飪課中
      D. 餐廳裡

2. D   Q: 洋蔥的備料方式為何？
      A. 切碎。
      B. 切片。
      C. 去皮切丁。
      D. 切半。

3. B   Q: 加入香料後的步驟為何？
      A. 加水和橄欖油。
      B. 將食材煮滾。
      C. 將食材在碗裡混合。
      D. 轉小火。

CHAPTER 05
餐廳用餐篇

教學重點

- ⊙ 餐廳用餐重點單字
- ⊙ 易混淆字：diners / dinners
- ⊙ [ɑ]、[ɔ]、[o] 的發音
- ⊙ 連音技巧：[h] 的消音

多益實戰

- ⊙ Part 1 照片描述
- ⊙ Part 2 應答問題
- ⊙ Part 3 簡短對話
- ⊙ Part 4 獨白對話

主題字彙與發音

MP3-041

聽聽看這些單字的正確發音，並比較英美腔調的不同。

---

cup (n.) 杯子
[kʌp]

glass (n.) 玻璃杯
[glæs]

saucer (n.) 碟子
[`sɔsə]

knife (n.) 刀子
[naɪf]

chair (n.) 椅子
[tʃɛr]

spoon (n.) 湯匙
[spun]

umbrella (n.) 遮陽傘
[ʌm`brɛlə]

fork (n.) 叉子
[fɔrk]

couple (n.) 情侶
[`kʌpəl]

napkin (n.) 餐巾（紙）
[`næpkɪn]

café (n.) 咖啡廳
[kæ`fe]

tablecloth (n.) 桌巾
[`tebəl͵klɑθ]

coffee (n.) 咖啡
[`kɑfi]

plate (n.) 盤子
[plet]

outdoor (a.) 戶外的，室外的
[`aut͵dɔr]

centerpiece (n.)（餐桌中央）擺飾
[`sɛntə͵pis]

view (n.) 風景，景觀
[vju]

salt (n.) 鹽巴
[sɔlt]

chat (v.) 聊天
[tʃæt]

pepper (n.) 胡椒
[`pɛpə]

主題易混淆字

MP3-042

聽力上也常會遇到的一個問題，就是有些字的發音非常相近，
在聽的時候，如果沒有整合前後文內容，很容易就聽錯。
以下我們整理了幾組容易弄錯的單字，請聽光碟朗讀，選出句中出現的字。

字音

1. café / coffee

2. glass / grass

3. desert / dessert

4. bar / ball

5. diners / dinners

字義

6. reservations
（餐廳）訂位 / 顧慮

7. toast 敬酒 / 烤土司

8. party（一群）餐客 / 派對

9. function 功能 / 聚會

10. rare 稀有的 / 三分熟的

解答

1. We should get together for **coffee** sometime.（咖啡）
2. Excuse me—this **glass** is dirty.（杯子）
3. Be careful—the **dessert** is very hot.（甜點）
4. I went to a **bar** with several co-workers last night.（酒吧）
5. The restaurant's salads are popular with **diners**.（用餐者）
6. After reading that review, I had **reservations** about going to the restaurant.（顧慮）
7. I'd like to propose a **toast** to our host.（敬酒）
8. How many people are there in your **party**?（餐客）
9. The hotel restaurant is a good place for a **function**.（聚會）
10. The restaurant has a great selection of **rare** wines.（稀有的）

單字聽讀力 | 聽懂 [ɑ]、[ɔ]、[o] 的發音

教學說明：
主題單字中，「tablecloth」、「coffee」、「saucer」，你知道如何正確發音嗎？在美語中，[ɑ]、[ɔ]、[o] 是非常容易混淆的幾個發音。如果不知道怎麼念對，就容易聽不懂。
現在就讓我們來聽聽正確的發音，並且跟著大聲念出來吧。

[ɑ]	chocolate	copy	cotton	lottery	carpenter
[ɔ]	short	autumn	caught	laundry	quarter
[o]	show	post	coat	low	toe

辨音測驗：
經過了剛才的發音練習，現在讓我們做個辨音小測驗，看看是不是聽懂更多了呢？請聽光碟播放，圈出每題中母音發音不同的字。

1. October   sort   corner   daughter

2. waffle   want   won't   wash

3. song   gone   more   often

4. phone   form   forty   warm

5. holiday   horse   cross   coffee

解答

1. October   sort   corner   (daughter)
    [o]   [o]   [o]   [ɔ]

2. waffle   want   (won't)   wash
    [ɑ]   [ɑ]   [o]   [ɑ]

3. song   (gone)   more   often
    [ɔ]   [ɑ]   [ɔ]   [ɔ]

4. (phone)   form   forty   warm
    [o]   [ɔ]   [ɔ]   [ɔ]

5. holiday   (horse)   cross   coffee
    [ɑ]   [o]   [ɑ]   [ɑ]

句子聽讀力 | 連音技巧：[h] 的消音

教學說明：

句子中出現 h 開頭的代名詞時，[h] 的聲音會被削弱，幾乎沒有聲音。例如：

I thought he was innocent.

Did you meet her?

句子中出現 h 開頭的助動詞及 who [hu] 時，[h] 的聲音會被削弱，幾乎沒有聲音。例如：

Where have you been?

The meeting has already begun.

[h] 開頭的代名詞或助動詞，若是在句首或作為加強語氣用字時，則不會被消音。例如：

It's not mine, it's his!

Has Ken arrived yet?

聽力小測驗：

聽懂了嗎？現依照 [h] 的連音規則，圈出 [h] 需被消音的字，作答完畢請聽光碟朗讀核對答案。

1. It's his pen, not my pen.

2. The flowers have all withered.

3. Did you tell her about the meeting?

4. Who did you take to the prom?

5. The movie had already started when we got there.

解答

1. It's _his_ pen, not my pen. （[h] 加強語氣用，不消音）

2. The flowers (have) all withered. （[h] 開頭之助動詞，需消音）

3. Did you tell (her) about the meeting? （[h] 開頭之代名詞，需消音）

4. W_h_o did you take to the prom? （[h] 在句首，不消音）

5. The movie (had) already started when we got there. （[h] 開頭之助動詞，需消音）

多益聽力實戰

PART 01
PHOTOGRAPHS 照片描述

MP3-047

請看圖片並聽光碟朗讀圖 1～4 的四段敘述，選出與圖片最相符的敘述。

1. _____

2. _____

3. _____

4. _____

PART 02
QUESTION-RESPONSE 應答問題

MP3-048

請聽光碟朗讀，並選出最適合的答案填在空格中。

1. _____ **2.** _____ **3.** _____ **4.** _____ **5.** _____

PART 03 簡短對話
CONVERSATION

請聽光碟朗讀從選項 A、B、C、D 中選出正確的答案。

_____ **1.** **What will the man do next week?**
  A. Take time off from work
  B. Take some customers out to eat
  C. Visit a foreign country
  D. Go on a date with the woman

_____ **2.** **What does the woman give the man?**
  A. Her business card
  B. The client's contact information
  C. The restaurant's business card
  D. Her phone number and address

_____ **3.** **What are the man and woman discussing?**
  A. A hotel
  B. A conference
  C. A client
  D. A restaurant

PART 04 簡短獨白
SHORT TALK

請聽光碟朗讀，並根據內容回答以下題目。

_____ **1.** **Who is the speaker?**
  A. A cook
  B. A waiter
  C. A salesman
  D. A bartender

_____ **2.** **What meal is probably being served?**
  A. Breakfast
  B. Lunch
  C. Dinner
  D. Tea

_____ **3.** **What will Rick probably do next?**
  A. Take the orders of the diners he's talking to
  B. Help other diners
  C. Pour wine for the diners
  D. Cook food for the diners

解答與解析

PART 01 照片描述 PHOTOGRAPHS

1. **C** A. The restaurant hasn't opened for business yet.
餐廳還沒開始營業。
B. The restaurant has been reserved.
餐廳已被預訂。
C. Someone has made a reservation for the table.
座位已經有人預訂了。
D. Someone has reservations about the table.
有人對座位有所顧慮。

2. **D** A. The waiter is pouring wine for the people.
服務生在替這些人倒紅酒。
B. The people have drunk the whole bottle of wine.
這些人喝掉整瓶紅酒。
C. The men and women are having toast.
那個男人和女人在吃烤土司。
D. The men and women are having a toast.
那些男女正在乾杯。

3. **A** A. The businesspeople are having a meeting over coffee.
那些商務人士邊喝咖啡邊開會。
B. The man and woman are chatting at the café.
那對男女在咖啡店聊天。
C. The man and woman are on a date at a restaurant.
那對男女在一間餐廳約會。
D. The secretary is making coffee for her boss.
那個秘書在替她的上司煮咖啡。

4. **B** A. The five people are having a party.
那五個人在開派對。
B. A party of five is sitting at the table.
有那五個人坐在桌邊。
C. The family is eating at home.
那一家人在家裡吃飯。
D. The restaurant guests are eating dinner.
餐廳裡的客人正在吃晚餐。

PART 02 應答問題 QUESTION-RESPONSE

1. **B** Q: Are you open for dinner on Monday?
   你們星期一晚餐時間有營業嗎？
   A. Diners are always welcome.
   用餐者隨時都歡迎。
   B. Actually, we're closed on Monday.
   其實，我們星期一不營業。
   C. Yes, we're open for lunch on Monday.
   有，我們星期一午餐時間有營業。

2. **A** Q: Are you full yet?
   你吃飽了沒？
   A. No, let's order dessert.
   還沒，我們來點甜點吧。
   B. Yes, I feel like dessert.
   飽了，我想吃甜點。
   C. Yes, I'm still hungry.
   飽了，我還很餓。

3. **B** Q: Do you serve wine?
   你們有賣葡萄酒嗎？
   A. Yes, we have beer and whisky.
   有，我們有啤酒和威士忌。
   B. Yes, we have red and white.
   有，我們有紅酒和白酒。
   C. Sorry, I don't drink.
   抱歉，我不喝酒。

4. **C** Q: Can I have another napkin, please?
   可以再給我一條餐巾嗎？
   A. You can take a nap later.
   你待會可以小睡一下。
   B. Sorry, we don't sell napkins.
   抱歉，我們沒有賣餐巾。
   C. Sure. I'll be right back.
   沒問題，我馬上拿來。

5. **A** Q: May I take your order?
   可以點餐了嗎？
   A. Sorry, we're not ready yet.
   抱歉，我們還沒選好。
   B. We didn't order this.
   我們沒有點這個。
   C. No, we're not finished yet.
   不，我們還沒用完餐。

PART 03 簡短對話 CONVERSATION

M: Have you been to that new restaurant in the hotel down the street?
你有去過街上那家飯店裡新開的餐廳嗎?

W: You mean the Japanese place? I think it's called Yoshi's. I had lunch there yesterday. It's pretty classy. The food is tasty and the service is excellent.
你是說那家日本料理嗎?那家店好像叫 Yoshi's。我昨天去那裡吃過午餐,滿高檔的。食物很好吃,服務也非常好。

M: That's what I wanted to hear. Some foreign clients are visiting next week, and I'd like to take them to a nice restaurant. Is it expensive?
那正是我想聽到的。下星期有幾個外國客戶來訪,我想帶他們去間好餐廳,那邊消費昂貴嗎?

W: The prices are actually pretty reasonable. I took one of their business cards. Here, you can have it. It has their phone number and address.
其實價錢還滿合理的。我有拿了張他們的名片。來,你拿去吧,上面有他們的電話和地址。

1. **B**   Q: 男士下星期將要做什麼?
   A. 休假
   B. 帶客戶外出用餐
   C. 出國
   D. 與女士去約會

2. **C**   Q: 女士給了男士什麼?
   A. 她的名片
   B. 客戶的連絡資料
   C. 餐廳的名片
   D. 她的電話和地址

3. **D**   Q: 男士與女士在討論的是?
   A. 一間飯店
   B. 一場大型研討會
   C. 一位客戶
   D. 一間餐廳

PART 04 簡短獨白 SHORT TALK

Hi. My name is Rick, and I'll be taking care of you this afternoon. First, let me tell you about today's specials. Our meat specials include roast lamb with mint sauce and steak with mushrooms and onions. If you're in the mood for seafood, we have baked salmon and spaghetti with clam sauce. We also have a goat cheese pizza with fresh garden vegetables, which is a favorite with our diners. All of our entrées come with soup and salad, and there's a wine list on the table if you'd like wine with your meal. Take your time looking at the menu, and just call me over when you're ready to order.

嗨，我叫瑞克，今天下午由我為你們服務。首先，讓我告訴你們今天的特餐。我們肉類特餐包括烤羊肉佐薄荷醬汁以及牛排搭配蘑菇洋蔥。如果你們想吃海鮮的話，我們有烤鮭魚與義大利麵配蛤蜊醬汁。我們也有羊奶起士比薩搭配新鮮蔬菜，這是我們最受歡迎的晚餐。我們所有的主菜都有附湯及沙拉，那邊桌上還有葡萄酒單，如果你的餐點想要搭配葡萄酒的話。慢慢看菜單，等你們準備好要點餐再叫我。

1. B　Q: 說話者是誰？
　　　A. 廚師
　　　B. 服務生
　　　C. 業務員
　　　D. 酒保

2. B　Q: 最可能提供的是哪一餐？
　　　A. 早餐
　　　B. 午餐
　　　C. 晚餐
　　　D. 下午茶

3. B　Q: 瑞克等下最可能做什麼？
　　　A. 為他所說話的用餐者點餐
　　　B. 協助其他用餐者
　　　C. 為點餐者倒酒
　　　D. 為用餐者烹煮食物

CHAPTER 06
商店篇

教學重點

⊙ 商店重點單字
⊙ 易混淆字：escalator / elevator
⊙ [a]、[ʌ]、[ɜ] 的發音
⊙ 子音的連音

多益實戰

⊙ Part 1 照片描述
⊙ Part 2 應答問題
⊙ Part 3 簡短對話
⊙ Part 4 獨白對話

主題字彙與發音

MP3-051

聽聽看這些單字的正確發音，並比較英美腔調的不同。

---

department store (n.) 百貨公司
[dɪ`pɑrtmənt stor]

receipt (n.) 發票，收據
[rɪ`sit]

grocery store (n.) 超市
[`grosəri stor]

section (n.) 區域
[`sɛkʃən]

supermarket (n.) 大超市
[`supɚˌmɑrkɪt]

crowded (a.) 擁擠的
[`kraʊdɪd]

shopping mall (n.) 購物中心
[`ʃɑpɪŋ mɔl]

empty (a.) 空的
[`ɛmpti]

cashier (n.) 收銀員
[kæ`ʃɪr]

entrance (n.) 入口
[`ɛntrəns]

cash register (n.) 收銀機
[kæʃ `rɛdʒɪstɚ]

exit (n.) 出口
[`ɛksɪt]

checkout lane (n.) 結帳走道
[tʃɛkaʊt len]

credit card (n.) 信用卡
[krɛdɪt kɑrd]

discount (n./v.) 折扣
[`dɪskaʊnt]

purchase (v./n.) 購買；購買的物品
[`pɝtʃəs]

shopping cart (n.) 購物推車
[ʃɑpɪŋ kɑrt]

storage (n.) 儲藏室
[`stɔrɪdʒ]

price tag (n.) 價格標籤
[praɪs tæg]

warehouse (n.) 倉庫
[`wɛrˌhaʊs]

主題易混淆字

MP3-052

聽力上也常會遇到的一個問題，就是有些字的發音非常相近，
在聽的時候，如果沒有整合前後文內容，很容易就聽錯。
以下我們整理了幾組容易弄錯的單字，請聽光碟朗讀，選出句中出現的字。

字音

1. escalator / elevator

2. prices / prizes

3. color / collar

4. browse / blouse

5. bag / back

字義

6. close 近的 / 打烊

7. exchange 兌換外幣 / 換貨

8. scale 磅秤 / 規模 / 刻度

9. produce 生產 / 蔬果

10. register 收銀機 / 註冊 / 登記（簿）

解答

1. We took the **elevator** to the second floor.（電梯）
2. There were excellent **prizes** at the store opening.（獎品）
3. I don't like the **color** of this shirt.（顏色）
4. Linda likes to **browse** in the ladies department.（閒逛）
5. The milk is in the **back**.（後面）
6. Do you know if the shop is **closed**?（打烊）
7. What is your store's **exchange** policy?（換貨）
8. The **scale** at the checkout counter is very accurate.（磅秤）
9. Can you tell me where the **produce** section is?（蔬果）
10. I think I left my purse at the **register**.（收銀機）

單字聽讀力 | 聽懂 [ɑ]、[ʌ]、[ɝ] 的發音

教學說明：
主題單字中，「shopping」、「purchase」，你知道如何正確發音嗎？在美語中，[ɑ]、[ʌ]、[ɝ] 是非常容易混淆的幾個發音。如果不知道怎麼念對，就容易聽不懂。
現在就讓我們來聽聽正確的發音，並且跟著大聲念出來吧。

[ɑ]	cop	shot	March	cart	odder
[ʌ]	cup	shut	much	cut	utter
[ɝ]	curb	shirt	merge	curt	further

辨音測驗：
經過了剛才的發音練習，現在讓我們做個辨音小測驗，看看是不是聽懂更多了呢？請聽光碟朗讀並選出正確的單字。

1. park / perk

2. burrow / borrow

3. stern / stun

4. puppy / poppy

5. clock / cluck

解 答

1. park

2. burrow

3. stun

4. poppy

5. cluck

句子聽讀力 | 子音的連音

MP3-055

教學說明：
英文句子中，一個母音結尾單字的下個字剛好是母音開頭，我們會在兩個字中間輕輕加上 [w] 或 [j] 幫助連音，讓句子聽起來比較流暢。若字尾母音是類似 [u] 或 [o] 的發音，用 [w] 來連音，若字尾母音為類似 [ɪ]、[aɪ] 或 [e] 的發音，則用 [j] 來連音。

聽聽看／念念看：
聽光碟朗讀，比較下列句子。

1. Who is it?

   Who ᵂis it?

2. It's quarter to eight.

   It's quarter to ᵂeight.

3. What day is it?

   What day ʲis it?

聽力小測驗：
請把需要用 [w] 或 [j] 連音的地方標示出來，作答完畢後聽光碟朗讀並核對答案。

MP3-056

1. Is this blue or grey?

2. Do you want coffee or tea?

3. See you in the evening.

4. I grew up here in Taipei.

5. He asked me a weird question.

解答

1. Is this bl**ue** ᵂor grey?

2. Do you want coff**ee** ʲor tea?

3. See yo**u** ᵂin the ʲevening.

4. I gr**ew** ᵂup here in Taipei.

5. He ʲasked me ʲa weird question.

多益聽力實戰

PART 01 照片描述
PHOTOGRAPHS

MP3-057

請看圖片並聽光碟朗讀圖 1 ～ 4 的四段敘述，選出與圖片最相符的敘述。

1. _____

2. _____

3. _____

4. _____

PART 02 應答問題
QUESTION-RESPONSE

MP3-058

請聽光碟朗讀，並選出最適合的答案填在空格中。

1. _____ **2.** _____ **3.** _____ **4.** _____ **5.** _____

請聽光碟朗讀從選項 A、B、C、D 中選出正確的答案。

____ **1.** **Where does the conversation probably take place?**
A. At a movie theater
B. At a subway station
C. At a store
D. At a parking lot

____ **2.** **Who is the woman?**
A. She is a customer.
B. She is a bookkeeper.
C. She is a cashier.
D. She is a bank clerk.

____ **3.** **How does the man pay for his purchase?**
A. With cash
B. With a credit card
C. With a check
D. With a discount card

請聽光碟朗讀，並根據內容回答以下題目。

____ **1.** **What does the store sell?**
A. Home appliances
B. Discount appliances
C. Office appliances
D. Used appliances

____ **2.** **When is the store usually closed?**
A. In the evenings
B. On Fridays and Saturdays
C. On holidays
D. On Mondays

____ **3.** **Which of the following is NOT on sale this week?**
A. Copiers
B. Printers
C. Fax machines
D. Computers

解答與解析

PART 01 照片描述 PHOTOGRAPHS

1. **D** A. The shoppers are loading their cart.
購物者正在把商品放上購物車。
B. There is a forklift on the island.
島上有一輛堆高機。
C. The man is giving directions to the checkout counter.
這位男士正在告訴人怎麼到結帳櫃臺。
D. The men are working in the warehouse.
這些男士正在倉庫裡工作。

2. **B** A. The cashier is adding up the man's items.
收銀員正在加總計算這位男士所買的物品。
B. The women are in line at the checkout.
幾位女士正在結帳處排隊。
C. The hardware store is very busy.
這間五金行很忙碌。
D. The shoppers are ordering groceries online.
購物者正在網路上訂購食物日用品。

3. **C** A. The couple is talking about vegetables.
這對夫妻正在談論蔬菜。
B. The farmer produces vegetables.
這個農夫生產蔬菜。
C. The shopper is in the produce section.
這個購物者正在生鮮區。
D. The man is going to buy the pepper.
這名男子正要買甜椒。

4. **B** A. There are many people on the elevators.
電梯上有很多人。
B. People are going up and down the escalators.
人們在手扶梯上上下下。
C. The shoppers are taking the stairs.
購物者在爬樓梯。
D. The passengers are going to their boarding gate.
乘客正前往登機處。

PART 02 應答問題 QUESTION-RESPONSE

1. `C` Q: Do you have this in a medium?
   這款有中號嗎？
   A. Yes, it's a medium.
   沒錯，這是中號。
   B. It only comes in medium.
   這款只有出中號。
   C. I'm afraid we're out of stock.
   恐怕已經沒貨了。

2. `B` Q: Do you have a dressing room?
   你們有試衣間嗎？
   A. The dresses are in that room.
   洋裝都在那一間。
   B. Yes, right this way.
   有的，請往這邊走。
   C. No, we don't sell dressing.
   沒有，我們沒有賣沙拉醬。

3. `B` Q: What's your return policy?
   你們對退換貨有什麼規定？
   A. It's a policy for the return of various products.
   這是一個與退換多種貨品相關的規定。
   B. Products can be returned within seven days for a refund.
   貨品可於七日內退還退費。
   C. Yes, you're welcome to return any time you like.
   是的，歡迎您隨時再來。

4. `C` Q: Can I use this coupon?
   我能使用這張折價券嗎？
   A. I don't know. Can you?
   我不知道耶。你可以嗎？
   B. I wouldn't recommend it.
   我不建議你這麼做。
   C. Sorry, it's expired.
   抱歉，這已經超過期限囉。

5. `A` Q: Can I exchange this for another item?
   我可以拿這個換另一個嗎？
   A. Sure, as long as you haven't used it.
   可以，只要沒有使用過。
   B. Yes, this is a good trade.
   對，換得很好。
   C. Only cash and credit cards are accepted.
   只接受現金和信用卡。

PART 03 簡短對話 CONVERSATION

W: All right. That'll be $78.93, sir. Do you have a discount card?

好，總共是七十八點九三元，先生。你有折價卡嗎？

M: Oh no, I don't have it with me. Let me give you my phone number—it's 523-8243.

糟糕，我沒帶。我給你我的電話－五二三八二四三。

W: OK. Let's see. Your new total is $77.36. Will that be cash or credit?

好，我看看。那你新的總額是七十七點三六元。你要用現金還是信用卡付款？

M: MasterCard.

萬事達卡。

W: OK. Paper or plastic?

好的，那要紙袋裝還是塑膠袋裝？

M: Paper, please.

請用紙袋。

1. C   Q: 這段對話可能發生在哪裡？
      A. 電影院
      B. 地鐵站
      C. 商店裡
      D. 停車場

2. C   Q: 這位女士是誰？
      A. 她是顧客。
      B. 她是記帳員。
      C. 她是收銀員。
      D. 她是銀行行員。

3. B   Q: 這位男子怎麼支付這筆購物款項？
      A. 用現金
      B. 用信用卡
      C. 用支票
      D. 用折價卡

PART 04 簡短獨白 SHORT TALK

Welcome to Homer's Appliances. This week only, we're offering discounts on selected items, including fax machines, copiers, printing paper and laptops. You're sure to appreciate our wide selection of equipment and supplies for your business needs. Our regular hours are Tuesday through Sunday from 10 a.m. to 10 p.m., but we'll be closed this Friday and Saturday for the national holiday. It is now 9:45 p.m., so please take your purchases to the checkout counter at the front of the store. Thank you for shopping at Homer's Appliances. We wish you a pleasant evening and hope to see you again soon.

歡迎光臨荷馬辦公用品店。只在這個星期，我們提供精選商品折扣活動，包括傳真機、影印機、列印紙，以及筆記型電腦。您一定會滿意我們為貴公司需求所準備多樣化的設備及用品。我們正常的營業時間為星期二至星期日上午十點至晚上十點，但這個星期五、六適逢國定假日休館。現在時間晚上九點四十五分，請將您所採購的物品帶至本店前方的結帳櫃臺。感謝您惠顧荷馬辦公用品店。祝您有個愉快的夜晚，希望很快您就能再度光臨。

1. **C**   Q: 這間店賣什麼東西？
   A. 家用品
   B. 折扣品
   C. 辦公室用品
   D. 二手用品

2. **D**   Q: 這間店一般會在什麼時候休館？
   A. 夜間
   B. 星期五及星期六
   C. 假日
   D. 星期一

3. **B**   Q: 以下何者這個星期沒有特價？
   A. 影印機
   B. 印表機
   C. 傳真機
   D. 電腦

CHAPTER **07**
展覽場篇

教學重點

⊙ 展覽場重點單字
⊙ 易混淆字：collection / correction
⊙ [u]、[ʊ] 的發音
⊙ [d] 的消音

多益實戰

⊙ Part 1 照片描述
⊙ Part 2 應答問題
⊙ Part 3 簡短對話
⊙ Part 4 獨白對話

主題字彙與發音

聽聽看這些單字的正確發音，並比較英美腔調的不同。

painting (n.) 繪畫
[`pentɪŋ]

booth (n.) 臨時攤位，座位
[buθ]

bench (n.) 長椅
[bɛntʃ]

carpet (n.) 地毯
[`karpɪt]

guide (n.) 導覽人員
[gaɪd]

salesperson (n.) 銷售員
[`selz͵pɝsən]

frame (n.) 畫框
[frem]

product (n.) 產品
[`pradʌkt]

skylight (n.) 天窗
[`skaɪ͵laɪt]

sign (n.) 告示，標示
[saɪn]

tour (n.) 導覽，遊覽
[tʊr]

display (v./n.) 展示，展覽品
[dɪ`sple]

arch (n.) 拱門
[artʃ]

customer (n.) 顧客
[`kʌstəmɚ]

explain (v.) 解說
[ɪks`plen]

logo (n.) 商標
[`logo]

gallery (n.) 畫廊，藝廊
[`gæləri]

case (n.) 櫃子
[kes]

exhibit (n.) 展覽
[ɪg`zɪbɪt]

collection (n.) 收藏（品）
[kə`lɛkʃən]

主題易混淆字

MP3-062

聽力上也常會遇到的一個問題，就是有些字的發音非常相近，
在聽的時候，如果沒有整合前後文內容，很容易就聽錯。
以下我們整理了幾組容易弄錯的單字，請聽光碟朗讀，選出句中出現的字。

字音

1. tool / tour

2. booth / both

3. collection / correction

4. bland / brand

5. view / few

字義

6. admission 入場費 / 入場許可

7. case 櫃子 / 箱子 / 案子

8. program 節目（單）/ 方案 / 課程

9. gallery 畫廊 / 頂層樓座

10. production 生產 / 產量 / （戲劇）演出

解答

1. Which **tour** would you recommend?（旅行團）
2. If they're cheap enough, why not rent **both**?（兩者皆要）
3. Have you seen this **collection** yet?（收藏品）
4. I don't like this **brand** of coffee.（品牌）
5. How many paintings are there to **view**?（觀賞）
6. Please note that **admission** is limited to those at least 18 years of age.（許可）
7. All the items in this **case** are on sale.（櫃子）
8. Copies of the **program** are available in the theater lobby.（節目單）
9. We couldn't see very well from the **gallery** seats.（頂層樓座）
10. When does the new **production** open?（演出）

單字聽讀力 │ 聽懂 [u]、[ʊ] 的發音

教學說明：

主題單字中，「booth」、「tour」，你知道如何正確發音嗎？在美語中，[u]、[ʊ] 是非常容易混淆的發音。如果不知道怎麼念對，就容易聽不懂。現在就讓我們來聽聽正確的發音，並且跟著大聲念出來吧。

| [u] | too | group | fruit | shoes | blue |
| [ʊ] | took | good | full | should | book |

辨音測驗：

經過了剛才的發音練習，現在讓我們做個辨音小測驗，看看是不是聽懂更多了呢？請聽光碟朗讀並選出正確的單字。

1. fool / full

2. pull / pool

3. look / Luke

4. suit / soot

5. cookie / kooky

解 答

1. full
2. pool
3. look
4. suit
5. kooky

句子聽讀力 | [d] 的消音

MP3-065

教學說明：

英文句子中，當字尾是 [d] 的字，緊接下一個為一子音開頭的單字時，[d]
會被消音，以增加說話時的流暢度。例如：

1. An old <u>c</u>ar.
  ×

2. She seemed <u>n</u>ice.
       ×

3. It moved <u>t</u>oward us.
       ×

但在 [h]、[l]、[w]、[r]、[s] 前的字尾是 [d]，則 [d] 不被消音。例如：

1. I have a bad <u>h</u>eadache.

2. Do you mind <u>w</u>alking?

3. Have you had <u>l</u>unch?

字尾是 [d] 的下一個字開頭為 [j]，兩音則合併，唸 [dʒ]。例如：

1. Had <u>y</u>ou two met before?
     [dʒ]

2. I'll lend <u>y</u>ou my notes.
       [dʒ]

3. Did <u>y</u>ou make this mess?
     [dʒ]

聽力小測驗：

MP3-066

請依照連音、消音規則，判別套色字母 [d] 的發音應為 A（[d] 無
變化）、B（[d] 被消音）或 C（[d] + [j] = [dʒ]）。作答完畢可
聽光碟核對答案。

1. We camped there before. _____

2. They seemed happy. _____

3. I've had it with you. _____

4. Would you like a Coke? _____

5. These are good strawberries. _____

6. Has he paid you yet? _____

7. I had a bad week. _____

8. She looked beautiful in the dress. _____

解答

1. B	2. A	3. A	4. C
5. A	6. C	7. A	8. B

多益聽力實戰

PART 01 照片描述
PHOTOGRAPHS

請看圖片並聽光碟朗讀圖 1～4 的四段敘述，選出與圖片最相符的敘述。

1. _____

2. _____

3. _____

4. _____

PART 02 應答問題
QUESTION-RESPONSE

請聽光碟朗讀，並選出最適合的答案填在空格中。

1. _____ **2.** _____ **3.** _____ **4.** _____ **5.** _____

PART 03 簡短對話
CONVERSATION

MP3-069

請聽光碟朗讀從選項 A、B、C、D 中選出正確的答案。

_____ **1.** What can be seen in the main gallery?
   A. Photographs
   B. Impressionist paintings
   C. Modern sculptures
   D. Pop art

_____ **2.** When will the spring lecture series begin?
   A. This month
   B. Next spring
   C. The following month
   D. The first of this month

_____ **3.** How can the man find out about the lecture series schedule?
   A. By speaking with an operator
   B. By visiting the Museum website
   C. By pressing one
   D. By pressing two

PART 04 簡短獨白
SHORT TALK

MP3-070

請聽光碟朗讀，並根據內容回答以下題目。

_____ **1.** How can you buy seats to the play?
   A. By calling 986-5657
   B. By visiting the website
   C. By sending an e-mail
   D. By visiting the box office

_____ **2.** When can a performance of _Death of a Salesman_ be seen?
   A. On Thursday evening
   B. On Sunday morning
   C. On Friday afternoon
   D. On Saturday afternoon

_____ **3.** Were can you read reviews of the play?
   A. On a website
   B. In a newspaper
   C. At the box office
   D. In a magazine

PART 01 照片描述 PHOTOGRAPHS

1. **D**   A. There are many people at the auction.
　　　拍賣會上有許多人。
   B. The paintings are nailed to the wall.
　　　畫都被釘在牆上。
   C. The class is on a field trip.
　　　這個班級在校外教學。
   D. The gallery is full of paintings.
　　　這個畫廊裡滿是畫作。

2. **B**   A. The man is serving customers.
　　　這位男士正在服務顧客。
   B. There is a man in front of the booth.
　　　攤位前有位男士。
   C. The women are paying their restaurant bill.
　　　女士們正在付吃飯的帳單。
   D. The door to the booth is open.
　　　攤位的門是打開的。

3. **C**   A. The class is visiting a historic castle.
　　　這個班級在參觀一個歷史悠久的城堡。
   B. The couple is at the museum with their children.
　　　這對夫妻與他們的孩子在博物館。
   C. The children are on a guided tour.
　　　這些孩子正在參與導覽。
   D. All the children are looking at the tool.
　　　所有的孩子都在看這個工具。

4. **B**   A. Both sides of the street are lined with shops.
　　　街道兩邊都佈滿了商店。
   B. The trade show hall is lined with booths.
　　　這個商展大廳排滿了參展攤位。
   C. The passengers are waiting for their flights.
　　　乘客正在等班機。
   D. The department store is having a big sale.
　　　百貨公司在大拍賣。

PART 02 應答問題 QUESTION-RESPONSE

1. **B**   Q: Are there guided tours available?
　　　有導覽嗎？
　　A. I'd rather see the exhibit on my own.
　　　我寧可自己參觀展覽。
　　B. Yes, you can sign up over there.
　　　有的，你可以在那邊登記參加。
　　C. Our guides are all qualified.
　　　我們所有導遊都是合格的。

2. **B**   Q: Can I have your business card?
　　　我可以跟你拿一張名片嗎？
　　A. Yes, I have a business card.
　　　是的，我有一張名片。
　　B. Sure, here you go.
　　　沒問題，拿去。
　　C. Yes, I'm in the card business.
　　　是的，我在卡片製造業工作。

3. **A**   Q: Can I pay for my ticket by credit card?
　　　可以用信用卡付款買票嗎？
　　A. Yes, we accept all major cards.
　　　可以，我們接受所有大廠牌的信用卡。
　　B. I'm sorry—we don't offer credit.
　　　對不起，我們不讓人賒帳。
　　C. Your credit card has been denied.
　　　你的信用卡被拒絕交易。

4. **C**   Q: How long will this exhibit be showing?
　　　這展覽的展期有多長？
　　A. Yes, it will.
　　　是的，它會展出。
　　B. Which one would you like to see?
　　　你想要看哪個展覽？
　　C. Until the end of next month.
　　　一直到下個月底。

5. **C**   Q: What are your hours?
　　　你們的營業時間是？
　　A. Sorry, I don't have any free time today.
　　　對不起，我今天沒有空。
　　B. Eight hours.
　　　八小時。
　　C. Tuesday through Sunday, eleven a.m. to five p.m.
　　　星期二到星期天，早上十一點到下午五點。

PART 03 簡短對話 CONVERSATION

W: Smith Museum of Art. How may I help you?
　史密斯美術館。有什麼能替你服務的嗎？

M: Hi. I was wondering about your current exhibits.
　嗨。我想了解你們目前的展覽。

W: We have a collection of French Impressionist paintings on view this month in our main gallery. Also on view is an exhibit of photographs by young American artists.
　我們這個月在主館有法國印象派繪畫收藏展出。另外正在進行的是美國年輕藝術家的攝影展。

M: That sounds interesting. Are there any activities this month?
　這聽起來很有趣。這個月有什麼活動嗎？

W: Well, our spring lecture series starts on the first of next month. This year there'll be lectures on pop art, modern sculpture and Russian Futurism. We also have art workshops for adults and children. For the lecture series schedule you can press one, and for information on the art workshops you can press two.
　嗯，下個月一號開始有春季的系列演講。今年會有普普藝術、現代雕塑及俄國未來派的演講。我們也有成人和兒童的藝術工作坊。如果要查詢這些演講的時間，可以按一，若要查詢藝術工作坊的資訊，可以按二。

1. **B**　　Q: 主館可以看到什麼？
　　　　　A. 照片
　　　　　B. 印象派繪畫
　　　　　C. 現代雕塑
　　　　　D. 普普藝術

2. **C**　　Q: 春季系列演講何時開始？
　　　　　A. 這個月
　　　　　B. 明年春季
　　　　　C. 下個月
　　　　　D. 這個月一號

3. **C**　　Q: 這個男人如何查到系列演講的時間表？
　　　　　A. 與接線生對話
　　　　　B. 造訪美術館網站
　　　　　C. 按下一
　　　　　D. 按下二

PART 04 簡短獨白 SHORT TALK

The Modern Theater Troupe's production of Arthur Miller's award-winning play, *Death of a Salesman*, is now in its fourth week, and is playing to packed houses. The director has been praised by critics for his innovative approach to this classic drama. The production will run until April 29, so be sure not to miss it. Performances begin at seven thirty p.m. Friday through Sunday and one thirty p.m. on Saturday and Sunday. For prices and other information, please call 986-5657. You can order tickets by e-mail at boxoffice@moderntheater.com. To read reviews, visit our website at moderntheater.com. Tickets are sure to sell out fast, so make sure you act today.

現代戲劇團的演出，亞瑟米勒得獎鉅作《推銷員之死》，現已上演第四週，且場場滿座。劇評家們對導演以創新方式處理這齣經典戲劇讚譽有嘉。這部戲將持續上演至四月二十九日，千萬別錯過此戲。開演時間為星期五到星期日的晚上七點半，以及星期六、星期日下午一點半。詢問票價及其他訊息，請撥 986-5657。您可寄電子郵件至 boxoffice@moderntheater.com 訂票。欲閱讀劇評請到我們的網站 moderntheater.com。戲票必將快速售罄，請於今日馬上行動！

1. **C** Q: 你可如何購買看戲座位？
   A. 去電 986-5657
   B. 造訪網站
   C. 寄送電子郵件
   D. 到售票口

2. **D** Q: 下列哪個時間可以看到《推銷員之死》？
   A. 星期四晚上
   B. 星期天早上
   C. 星期五下午
   D. 星期六下午

3. **A** Q: 你可在哪看到劇評？
   A. 在網站上
   B. 在報紙上
   C. 在售票口
   D. 在雜誌上

教學重點

⊙ 國際旅遊重點單字
⊙ 易混淆字：phrases / phases
⊙ [m]、[n] 的發音
⊙ 音節介紹：減少音節

多益實戰

⊙ Part 1 照片描述
⊙ Part 2 應答問題
⊙ Part 3 簡短對話
⊙ Part 4 獨白對話

主題字彙與發音

聽聽看這些單字的正確發音，並比較英美腔調的不同。

plane (n.) 飛機
[plen]

weigh (v.) 秤重
[we]

flight (n.) 班機
[flaɪt]

cart (n.) 手推車
[kart]

board (v.) 登機
[bɔrd]

terminal (n.) 航廈
[`tɜmɪnəl]

immigration (n.) 入境（處）
[ˌɪmɪ`greʃən]

declare (v.) 申報
[dɪ`klɛr]

destination (n.) 目的地
[ˌdɛstə`neʃən]

passport (n.) 護照
[`pæsˌpɔrt]

boarding gate (n.) 登機門
[`bɔrdɪŋ get]

visitor information center (n.)
遊客中心
[`vɪzɪtə ˌɪnfɔr`meʃən `sɛntə]

tourist (n.) 觀光客
[`tʊrɪst]

baggage claim (n.) 行李提領
[`bægɪdʒ klem]

reservation (n.) 訂位
[ˌrɛzə`veʃən]

security check (n.) 安全檢查
[sə`kjʊrəti tʃɛk]

luggage (n.) 行李
[`lʌgɪdʒ]

visa (n.) 簽證
[`vizə]

sight (n.) 景點
[saɪt]

主題易混淆字

聽力上也常會遇到的一個問題，就是有些字的發音非常相近，
在聽的時候，如果沒有整合前後文內容，很容易就聽錯。
以下我們整理了幾組容易弄錯的單字，請聽光碟朗讀，選出句中出現的字。

字音

1. tip / trip

2. diver / driver

3. fare / far

4. hotel / hostel

5. plans / planes

6. phrases / phases

字義

7. immigration 移民 / 入境（處）

8. declare 宣佈 / 申報

9. sight 視覺 / 景點

10. package 套裝（旅遊）/ 包裹

解答

1. How much was the **trip**?（旅程）
2. The **driver** was very professional.（司機）
3. Is the hotel **far** from here by taxi?（遠）
4. A bed at the **hostel** is quite cheap.（青年旅社）
5. We changed **planes** in Hong Kong before arriving in Singapore.（班機）
6. You should learn a few **phrases** in the local language.（片語）
7. There was a long line at **immigration**.（入境（處））
8. Do you have any items to **declare**?（申報）
9. Is that **sight** included on the tour?（景點）
10. Does the five-day **package** include airfare?（套裝（旅遊））

單字聽讀力 | 聽懂 [m]、[n] 的發音

教學說明：

[m] 發音時，空氣會從鼻腔送出，嘴唇是閉合的。這個發音常看到的拼寫可能是 m、mm、mb 或 mn。

[m] mice   warm   smear   dimmer   market   summer   dumb   column   farmer

[n] 發的發音和 [m] 位置非常相似，空氣也會從鼻腔送出，但發 [n] 時，嘴唇微張的，舌尖會輕輕頂著上排牙齒後方。這個發音常看到的拼寫可能是 n、nn 或 kn。

[n] nice   warn   sneer   dinner   listen   knowledge   cannon   knob   snow   sun   ton   sinner   thin

另一個容易和 [n] 混淆的音是 [ŋ]。發 [ŋ] 這個音時聲音也會從鼻腔送出，但舌頭不在上排牙齒後方，而是平放。這個發音常看到的拼寫可能是 ng 或 n，（後方拼字通常接 k 和 g）。

[ŋ] sung   tongue   singer   thing   ring   finger   shrink   strong   tinker

辨音測驗：

經過了剛才的發音練習，現在讓我們做個辨音小測驗，看看是不是聽懂更多了呢？請聽光碟朗讀每題句子，並選出正確單字。

1. warm / worn
2. singers / sinners
3. dinner / dimmer
4. ran / rang
5. moon / noon

解答

1. My jacket is really (worn).
2. The church was full of (singers).
3. Do you know where I can get a light (dimmer)?
4. The clock (rang) for a long time.
5. The (moon) was really bright yesterday.

句子聽讀力 | 音節介紹：減少音節

教學說明：

一個英文字可能會有一個或多個音節。一個音節可能由一個～多個音組成，其中一定要有一個母音。以下是一個音節可能出現的發音排列方式：

（C：Consonant 子音；V：Vowel 母音）

V	CV	VC	CVC
eye oh ah	foe pie bow too	egg in ought up	sit fog porch cab

根據這個規則，可得知一個字有幾個母音，就有幾個音節。

一個音節：pack storm clear bit

二個音節：apple monkey unless foreign

三個音節：computer dinosaur period horizon

四個音節：television automatic incredible conversation

有些字的實際發音會比字面的拼字少音節。因此，判斷音節時，還是要以音標內容為主。

cho-co-late（三音節）→ [ˋtʃɑklət]（二音節）：

從字面上看起來，chocolate 這個字似乎有三個音節，但實際發音只有兩個母音，因此也只有兩個音節。再看以下例子：

- di-ffe-rent（三音節）→ [ˋdɪfrənt]（二音節）
- com-for-ta-ble（四音節）→ [ˋkʌmftəbəl]（三音節）
- in-te-res-ting（四音節）→ [ˋɪntrəstɪŋ]（三音節）
- ge-ne-ral（三音節）→ [ˋdʒɛnrəl]（二音節）

聽力小測驗

英文中的繞口令句子（tongue twister）中，通常是以幾個相同數目音節的字組成。請聽光碟中的句子，並判斷每個句子的音節數。

例如： **6** Clean clams crammed in clean cans.

1. ____ Peter Piper picked a peck of pickled peppers.

2. ____ She sells seashells by the seashore.

3. ____ The sixth sick sheik's sixth sheep's sick.

4. ____ Rubber baby buggy bumpers.

解答

1. **12** Peter Piper picked a peck of pickled peppers.
2. **8** She sells seashells by the seashore.
3. **7** The sixth sick sheik's sixth sheep's sick.
4. **8** Rubber baby buggy bumpers.

多益聽力實戰

PART 01 PHOTOGRAPHS 照片描述

請看圖片並聽光碟朗讀圖 1 ～ 4 的四段敘述，選出與圖片最相符的敘述。

1. _____

2. _____

3. _____

4. _____

PART 02 QUESTION-RESPONSE 應答問題

請聽光碟朗讀，並選出最適合的答案填在空格中。

1. _____ **2.** _____ **3.** _____ **4.** _____ **5.** _____

PART 03 簡短對話
CONVERSATION

請聽光碟朗讀從選項 A、B、C、D 中選出正確的答案。

_____ **1.** **What does the woman offer the man?**
A. A meal
B. A drink
C. A magazine
D. A snack

_____ **2.** **Who is the man talking to?**
A. A waiter
B. A flight attendant
C. A pilot
D. A travel agent

_____ **3.** **When will the man arrive in San Francisco?**
A. At 10:00
B. In one hour
C. At 9:30
D. In 30 minutes

PART 04 簡短獨白
SHORT TALK

MP3-080

請聽光碟朗讀，並根據內容回答以下題目。

_____ **1.** **Who is the speaker?**
A. A teacher
B. A travel agent
C. A driver
D. A diver

_____ **2.** **What will the second stop on the tour be?**
A. A local pub
B. A sheep farm
C. Shetland Church
D. St. Andrews

_____ **3.** **If passengers have questions, what should they do?**
A. Ask their travel agent
B. Wait until the tour is over
C. Fasten their seatbelts
D. Raise them before the tour

PART 01 照片描述 PHOTOGRAPHS

1. **C** A. The flight has been delayed.
班機誤點了。
B. The plane has just landed.
飛機才剛降落。
C. The flight is now boarding.
此班機目前正在登機。
D. The passengers are getting off the plane.
旅客正在下飛機。

2. **A** A. The stewardess is checking the overhead bin.
空服小姐在檢查上方置物艙。
B. The plane will be taking off soon.
飛機即將起飛。
C. The passenger is checking her luggage.
旅客正在托運行李。
D. The woman can't find her suitcase.
女士找不到她的行李箱。

3. **D** A. The man is helping the customer with his purchase.
男士正在幫顧客結帳。
B. The clerk is folding the customer's laundry.
店員正在幫顧客折送洗衣物。
C. The man is packing for his flight.
男士正為搭機在打包。
D. The customs agent is examining the luggage.
海關人員正在檢查行李。

4. **A** A. The passengers are waiting for their luggage.
旅客正在等待行李。
B. The departure hall is full of passengers.
離境大廳擠滿了旅客。
C. The passengers are going through airport security.
旅客正在通過機場安檢。
D. The passengers are having their luggage weighed.
旅客將他們的行李過磅。

PART 02 應答問題 QUESTION-RESPONSE

1. [A] Q: Do I need a visa to visit Thailand?
去泰國需要簽證嗎？
A. Only if you plan on staying longer than 30 days.
如果你預計停留超過三十天的話才要。
B. Yes. All Thai citizens require visas.
要。每個泰國公民都需要簽證。
C. Only if you want to visit for less than two weeks.
如果你停留不到兩週的話才要。

2. [B] Q: Could you bring me a blanket, please?
請幫我拿一條毯子好嗎？
A. No, thanks. I'm not cold.
不用，謝謝。我不會冷。
B. Sure. I'll be right back.
沒問題。我馬上回來。
C. Yes, I brought you a blanket.
是的，我已經幫你拿了一條毯子。

3. [B] Q: May I see your passport and boarding pass, please?
請給我看你的護照和登機證好嗎？
A. No, thank you.
不了，謝謝。
B. Here you go.
拿去吧。
C. That won't be necessary.
沒那個必要。

4. [C] Q: How big are your tour groups?
你們旅行團有多少人？
A. Yes, they're quite large.
是的，他們滿大的。
B. I can put you in a smaller group if you like.
如果你要的話，我可以安排你到人數比較少的旅行團。
C. Usually between 10 and 20 people.
通常是十到二十人。

5. [B] Q: I'd like to report a missing passport.
我要掛失護照。
A. OK. Here's the passport application form.
好的。這是申請護照的表格。
B. All right. Fill out this form, please.
好的。請填寫這份表格。
C. I see. I'll need to see your passport first.
了解。我要先看看你的護照。

PART 03 簡短對話 CONVERSATION

W: Can I get you another beverage, sir?
先生，要再幫你拿一杯飲料嗎？

M: But won't we be landing soon? It says on my ticket that the flight arrives in San Francisco at 9:30.
但我們不是快要降落了？我的機票上寫這班飛機九點三十分會到達舊金山。

W: Didn't you hear the captain's announcement? Due to bad weather, we won't be landing for another half hour.
你沒聽到機長剛才的廣播嗎？因為天候不佳，我們還要再半小時才會降落。

M: Oh, no. I hope I don't miss my shuttle. It's supposed to pick me up at 11:00. Taxis are really expensive!
糟糕！希望我不會錯過我的接駁車。接駁車十一點會來接我。搭計程車的話真的很貴！

1. **B**   Q: 女士提供給男士什麼？
    A. 一份餐點
    B. 一杯飲料
    C. 一本雜誌
    D. 一份點心

2. **B**   Q: 男士講話的對象是？
    A. 服務生
    B. 空服員
    C. 飛行員
    D. 旅行社職員

3. **D**   Q: 男士何時會到達舊金山？
    A. 十點
    B. 一小時之後
    C. 九點三十分
    D. 三十分鐘之後

PART 04 簡短獨白 SHORT TALK

Hello, everybody. My name is Gusy and I'll be your driver and tour guide today. After a quick stop for breakfast at a local pub, we'll be visiting several historic churches in the area, starting with St. Andrew's, and including Shetland Church and St. Paul's. Next, we'll visit a sheep farm, where we'll learn how wool is turned into yarn. After a lunch stop at another pub, we'll go for a short boat ride on a traditional canal, which is still being used to this day. We'll end the tour with a stop at the Bradford Museum, which has works of art both ancient and modern. Please note that there's no eating in the vehicle, and please keep your windows closed at all times. If you have any questions, save them for the end of the tour. Now everyone fasten your seatbelts and we'll be on our way.

哈囉大家好。我叫葛絲，我今天會當各位的司機與導遊。在當地酒吧吃過簡單的早餐，稍做停留之後，我們將會參觀幾個這附近歷史悠久的教堂，從聖安德魯教堂開始，包括雪特蘭教堂及聖保羅教堂。接下來，我們會參觀一個綿羊農場，在那裡會看到羊毛如何變成毛線。在另一個酒吧用過午餐後，我們會前往搭一小段船，是在一個沿用至今的傳統運河上。我們會在布萊得佛博物館結束今天的遊覽行程，此博物館有現代與古代的藝術品。請注意在車上不可飲食，請保持窗戶一直關著。如果你有任何問題，請保留到行程最後。現在請各位繫緊安全帶我們即將出發。

1. C　Q: 說話者是誰？
A. 老師
B. 旅行社職員
C. 司機
D. 潛水者

2. D　Q: 旅程的第二站是哪裡？
A. 當地酒吧
B. 綿羊農場
C. 雪特蘭教堂
D. 聖安得魯教堂

3. B　Q: 如果乘客有問題，他們該做什麼？
A. 問旅行社職員
B. 等旅程結束
C. 繫緊安全帶
D. 在旅程前提出來

CHAPTER 09
機場篇

教學重點

⊙ 機場重點單字
⊙ 易混淆字：aboard / abroad
⊙ [ɑr]、[ɜr] 的發音
⊙ 輕音字：代名詞及所有格

多益實戰

⊙ Part 1 照片描述
⊙ Part 2 應答問題
⊙ Part 3 簡短對話
⊙ Part 4 獨白對話

主題字彙與發音

MP3-081

聽聽看這些單字的正確發音，並比較英美腔調的不同。

check in (v.) 登記，報到
[tʃɛk ɪn]

concourse (n.) 機場大廳
[`kɑnkors]

line (n.)（排隊）隊伍
[laɪn]

counter (n.) 櫃枱
[`kaʊntɚ]

monitor (n.) 顯示螢幕
[`mɑnɪtɚ]

ticket agent (n.) 售票員，票務
[`tɪkɪt `edʒənt]

plane ticket (n.) 機票
[plen `tɪkɪt]

compartment (n.) 置物箱
[kəm`pɑrtmənt]

non-smoking (a.) 禁煙的
[ˌnɑn`smokɪŋ]

carry-on luggage (n.) 隨身行李
[`kæriˌɑn `lʌgɪdʒ]

tarmac (n.) 停機坪
[`tɑrˌmæk]

ramp (n.)（登機、登船）活動扶梯
[ræmp]

layover (n.) 轉機
[`leˌovɚ]

airplane (n.) 飛機，簡稱 plane
[`ɛrˌplen]

engine (n.) 引擎
[`ɛndʒən]

wing (n.) 機翼
[wɪŋ]

nose (n.) 機鼻
[noz]

cockpit (n.) 駕駛艙
[`kɑkˌpɪt]

landing gear (n.) 起落架
[`lændɪŋ gɪr]

ground crew (n.) 地勤人員
[graʊd kru]

主題易混淆字

MP3-082

聽力上也常會遇到的一個問題，就是有些字的發音非常相近，
在聽的時候，如果沒有整合前後文內容，很容易就聽錯。
以下我們整理了幾組容易弄錯的單字，請聽光碟朗讀，選出句中出現的字。

字音

1. customs / customers

2. aboard / abroad

3. wait / weigh

4. flight / fight

5. cart / card

6. board / bored

字義

7. terminal 終端機 / 航廈

8. line 隊伍 / 路線

9. monitor 螢幕 / 監看

10. check 托運 / 檢查

解答

1. We stood in the **customs** line for nearly an hour.（海關）
2. It's time to go **aboard**.（上（飛機、船））
3. How long did you **wait** for your luggage?（等待）
4. Did you watch the **fight** on TV last night?（鬥毆）
5. You get your money back when you return the **cart**.（手推車）
6. I always get **bored** on long flights.（無聊的）
7. Which **terminal** should I drop you off at?（航廈）
8. You can take the Green **Line** to the airport.（路線）
9. Do you see our flight on the **monitor**?（螢幕）
10. Did they **check** your luggage when you went through customs?（托運）

單字聽讀力 | 聽懂 [ɑr]、[ɛr] 的發音

MP3-083

教學說明：

主題單字中，「cart」、「airplane」，你知道如何正確發音嗎？在美語中，[ɑr]、[ɛr] 是非常容易混淆的發音。如果不知道怎麼念對，就容易聽不懂。

現在就讓我們來聽聽正確的發音，並且跟著大聲念出來吧。

| [ɑr] | far | car | march | star | heart |
| [ɛr] | fair | care | mare | stair | hair |

辨音測驗：

MP3-084

經過了剛才的發音練習，現在讓我們做個辨音小測驗，看看是不是聽懂更多了呢？請聽光碟朗讀並圈出正確的單字。

1. scared / scarred

2. far / fair

3. bar / bear

4. cars / cares

5. stars / stairs

解答

1. The experience scarred him for life.
2. It isn't very fair.
3. Is there a bar around here?
4. Jason doesn't have any cars.
5. It's too dark to see the stairs.

句子聽讀力 | 輕音字：代名詞及所有格

教學說明：
我們都知道英文單字有分輕音節和重音節，英文句子也一樣，有些字會是
重音，有些字在句子裡不需強調，所以也不用把整個字的發音完整唸出。
先介紹代名詞及所有格這兩種詞性，落在句子輕音節時發音上的變化。

聽聽看／念念看：

代名詞	重音發音	輕音發音
you	[ju]	[jə]
he	[hi]	[i]
him	[hɪm]	[ɪm]
her	[hɜ]	[ɜ]
us	[ʌs]	[əs]
them	[ðɛm]	[ðəm]

所有格	重音發音	輕音發音
your	[jɔr]	[jər]
his	[hɪz]	[ɪz]
their	[ðɛr]	[ðər]

聽力小測驗：

請圈出下列句子套色字處需改變發音成為輕音節的字。作答完畢
後請聽光碟朗讀答案並試著跟讀。

1. A: Are you going to talk to him?

　　B: No, I think he should talk to me first.

2. A: Get your feet off the coffee table!

　　B: But you have your feet on the table.

3. A: Did you give her the keys?

B: Her? I thought you told me to give them to him.

4. A: Is that them over there?

B: I'm not sure—Let's wave to them.

5. A: Did they give you their address?

B: No, but they gave me their phone number.

解答

1. A: Are you going to talk to him?

B: No, I think he should talk to me first.

2. A: Get your feet off the coffee table!

B: But you have your feet on the table.

3. A: Did you give her the keys?

B: Her? I thought you told me to give them to him.

4. A: Is that them over there?

B: I'm not sure—Let's wave to them.

5. A: Did they give you their address?

B: No, but they gave me their phone number.

多益聽力實戰

PART 01 PHOTOGRAPHS 照片描述

請看圖片並聽光碟朗讀圖 1 ～ 4 的四段敘述，選出與圖片最相符的敘述。

1. _____

2. _____

3. _____

4. _____

PART 02 QUESTION-RESPONSE 應答問題

請聽光碟朗讀，並選出最適合的答案填在空格中。

1. _____ **2.** _____ **3.** _____ **4.** _____ **5.** _____

PART 03 簡短對話
CONVERSATION

MP3-089

請聽光碟朗讀從選項 A、B、C、D 中選出正確的答案。

_____ **1.** **Where does the woman work?**
A. At a travel agency
B. At the post office
C. At a hotel
D. At a delivery company

_____ **2.** **Why does the man call the woman?**
A. Because he needs to make a reservation
B. Because his delivery needs to be picked up
C. Because he hasn't received his ticket yet
D. Because he wants his money back

_____ **3.** **Why isn't Mr. Silverberg at the office?**
A. He's resting at home.
B. He's at a business meeting.
C. He doesn't work there any more.
D. He's out running errands.

PART 04 簡短獨白
SHORT TALK

MP3-090

請聽光碟朗讀，並根據內容回答以下題目。

_____ **1.** **Who is making this announcement?**
A. The ground staff
B. A pilot
C. A flight attendant
D. An engineer

_____ **2.** **Passengers are allowed to use their cell phones under which of the following conditions?**
A. Their phones are in an overhead bin.
B. They can reach their phones without getting up.
C. They make a local call.
D. They have a connecting flight.

_____ **3.** **When is this announcement made?**
A. At 8:40 a.m.
B. At 8:20 p.m.
C. While the plane is landing
D. After the plane has landed

PART 01　照片描述 PHOTOGRAPHS

1. **D** A. Check-in for the fight has already begun.
　　　　拳擊賽已經開始報到。
　　　B. The passengers are waiting for their flight.
　　　　乘客們在等待他們的班機。
　　　C. Friends and relatives are waiting in the arrival hall.
　　　　親朋好友在入境大廳等待著。
　　　D. The passengers are checking in for their flight.
　　　　乘客們正在做登機報到手續。

2. **C** A. The passengers are boarding the plan.
　　　　乘客們正在登上計畫。
　　　B. The plane is taking off from the runway.
　　　　飛機正從跑道上起飛。
　　　C. Passengers are walking up the ramp.
　　　　乘客們正走上活動扶梯。
　　　D. The cargo plane is parked on the tarmac.
　　　　貨機正停在停機坪上。

3. **B** A. The tourists are taking pictures.
　　　　觀光客在拍照。
　　　B. The tourists are sightseeing.
　　　　觀光客在遊覽風景。
　　　C. The hikers are climbing the mountain.
　　　　登山客正在爬山。
　　　D. The travelers are waiting for their boat.
　　　　遊客正在等船。

4. **D** A. Patients are being admitted to the hospital.
　　　　病患正在登記住院。
　　　B. People are waiting in line at the health clinic.
　　　　人們在醫療診所排隊等待。
　　　C. People are immigrating into the country.
　　　　人們正移民至這個國家。
　　　D. There are long lines at immigration.
　　　　入境處排很長的隊。

PART 02 應答問題 QUESTION-RESPONSE

1. **A** Q: Any luggage to check, sir?
先生，有行李要托運嗎？
A. Yes—these two suitcases.
有，這兩個行李箱。
B. I checked them before I came.
我來之前已經檢查過了。
C. Yes. They're ready for inspection.
有。它們準備好送檢了。

2. **A** Q: What's the exchange rate?
匯率是多少？
A. It's 92 yen per dollar.
九十二日圓兌一美元。
B. We take most major currencies.
大部分的主要貨幣我們都收。
C. Yes, you can change money here.
是的，你可以在此處換錢。

3. **A** Q: How long is the layover?
轉機的時間要多久？
A. A little over two hours.
兩個小時多一點點。
B. About 300 miles.
約三百英里
C. You can stay as long as you like.
你想待多久都可以。

4. **C** Q: Is that a non-smoking flight?
那是禁菸的班機嗎？
A. Yes, it's OK if you smoke.
是的，你可以吸菸。
B. Please put out your cigarette, sir.
請將香菸熄滅，先生。
C. All of our flights are non-smoking.
我們全部的班機都禁菸。

5. **B** Q: Can I take this as a carry-on?
我可以把這個當作隨身行李嗎？
A. No, it's smaller than our minimum size requirement.
不行，這比我們的最小體積限制還要小。
B. Yes, it's small enough to fit in the overhead compartment.
可以，這夠小，能容納於我們的艙頂置物箱裡。
C. Yes, it's small enough for me to put under the seat.
可以，這夠小，我可以擺在座位底下。

PART 03 簡短對話 CONVERSATION

M: Hi, my name is Daniel Jackson. I'm calling because I have a flight tomorrow and haven't received my ticket in the mail yet. I got the original ticket from Mr. Silverberg last week, but the date was wrong. So I called and spoke to a Mr. Callahan, who told me a new ticket would be sent right away.

嗨，我的名字是丹尼爾傑克森。我打來是因為我明天要搭機了，但卻還沒收到郵寄給我的機票。上禮拜我收到西爾弗伯格先生原先寄來的機票，但是上面的日期是錯的，所以我打電話去，跟一位卡拉罕先生講話，他告訴我會馬上寄出新的機票。

W: I see. I'm sorry to hear you haven't received your ticket yet. Mr. Callahan is at home with a cold, and Mr. Silverberg has left the company, but I'll try to straighten this out for you.

我瞭解了。我很抱歉你還沒收到機票。卡拉罕先生因感冒人在家中，而西爾弗伯格先生已經離職了。但我會試著解決你的問題。

M: I'd appreciate it. I have a really important business meeting tomorrow, so I can't afford to miss this flight.

非常感謝。我明天有場非常重要的商務會議，所以我可擔不起錯過這班飛機。

W: OK, I'm looking at your file. The ticket was only mailed yesterday. I'll issue another one for you immediately and have it sent to you by express delivery. You should receive it by 4:00 this afternoon.

好的，我正在看你的檔案。機票是昨天才寄送出去的。我現在立即開另一張票快遞過去給你，應該今天下午四點前你就會收到了。

1. **A** Q: 此女人在哪裡工作？
    A. 旅行社
    B. 郵局
    C. 飯店
    D. 快遞公司

2. **C** Q: 男人為何打電話給女人？
    A. 因為他要訂票
    B. 因為他需要領取他的貨件
    C. 因為他還沒有收到機票
    D. 因為他想要退錢

3. **C** Q: 為何西爾弗伯格先生不在辦公室裡？
    A. 他正在家中休息。
    B. 他正在開會。
    C. 他不在那邊工作了。
    D. 他正外出辦事。

PART 04 簡短獨白 SHORT TALK

Ladies and Gentlemen, this is your captain speaking. We have landed in New York and will be at the gate shortly. The local time is 8:20 a.m., and the outside temperature is 84 degrees. At this time, you are welcome to use your cell phone if it is accessible. Please keep your seatbelts fastened until the seatbelt sign is turned off. Be careful when opening overhead bins, as items tend to move during flight. If this is your final destination, please proceed to Carousel Two to claim your luggage. If you have a connecting flight, our ground staff will be available at the gate to assist you. Thank you for flying Friendly Air, and we hope to see you again soon.

各位先生女士,我是你們的機長。我們已經於紐約降落,即將到達機門。當地時間是早上八點二十分,外面溫度是八十四度。現在你們可以使用行動電話,如果收得到訊號的話。在安全帶號誌熄滅前請繫好安全帶。由於飛行期間物品會移動,打開上方置物艙時請小心。如果此處是您的終點站,請前往二號行李轉盤提領行李。如果您要轉機,我們的地勤人員將在機門處協助您。感謝您搭乘友善航空,希望很快能再度與你相見。

1. **B** Q: 這段廣播是誰在講話?
    A. 地勤人員
    B. 飛行員
    C. 空服人員
    D. 工程師

2. **B** Q: 旅客在下列哪種情況下可以使用行動電話?
    A. 他們的手機放在艙頂置物箱。
    B. 他們不用起身就可以拿到手機。
    C. 他們打市內電話。
    D. 他們要轉機。

3. **D** Q: 這段廣播是在何時播出的?
    A. 早上八點四十分
    B. 晚上八點二十分
    C. 飛機降落途中
    D. 飛機已經降落後

CHAPTER 10
交通工具篇

教學重點

⊙ 交通工具重點單字
⊙ 易混淆字：truck / track
⊙ 子音 [b] [p]、[t] [d] 的發音
⊙ 輕音字：be 動詞和助動詞

多益實戰

⊙ Part 1 照片描述
⊙ Part 2 應答問題
⊙ Part 3 簡短對話
⊙ Part 4 獨白對話

主題字彙與發音

MP3-091

聽聽看這些單字的正確發音,並比較英美腔調的不同。

subway (n.) 地鐵
[`sʌb,we]

station (n.) 車站
[`steʃən]

return ticket (n.) 來回票
[rɪ`tɜn `tɪkɪt]

train (n.) 火車
[tren]

dock (n.) 碼頭,船塢
[dɑk]

escalator (n.) 手扶梯
[`ɛskə,letə]

lifeboat (n.) 救生船或飛機
[`laɪf,bot]

sign (n.) 標誌,指示牌
[saɪn]

porthole (n.) 船或飛機的舷窗
[`pɔrt,hol]

platform (n.) 月台
[`plæt,fɔrm]

ship (n.) 船
[ʃɪp]

descend (v.) 下降
[dɪ`sɛnd]

cabin (n.) 坐艙,船艙
[`kæbɪn]

arrive (v.) 到達
[ə`raɪv]

sail (v.) 航行
[sel]

wait (v.) 等候
[wet]

port (n.) 港口
[pɔrt]

roof (n.) 屋頂
[ruf]

depart (v.) 啟航,出發
[dɪ`pɑrt]

commute (v.) 通勤
[kə`mjut]

主題易混淆字

聽力上也常會遇到的一個問題，就是有些字的發音非常相近，
在聽的時候，如果沒有整合前後文內容，很容易就聽錯。
以下我們整理了幾組容易弄錯的單字，請聽光碟朗讀，選出句中出現的字。

字音

1. bus / boss

2. truck / track

3. load / road

4. cab / cap

5. proceed / precede

字義

6. cabin 客艙 / 小屋

7. wheel 車輪 / 方向盤

8. toll（路，橋等的）通行費 /
   損失 / 傷亡人數

9. coach 巴士 / 經濟艙 /（火車）
   一般座位車廂

10. gas 氣體 / 瓦斯 / 汽油

解答

1. I can't believe Robert got hit by a **bus**.（公車）
2. Most of the freight is transported by **truck**.（卡車）
3. Where does this **road** go?（路）
4. Have you seen Henry's new **cap**?（帽子）
5. Please **proceed** to the boarding gate immediately.（前往）
6. How much is it to rent a **cabin** at the resort?（小屋）
7. Keep your hands on the **wheel** at all times.（方向盤）
8. Drunk driving is taking a heavy **toll** on our nation's roads.（傷亡人數）
9. I usually fly **coach** to save money.（經濟艙）
10. We ran out of **gas** and had to call a tow truck.（汽油）

單字聽讀力 | 聽懂子音 [b] [p]、[t] [d] 的發音

MP3-093

教學說明：

主題單字中，「ship」、「port」，你知道如何正確發音嗎？講話時，字尾的 [b] 或 [p] 只要做出嘴型，幾乎不需要發出聲音，所以聽起來像被省略沒有聲音。例如「Stop!」、「Hey Bob!」。

現在就讓我們來聽聽正確的發音，並且跟著大聲念出來吧。

[b]　bat　rabid　slab

[p]　pat　rapid　slap

另外，講話時，字尾的 [t] 或 [d] 也是只要做出嘴型，幾乎不需要發出聲音，所以聽起來像被省略沒有聲音。例如「Please turn on the light.」、「It's at the end of the road.」。

[t]　tip　wrote　town

[d]　dip　road　down

[t] 夾在兩個母音間時，聽起來會像 [d]，例如「writer」、「butter」。而 [t] 或 [d] 夾在兩個子音間時，則省略不發音。例如「exactly」、「sounds」。

辨音測驗：

MP3-094

經過了剛才的發音練習，現在讓我們做個辨音小測驗，看看是不是聽懂更多了呢？請聽光碟朗讀並圈出正確的單字。

1. wide / white

2. tip / dip

3. cap / cab

4. pack / back

5. dock / talk

解答

1. The beach at the resort was very (white).

2. Did you try the (tip) I told you about?

3. How much did the (cab) cost?

4. It took Mark a long time to (back) up the car.

5. We went to the (dock) on Saturday.

句子聽讀力 ｜ 輕音字：be 動詞和助動詞

MP3-095

教學說明：

be 動詞不論在句首或句中都屬於輕音字，而且經常使用縮寫，但在否定句中會唸重音。強調語氣、凸顯對比的時候也念重音。

聽聽看／念念看：

be 動詞	重音發音	輕音發音
am	[æm]	[əm]
is	[ɪz]	[ɪz]
are	[ɑr]	[ə/ɚ]
were	[wɜ]	[wə]
was	[wɑz]	[wəz]

Wh- 疑問句中的助動詞屬於輕音字，have、has 的第一個字甚至不發音。跟 be 動詞一樣，在否定句與強調語氣、凸顯對比時會唸重音。

助動詞	重音發音	輕音發音
do	[du]	[də]
does	[dʌz]	[dəz]
will	[wɪl]	[wəl]
has	[hæz]	[əs]
have	[hæv]	[əv]
can	[kæn]	[kən]

聽力小測驗：
聽光碟朗讀並圈出每題正確的 be 動詞或助動詞。

MP3-096

1. How many people are/were at the office?

2. Is/Was that the tallest building in the city?

3. Steve can/can't play the guitar.

4. That has/is to be the worst meal I've ever had!

5. What _____ he do for a living?

6. What _____ you want for your birthday?

7. Why _____ you stopped coming to class?

8. Where _____ you go on your vacation?

解答

1. How many people were at the office?
2. Is that the tallest building in the city?
3. Steve can't play the guitar.
4. That has to be the worst meal I've ever had!
5. What **does** he do for a living?
6. What **do** you want for your birthday?
7. Why **have** you stopped coming to class?
8. Where **did** you go on your vacation?

多益聽力實戰

請看圖片並聽光碟朗讀圖 1 ～ 4 的四段敘述，選出與圖片最相符的敘述。

1. _____

2. _____

3. _____

4. _____

PART 02 QUESTION-RESPONSE 應答問題

請聽光碟朗讀，並選出最適合的答案填在空格中。

1. _____ **2.** _____ **3.** _____ **4.** _____ **5.** _____

PART 03 簡短對話
CONVERSATION

請聽光碟朗讀從選項 A、B、C、D 中選出正確的答案。

_____ **1.** **Where does this conversation likely take place?**
A. On a public bus
B. In a car
C. At a subway station
D. On a subway train

_____ **2.** **What relationship do the speakers probably have?**
A. They are a couple.
B. They are co-workers.
C. They are neighbors.
D. They are roommates.

_____ **3.** **According to the man, why does he stop driving?**
A. Because gas is too expensive
B. Because he often got stuck in traffic
C. Because had trouble finding parking spaces
D. Because it is bad for the environment

PART 04 簡短獨白
SHORT TALK

請聽光碟朗讀,並根據內容回答以下題目。

_____ **1.** **Where does this announcement take place?**
A. A bus station
B. A train station
C. A cruise ship
D. An airport

_____ **2.** **Which direction is Ridgeville from the station?**
A. To the west
B. To the south
C. To the north
D. To the east

_____ **3.** **What should passengers do if they miss the train to Oakdale?**
A. Take the 3:20 train
B. Take the next train to Ridgeville
C. Catch the next train at 3:15
D. Proceed to platform 2

PART 01 照片描述 PHOTOGRAPHS

1. **B**   A. The dock is crowded with people.
碼頭上擠滿了人。
B. The people are going up the ramp.
人們正往活動扶梯上走。
C. Passengers are boarding the sailboat.
旅客們正在登上這艘帆船。
D. The ship is sailing into the port.
這艘船正進入港口。

2. **D**   A. People are riding the elevator.
人們正在搭乘電梯。
B. The cable car is entering the station.
纜車正駛進車站。
C. People are getting off the train.
人們正從火車上下車。
D. Passengers are waiting for the train.
旅客們正在等候火車。

3. **C**   A. The student is going to school.
這個學生正要去上學。
B. The girl is waiting for the boss.
這個女孩在等老闆。
C. The girl is standing at a bus stop.
這個女孩站在公車站牌旁。
D. The weather is very cold.
天氣非常冷。

4. **D**   A. The track is painted white.
軌道漆成白色。
B. The vehicle is driving on the road.
這輛車行駛在路上。
C. The truck is carrying a heavy load.
這台卡車載貨很重。
D. The truck is parked in the lot.
這台卡車停在停車場。

PART 02 應答問題 QUESTION-RESPONSE

1. **B** Q: Can I get there by subway?
  我可以搭地鐵到那裡嗎？
  A. There's a station on the corner.
    車站就在轉角。
  B. No, you'll have to take a bus.
    不能，你必須搭公車去。
  C. Yes, it's under construction.
    可以，它在建造當中。

2. **A** Q: Are we running low on gas?
  我們是不是快沒油了？
  A. Yes, we need to fill up soon.
    對，我們要快去加油了。
  B. Yes, gas is cheaper now.
    對，油價現在比較便宜。
  C. The tank holds twenty gallons.
    油箱可以裝二十加侖的油。

3. **B** Q: When is the last train to Richmond?
  到瑞奇蒙的最後一班火車是幾點？
  A. There are ten trains a day.
    一天有十班火車。
  B. Eleven p.m.
    晚上十一點。
  C. Yes, you can take the train.
    對，你可以搭火車。

4. **B** Q: Did you buy a return ticket?
  你有買來回票嗎？
  A. Yes, I'd like a return ticket.
    是的，我想買一張來回票。
  B. No, just one-way.
    沒有，只買單程。
  C. You can't return the ticket.
    你不能退票。

5. **C** Q: Do you have a driver's license?
  你有駕照嗎？
  A. Yes, I know how to drive.
    對，我會開車。
  B. I'm a very good driver.
    我是個優良駕駛。
  C. Yes, but it's expired.
    有，但是過期了。

PART 03 簡短對話 CONVERSATION

W: Hey, Tom! I didn't know you took public transportation.
嘿，湯姆！我不知道你都搭車。

M: Well, I used to drive, but I got tired of paying so much at the pump. And parking is so expensive too.
嗯，我以前都是開車，但是我覺得付那麼多油錢很煩。停車費也超貴。

W: Yeah. Not to mention getting stuck in traffic.
就是說。更別提被塞在車陣中了。

M: That's a benefit I didn't even think of. So which stop is closest to our building?
這個好處我倒沒想到。離我們公司最近的是哪一站？

W: Fremont Station—it's just a two minute walk from there. And Richmond Station is across the street from my apartment, which is super convenient.
佛利蒙站——從那邊走去只要兩分鐘。而且瑞奇蒙站就在我家對面，超方便的。

M: That is convenient. Hey, we're almost there.
真的很方便。嘿，我們快到了。

1. D Q: 這對話最有可能發生在哪裡？
   A. 公車上
   B. 汽車內
   C. 地鐵站
   D. 地鐵上

2. B Q: 兩位說話者是什麼關係？
   A. 他們是情侶。
   B. 他們是同事。
   C. 他們是鄰居。
   D. 她們是室友。

3. A Q: 根據男人所說的話，他為何不再開車？
   A. 因為油錢太貴
   B. 因為常遇到塞車
   C. 因為停車位很難找
   D. 因為不環保

PART 04 簡短獨白 SHORT TALK

Attention passengers, the two fifteen train to Oakdale is running on schedule, and will be arriving on platform two in five minutes. Oakdale bound passengers should proceed to platform two immediately. For those who can't make it to the platform in time, another train leaves in one hour. The two twenty train to Ridgeville, leaving from platform one, is running ten minutes late due to bad weather, and we apologize to passengers for the delay. All eastbound trains depart from platform one, and all westbound trains depart from platform two.

旅客請注意，兩點十五分到奧克戴爾的火車將準時進站，五分鐘後將會到達第二月台，前往奧克戴爾方向的旅客應立即前往第二月台。無法及時趕到月台的旅客，還有另一班火車在一個小時後出發。第一月台發車，兩點二十分到瑞吉維爾的火車因為天候不佳，將晚十分鐘出發，我們為班車誤點感到非常抱歉。所有東向火車都在第一月台發車，西向的則都在第二月台發車。

1. B Q: 這段廣播是在哪裡聽到的？
A. 公車站
B. 火車站
C. 郵輪
D. 機場

2. D Q: 瑞吉維爾是在車站的哪個方向？
A. 西方
B. 南方
C. 北方
D. 東方

3. C Q: 旅客若錯過到奧克戴爾的火車該怎麼辦？
A. 搭三點二十分的火車
B. 搭去瑞吉維爾的火車
C. 改搭下一班三點十五分的火車
D. 前往第二月台

CHAPTER 11
飯店篇

教學重點

- ⊙ 飯店重點單字
- ⊙ 易混淆字：towel / tower
- ⊙ [k] [g]、[f] [v] 的發音
- ⊙ 輕音節母音變化

多益實戰

- ⊙ Part 1 照片描述
- ⊙ Part 2 應答問題
- ⊙ Part 3 簡短對話
- ⊙ Part 4 獨白對話

主題字彙與發音

MP3-101

聽聽看這些單字的正確發音，並比較英美腔調的不同。

front desk (n.) 接待櫃台
[frʌnt dɛsk]

receptionist (n.) 櫃台接待員
[rɪˋsɛpʃənɪst]

bellhop (n.) 提行李的服務生
[ˋbɛlˏhɑp]

lobby (n.) 大廳
[ˋlɑbi]

guest (n.) 客人
[gɛst]

reservation (n.) 預訂
[ˏrɛzɚˋveʃən]

concierge (n.)
飯店迎賓員／高級服務員
[ˏkɑnsiˋɛrʒ]

suite (n.) 套房
（指有會客區或小客廳的房間）
[swit]

valet (n.) 代客停車服務員
[ˋvæˏle]

revolving door (n.) 旋轉門
[rɪˋvɑlvɪŋ dɔr]

elevator (n.) 電梯
[ˋɛləˏvetɚ]

maid (n.) 清潔女工
[med]

tip (v.) 給小費 (n.) 小費
[tɪp]

hallway (n.) 走廊
[ˋhɔlˏwe]

door attendant (n.)
門房；門口服務員
[dɔr əˋtɛndənt]

occupancy (n.) 居住；佔用
[ˋɑkjəpənsi]

clerk (n.) 職員；店員
[klɝk]

suitcase (n.) 行李箱
[ˋsutˏkes]

vase (n.) 花瓶
[ves]

coupon (n.) 招待券
[ˋkupɑn]

主題易混淆字

MP3-102

聽力上也常會遇到的一個問題,就是有些字的發音非常相近,
在聽的時候,如果沒有整合前後文內容,很容易就聽錯。
以下我們整理了幾組容易弄錯的單字,請聽光碟朗讀,選出句中出現的字。

字音

1. suites / suits

2. towel / tower

3. mate / maid

4. bed / bet

5. guess / guest

字義

6. reservations（餐廳）訂位 / 顧慮

7. check out 退房 / 看看

8. function 功能 / 聚會

9. reception 櫃台 / 宴會,接待會

10. floor 地板 / 樓層

解答

1. The **suits** here are very expensive.（西裝）
2. How much did the **tower** cost?（大樓）
3. Is that the **mate** you were talking about?（朋友）
4. How many **bets** did you make today?（賭注）
5. Would you like to take a **guess**?（猜測）
6. After reading that review, I immediately made **reservations** for the restaurant.（訂位）
7. Is it OK if we **check out** the room first?（看看）
8. The hotel restaurant is a good place for a **function**.（聚會）
9. The **reception** is being held on the first floor.（宴會）
10. Have you ever slept on the **floor**?（地板）

單字聽讀力　聽懂 [k] [g]、[f] [v] 的發音

MP3-103

教學說明：

主題單字中，「clerk」、「guest」，你知道如何正確發音嗎？講話時，[k] 的拼寫可能是 c、k、cc、ck 或 ch。[kw] 則拼成 qu，[ks] 是 x。kn 出現在字首時 k 不發音。

現在就讓我們來聽聽正確的發音，並且跟著大聲念出來吧。

[k]	ba**ck**	fro**ck**	**c**ap	**c**ould	bi**ck**er
[k]	**c**omi**c**	lo**ck**	so**cc**er	**k**angaroo	**ch**emist
[kw]	**qu**een				
[ks]	ta**x**i				
不發音	**kn**ife				

[g] 的拼寫可能是 g、gg、gh 或 gu。gn 若放在一起，g 則不發音。

[g]	ba**g** fro**g** **g**ap **g**ood bi**gg**er **g**arden lu**gg**age **gh**ost **g**uest	
不發音	forei**gn**	

[f] 的拼寫可能是 f、ff、ph 或 gh。[v] 的拼寫大部分都是 v，但少數時候可能是 f，譬如 of [əv]。

[f]	**f**ew	grie**f**	sa**f**er	**f**ace	belie**f** after
	co**ff**ee	autogra**ph**	lau**gh**		
[v]	**v**iew	grea**v**e	sa**v**er	**v**ase	belie**v**e

辨音測驗：

MP3-104

經過了剛才的發音練習，現在讓我們做個辨音小測驗，看看是不是聽懂更多了呢？請聽光碟朗讀並圈出正確的單字。

1. cold / gold
2. belief / believe
3. class / glass
4. block / blog
5. file / vial

解答

1. How can I get rid of my (cold)?
2. Michael's story is hard to (believe).
3. Which (glass) do you like best?
4. There's a new restaurant on the (block).
5. Do you remember where you put the (vial)?

句子聽讀力 ｜ 輕音節母音變化

MP3-105

教學說明：

先前介紹過七種經常在句子中會變成「輕音字」的字組：代名詞、所有格、be 動詞、助動詞、冠詞、連接詞和介系詞。這些「輕音字」的變化都落在母音上，也就是把所有母音都變成 [ə] 或 [ɪ]。這樣的規則不只適用在「輕音字」，也適用在一個單字的「輕音節」。

聽聽看／念念看：

1. banana [bə`nænə]：三個音節，第二節重音的 a 唸 [æ]，另外兩個輕音的 a 則唸成 [ə]。

2. regret [rɪ`grɛt]：兩音節，第二節重音的 e 唸 [ɛ]，輕音節的 e 唸 [ɪ]。

母音字母位於輕、重音節發音對照大致如下：

字母	重音	輕音	
a	[æ]、[ɑ]、[e]	[ə]	[i]
e	[ɛ]、[i]		
i	[ɪ]、[aɪ]		
o	[ɑ]、[o]、[ʌ]	[ə]	[i]
u	[ʌ]、[ʊ]、[u]		

由於這樣的變化，有些字連音之後會跟別的字發音一樣。

例如： Is this the way to the school? [we-tə]

　　　　Can you wait a minute? [we-tə]

聽力小測驗：

將 1 ～ 4、a ～ d 有相同發音的句子配對。找出句子中相同發音的字並畫上底線（作答完畢可聽光碟核對答案）。

MP3-106

1. _____ I've lived here for a long time.

2. _____ Jennifer has a loud voice.

3. _____ We weren't hungry at all.

4. _____ Vicky screams every time she sees an insect.

a. I'm not allowed to stay out late.

b. Can I come along with you?

c. Spring is my favorite season.

d. Dana wants to go out with a tall guy.

解答

1. I've lived here for **a long** time.
b Can I come **along** with you?

2. Jennifer has **a loud** voice.
a I'm not **allowed** to stay out late.

3. We weren't hungry **at all**.
d Dana wants to go out with **a tall** guy.

4. Vicky screams every time she **sees an** insect.
c Spring is my favorite **season**.

多益聽力實戰

請看圖片並聽光碟朗讀圖 1～4 的四段敘述，選出與圖片最相符的敘述。

1. _____

2. _____

3. _____

4. _____

PART 02 QUESTION-RESPONSE 應答問題

MP3-108

請聽光碟朗讀，並選出最適合的答案填在空格中。

1. _____　　**2.** _____　　**3.** _____　　**4.** _____　　**5.** _____

PART 03 簡短對話
CONVERSATION

請聽光碟朗讀從選項 A、B、C、D 中選出正確的答案。

____ **1.** **How long will the woman stay at the hotel?**
A. 14 days
B. Until Thursday
C. One week
D. Six nights

____ **2.** **When did she make her reservation?**
A. Two weeks ago
B. Four days ago
C. Monday night
D. Yesterday

____ **3.** **What does the man offer the woman?**
A. Tickets to a performance
B. Free drinks
C. Tickets for free food
D. Extra nights at the hotel

PART 04 簡短獨白
SHORT TALK

MP3-110

請聽光碟朗讀，並根據內容回答以下題目。

____ **1.** **Who is the audience for this message?**
A. Foreign citizens
B. Students
C. Vacationers
D. Business travelers

____ **2.** **Why would a caller visit the Tropical Sun Resorts website?**
A. To make or cancel a room reservation
B. To find out what types of rooms are available
C. To look at pictures of resort facilities
D. To find out about special package deals

____ **3.** **What should a caller do to talk to an operator?**
A. Press three
B. Press four
C. Call back later
D. Wait on the line

PART 01 照片描述 PHOTOGRAPHS

1. **B**   A. The passengers are checking in for their flight.
          乘客們正在辦理登機手續。
       B. There are many guests in the hotel lobby.
          飯店大廳裡有很多客人。
       C. The passengers are buying tickets at the station.
          乘客們正在車站買票。
       D. All the guests have luggage with them.
          每一位客人都有帶行李。

2. **C**   A. The guest is tipping the bellhop.
          客人正在給行李員小費。
       B. The receptionist is helping a guest check in.
          櫃臺接待員正在幫客人辦住房手續。
       C. The woman is dragging her suitcase behind her.
          女士正在拖行她後方的行李。
       D. The clerk is showing a suite to the guest.
          服務員正在帶客人參觀套房。

3. **A**   A. The maid is making the bed.
          女僕正在整理床鋪。
       B. The girl is changing her sheets.
          女孩在換她的床單。
       C. The waitress is spreading the tablecloth.
          女服務生在鋪桌巾。
       D. The mate is bending over.
          這位伙伴正彎下腰。

4. **D**   A. The girl is borrowing her father's car.
          這女孩正在跟父親借車。
       B. The woman is going to a reception.
          這女人要去一個接待會。
       C. The woman is checking out her room.
          這女人在退房。
       D. The clerk is handing the woman her key.
          服務員正把鑰匙交給這女人。

PART 02 應答問題 QUESTION-RESPONSE

1. **A** Q: Is a deposit required?
需要付押金嗎？

A. Yes, it'll be charged to your credit card.
是的，費用會從你的信用卡扣。

B. Yes, you can pay it when you check out.
是的，你可以退房後再付。

C. No, taxes are included in the room rate.
不用，房價已經有含稅了。

2. **B** Q: Can I upgrade to a suite?
我可以升級到套房嗎？

A. Yes, we can have it cleaned for you.
是的，我們可以為你打掃乾淨。

B. Sorry, they're all booked.
抱歉，都被訂滿了。

C. Yes, but the rent is higher.
可以，但租金比較高。

3. **A** Q: Do you have room service?
你們有提供客房服務嗎？

A. No, but our restaurant is open till midnight.
沒有，但我們餐廳一直營業到半夜十二點。

B. We provide convenient services for our guests.
我們為顧客提供便利的服務。

C. Yes, maid service is included.
是的，有包含清房服務。

4. **C** Q: The sheets in my room are dirty!
我房間的床單很髒。

A. In that case, you should have them washed right away.
如果是那樣的話，你應該立刻送洗。

B. You can be sure that I won't be staying here again.
我可以跟你保證我再也不會住這裡了。

C. Sorry—we'll send someone to change them right away.
抱歉，我們會立刻派人去更換。

5. **B** Q: How much are your cheapest rooms?
你們最便宜的房價是？

A. Our rooms are very cheap.
我們的房價非常便宜。

B. Singles start at 40 Euros.
單人房由四十歐元起跳。

C. Do you have a reservation?
你有訂房嗎？

PART 03 簡短對話 CONVERSATION

M: I apologize, ma'am, but we don't have any record of your reservation.
很抱歉，女士。但我們並沒有任何關於妳的訂房紀錄。

W: How is that possible? I made an online reservation 14 days ago. I reserved a double room for Monday night through Sunday night. Here, I printed out the receipt.
怎麼可能？我十四天前就在線上預約了。我訂了星期一到星期天晚上的雙人房。這裡，我印了收據。

M: I'm so sorry. All the doubles are full, so I'll put you in a suite for three nights. Then I can move you into a double on Thursday. Also, to show our apology, I'd like to give you these drink coupons that can be used in our restaurant or piano lounge.
真的很抱歉。雙人房已經客滿了，所以我先安排妳住三天的套房，然後星期四再幫妳換到雙人房。為了表示我們的歉意，我會給妳這些可以在餐廳或鋼琴酒吧使用的飲料招待券。

W: OK, that sounds reasonable. And thanks for the coupons.
好吧，聽起來很合理。謝謝你的招待券。

1. `C` Q: 女士會在飯店住多久？
A. 十四天
B. 到星期四
C. 一個星期
D. 六個晚上

2. `A` Q: 女士是什麼時候做了預約？
A. 兩個星期前
B. 四天前
C. 星期一晚上
D. 昨天

3. `B` Q: 男士提供了什麼給女士？
A. 表演的觀賞券
B. 免費的飲料
C. 食物的免費招待券
D. 額外的住宿天數

PART 04 簡短獨白 SHORT TALK

Hello. You've reached Tropical Sun Resorts, the ideal destination for fun in the sun vacations. To browse our resorts around the world, look at photos of our resort facilities and find addresses and contact information, please visit our website. For room options and rates, please press one. To make, change or cancel a reservation, please press two. For information about package deals, please press three. To hear this message again, please press four. To speak to one of our operators, please press zero. Calls are answered in the order they are received, so please remain on the line and the next available operator will assist you. Thank you for calling Tropical Sun Resorts.

哈囉。這裡是熱帶陽光度假村,享受陽光度假最理想的去處。要瀏覽我們度假村全球據點、看度假村設施圖片及連絡資訊,請上我們的網站。房型和房價,請按一。欲預約、更改、取消訂房,請按二。套裝行程資訊,請按三。重聽請按四。和客服人員通話,請按零。我們會依來電順序處理,請稍候我們會有客服人員為您協助。謝謝您來電熱帶陽光度假村。

1. **C** Q: 這段話的是說給誰聽的?
A. 外國公民
B. 學生
C. 度假者
D. 商務旅客

2. **C** Q: 打電話的人上熱帶陽光度假村的網站可以做什麼?
A. 訂房或取消訂房
B. 了解有哪些不同的房間類型
C. 看度假村設施的照片
D. 了解特殊套裝行程

3. **D** Q: 要跟客服人員說話要怎麼做?
A. 按三
B. 按四
C. 稍候再播
D. 在線上等候

CHAPTER 12
街景篇

教學重點

⊙ 街景重點單字
⊙ 易混淆字：circle / cycle
⊙ [ɪ]、[i] 的發音
⊙ 連音技巧：[t] 的消音

多益實戰

⊙ Part 1 照片描述
⊙ Part 2 應答問題
⊙ Part 3 簡短對話
⊙ Part 4 獨白對話

主題字彙與發音

MP3-111

聽聽看這些單字的正確發音，並比較英美腔調的不同。

crosswalk (n.) 行人穿越道
[`krɔs,wɔk]

shoulder (n.) 路肩
[`ʃoldə]

pedestrian (n.) 行人
[pə`dɛstriən]

dividing line (n.) 分隔車道線
[dɪ`vaɪdɪŋ laɪn]

van (n.) 箱型車
[væn]

divider (n.) 分隔物
[də`vaɪdə]

intersection (n.) 交叉路口
[`ɪntə,sɛkʃən]

skyscraper (n.) 摩天大樓
[`skaɪ,skrepə]

sidewalk (n.) 人行道
[`saɪd,wɔk]

freeway (n) 高速公路
[`fri,we]

curb (n.) 路邊，人行道邊緣
[kɝb]

hill (n.)（道路的）斜坡
[hɪl]

taxi (n.) 計程車
[`tæksi]

exit sign (n.) 出口告示
[`ɛksɪt saɪn]

street sign (n.) 路牌
[strit saɪn]

overpass (n.) 高架橋
[`ovə,pæs]

traffic light (n.) 紅綠燈
[`træfɪk laɪt]

lane (n.) 車道
[len]

block (n.) 街區
[blɑk]

fence (n.) 護欄，柵欄
[fɛns]

主題易混淆字

MP3-112

聽力上也常會遇到的一個問題，就是有些字的發音非常相近，
在聽的時候，如果沒有整合前後文內容，很容易就聽錯。
以下我們整理了幾組容易弄錯的單字，請聽光碟朗讀，選出句中出現的字。

字音

1. cross / across

2. van / fan

3. curve / curb

4. lock / block

5. circle / cycle

字義

6. light 交通號誌 /（路）燈

7. sign 路牌 / 手勢

8. meters 停車收費器 / 公尺

9. lanes 小巷 / 車道

10. jam 困境 / 塞車

解答

1. Be careful when you **cross** the street.（越過）
2. I bought a new **fan** yesterday.（風扇）
3. You're too close to the **curb**.（人行道邊）
4. It looks like that **lock** has been picked.（鎖）
5. There's a traffic **circle** up ahead.（圓環）
6. Make a right at the next **light**.（紅綠燈）
7. Do you understand **sign** language?（手勢）
8. How many **meters** is the parking space?（公尺）
9. Always signal before switching **lanes**.（車道）
10. His parents helped him get out of a **jam**.（困境）

單字聽讀力 | 聽懂 [ɪ]、[i] 的發音

MP3-113

教學說明：

主題單字中，「exit」、「freeway」，你知道如何正確發音嗎？在口語中，
[ɪ]、[i] 是非常容易混淆的發音。如果不知道怎麼念對，就容易聽不懂。
現在就讓我們來聽聽正確的發音，並且跟著大聲念出來吧。

| [ɪ] | chip | fit | live | fill | sit |
| [i] | cheap | feet | leave | feel | seat |

辨音測驗：

MP3-114

經過了剛才的發音練習，現在讓我們做個辨音小測驗，看看是不
是聽懂更多了呢？聽光碟朗讀每題兩個單字，若聽到同一字唸兩
次，請選 S (same)，若為不同字請選 D (different)。

1. S / D

2. S / D

3. S / D

4. S / D

5. S / D

解答

1. D (eat / it)
2. D (wheel / will)
3. S (team / team)
4. D (filled / field)
5. S (live / live)

句子聽讀力 | 連音技巧：[t] 的消音

教學說明：

當字尾是 [t] 且跟著的下一個字的開頭也為子音（h 除外），[t] 會被省略，以增加講話時的流暢度。

請聽光碟播放下列句子，注意 t 的發音。

1. He drank too much last night.
×

2 I collect coins.
×

3. He was left behind.
×

當字尾是 [t] 且跟著的下一個字的開頭音為 [j]，則會把兩個音加起來變成 [tʃ]。

1. Has Mr. James left yet?
[tʃ]

2. I can't let you go.
× [tʃ]

3. It was bought last year.
× [tʃ]

聽力小測驗：

聽光碟朗讀，判別套色字母的子音 [t] 發音應為 A（[t] 無變化）、B（[t] 被消音）或 C（[t] + [j] = [tʃ]）。

1. ____ Take a left turn.

2. ____ Sarah's having the baby next year.

3. ____ The dog bit her leg.

4. ____ I expect an answer soon.

5. ____ She's a fat girl.

6. _____ Just use your common sense.

7. _____ I'll have a soft drink.

8. _____ It's in first gear.

9. _____ We crossed over the road.

10. _____ What you did is wrong.

解答

1. B	**2.** C	**3.** A	**4.** A	**5.** B
6. C	**7.** B	**8.** B	**9.** A	**10.** C

多益聽力實戰

PART 01 照片描述
PHOTOGRAPHS

請看圖片並聽光碟朗讀圖 1～4 的四段敘述，選出與圖片最相符的敘述。

1. _____

2. _____

3. _____

4. _____

PART 02 應答問題
QUESTION-RESPONSE

請聽光碟朗讀，並選出最適合的答案填在空格中。

1. _____ **2.** _____ **3.** _____ **4.** _____ **5.** _____

PART 03 簡短對話
CONVERSATION

MP3-119

請聽光碟朗讀從選項 A、B、C、D 中選出正確的答案。

_____ **1.** **What problem does the woman have?**
A. She's out of gas.
B. Her car broke down.
C. She is lost.
D. She needs directions.

_____ **2.** **Where does the woman want to go?**
A. To the convenience store
B. To the petrol station
C. To the shopping center
D. To the post office

_____ **3.** **What should the woman do when she gets to Post Street?**
A. Turn left
B. Turn right
C. Find a parking space
D. Drive three blocks

PART 04 簡短獨白
SHORT TALK

MP3-120

請聽光碟朗讀，並根據內容回答以下題目。

_____ **1.** **Who is most likely listening to this report?**
A. Vehicle drivers
B. Subway passengers
C. Housewives
D. Bus passengers

_____ **2.** **How many intersections are closed?**
A. Four
B. Five
C. Three
D. Six

_____ **3.** **When will the repaving project probably be completed?**
A. In early July
B. By November 15th
C. In mid-September
D. On May 15th

解答與解析

PART 01 照片描述 PHOTOGRAPHS

1. **C** A. The street is under construction.
街道施工中。
B. There is a fan on the street.
街上有一個電扇。
C. Several pedestrians are crossing the street.
好幾位行人在過馬路。
D. There are many cars parked on the street.
街上停了許多汽車。

2. **B** A. The vehicles are driving down the lane.
車輛正順著小巷開。
B. Most of the vehicles are driving downhill.
大部分的車輛都向下坡行駛。
C. The freeway has four lanes in each direction.
高速公路雙向皆有四個車道。
D. There is lots of traffic on the overpass.
高架橋上車潮眾多。

3. **B** A. Lots of cars are parked next to the curve.
很多車停在彎道旁。
B. There are parking meters along the curb.
路邊有停車計時器。
C. The cars are parked meters apart.
這些車停車距離相隔數公尺。
D. There are free parking spaces on the street.
街上有免費停車位。

4. **D** A. Lots of cars are driving onto the island.
很多車正開往島上。
B. People are riding on the cycle path.
人們在自行車道上騎車。
C. The vehicles are stuck in a traffic jam.
汽車塞在車陣中。
D. Cars are driving around the traffic circle.
車子正順著圓環而行。

PART 02 應答問題 QUESTION-RESPONSE

1. **A** Q: Should I turn left or right up ahead?
我應該在前面左轉還是右轉？

A. Let me look at the map.
讓我看一下地圖。

B. Yes, that's the right way.
對，那是對的路。

C. Yes, I think you should turn left.
對，我想你應該要左轉。

2. **B** Q: You just ran a red light!
你剛剛闖紅燈了！

A. I wasn't running, I was walking.
我沒有跑啊，我是用走的。

B. Oops, I didn't see it.
哎呀，我剛剛沒注意到。

C. You really should be more careful.
你應該要更小心謹慎。

3. **C** Q: Do you commute to work?
你通勤上班嗎？

A. Yes, I have a full-time job.
對，我有一個全職的工作。

B. No, I live too far away.
沒有，我家住太遠了。

C. No, I live right around the corner.
沒有，我就住附近。

4. **C** Q: Are the buses very frequent?
公車的班次很頻繁嗎？

A. I'm not sure, but they come pretty often.
我不確定耶，但它們還蠻常來的。

B. Yes, there are lots of bus stops around here.
是的，這裡有很多公車站牌。

C. Yes, one comes every five minutes or so.
是的，差不多每五分鐘就會來一班。

5. **B** Q: Why is the street closed to traffic?
為什麼這條街封閉了？

A. There's just too much traffic.
車流量太大了。

B. There's construction up ahead.
那邊前面在施工。

C. Yes, we'll have to take another street.
是的，我們必須要走另一條路。

PART 03 簡短對話 CONVERSATION

W: Excuse me. Do you know where the nearest petrol station is?
不好意思。你知道最近的加油站在哪裡嗎？

M: Uh, let's see. Yeah, there's one not too far from here. Just turn right at the convenience store up ahead, drive three blocks, and then make a left.
呃，我看看。對了，有一個加油站離這邊不遠。在前面的便利商店右轉，開過三個路口再左轉。

W: Do you know what street that is?
你知道那條街的街名嗎？

M: Yes. That's Post Street. The station is half a block down, across from the shopping center.
知道。是郵政街。加油站在轉進郵政街離下個路口一半的地方，在購物中心對面。

1. **D**   Q: 那女人遇到什麼問題？
      A. 她的車沒油了。
      B. 她的車拋錨了。
      C. 她迷路了。
      D. 她需要問路。

2. **B**   Q: 那女人想去哪？
      A. 便利商店
      B. 加油站
      C. 購物中心
      D. 郵局

3. **A**   Q: 那女人到郵政街之後要做什麼？
      A. 左轉
      B. 右轉
      C. 找車位
      D. 開過三個路口

PART 04 簡短獨白 SHORT TALK

Good morning, commuters. This is Dan Mathers with a special May 15th traffic report. Due to a repaving project, Memorial Drive is only open to one lane of traffic in each direction from Sixth Street to the Fox River Bridge. The intersections of Front Street, Third Street and Fourth Street are also closed. Prospect Avenue west of Memorial is closed to traffic as well. The truck route detour is on I-90 and U.S. 42. The local detour is Mason Street from Prospect to Spencer Street, Spencer from Mason to Badger, and Badger from Spencer to Prospect. Stage one is expected to be completed in early July, stage two in mid-September, and the final stage by November 15th.

通勤族們早安！我是丹馬瑟斯，為您帶來五月十五日的交通特報。由於道路重鋪計畫，第六街往福斯河大橋方向的紀念大道往來均只有單一車道通車。前街、第三街和第四街的路口也是封閉的。紀念大道以西的展望大道也不開放通行。貨車可繞道走九十號州際公路與四十二號快速道路。本地居民可改道，從展望大道轉梅森街到史賓賽街，轉貝傑街再接回展望大道。第一階段預計於七月上旬告一段落，第二階段在九月中旬完成，最後階段於十一月十五日前竣工。

1. A 　Q: 這個報導的收聽族群會是？
　　　A. 開車族
　　　B. 地鐵乘客
　　　C. 家庭主婦
　　　D. 公車乘客

2. C 　Q: 有幾個路口是封閉的？
　　　A. 四個
　　　B. 五個
　　　C. 三個
　　　D. 六個

3. B 　Q: 道路重鋪計畫可能會在何時完成？
　　　A. 七月上旬
　　　B. 十一月十五日前
　　　C. 九月中旬
　　　D. 五月十五日

CHAPTER 13
機械設備篇

教學重點

- ⊙ 機械設備重點單字
- ⊙ 易混淆字：manufacture / manufacturer
- ⊙ [tr]、[tʃ] 的發音
- ⊙ 重音：主詞、動詞

多益實戰

- ⊙ Part 1 照片描述
- ⊙ Part 2 應答問題
- ⊙ Part 3 簡短對話
- ⊙ Part 4 獨白對話

主題字彙與發音

聽聽看這些單字的正確發音，並比較英美腔調的不同。

---

equipment (n.) 設備，裝備
[ɪˋkwɪpmənt]

facility (n.) 設施，工具；場所
[fəˋsɪləti]

mechanical (a.) 機械的
[məˋkɛnɪkəl]

technician (n.) 技師
[tɛkˋnɪʃən]

electrical (a.) 電力的
[ɪˋlɛktrɪkəl]

manufacture (n./v.) 製造
[ˌmænjəˋfæktʃɚ]

forklift truck (n.) 堆高機
[ˋfɔrkˌlɪft trʌk]

automation (n.) 自動化
[ˌɔtəˋmeʃən]

stacker (n.) 堆貨機
[ˋstækɚ]

tray (n.)（機械設備）的拖盤
[tre]

assemble (v.) 組裝
[əˋsɛmbəl]

console (n.) 控制台
[ˋkɑnsol]

transmission (n.) 變速箱
[transˋmɪʃən]

gear (n.) 齒輪
[gɪr]

maintenance (n.) 保養
[ˋmentənəns]

switch (n./v.) 更換，切換
[swɪtʃ]

production (n.) 生產
[prəˋdʌkʃən]

operator (n.) 作業員
[ˋɑpɚˌretɚ]

factory (n.) 工廠
[ˋfæktəri]

warehouse (n.) 倉庫
[ˋwɛrˌhæus]

主題易混淆字

聽力上也常會遇到的一個問題，就是有些字的發音非常相近，
在聽的時候，如果沒有整合前後文內容，很容易就聽錯。
以下我們整理了幾組容易弄錯的單字，請聽光碟朗讀，選出句中出現的字。

字音

1. devise / device

2. manufacture / manufacturer

3. production / protection

4. console / council

5. fax / fix

字義

6. facility 設備 / 場所

7. transmission 傳輸 / 變速箱

8. charge 充電 / 收費

9. switch（打開關掉）開關 / 更換

10. gear 齒輪 / 裝備

解答

1. What is this **device** used for?（裝置）
2. Their main business is the **manufacture** of office equipment.（製造）
3. Our factory workers wear these hard hats for **protection**.（保護）
4. Several engineers sat in front of the **console**.（控制台）
5. Were you able to **fax** the mechanical diagrams on time?（傳真）
6. How many people work at the production **facility**?（場所）
7. It would be very expensive to install a new **transmission**.（變速箱）
8. How much did they **charge** you for the battery?（收費）
9. I **switched** to an electric stove for safety reasons.（更換）
10. The **gears** need to be oiled regularly.（齒輪）

單字聽讀力 | 聽懂 [tr]、[tʃ] 的發音

MP3-123

教學說明：

主題單字中，「transmission」、「switch」，你知道如何正確發音嗎？在美語中，[tr]、[tʃ] 是非常容易混淆的幾個發音。[tr] 是由 [t] 和 [r] 連音組合而成的有聲子音，後方通常會跟著一個母音，常見的拼字即為 tr。

現在就讓我們來聽聽正確的發音，並且跟著大聲念出來吧。

[tr]   train   trick   trunk   control   attracted

[tʃ] 的發音是從嘴巴送出氣體，不會振動聲帶。常看到的拼寫可能是 ch、t 或 tch

[tʃ]   chain   chick   chunk   future   scotch

辨音測驗：

經過了剛才的發音練習，現在讓我們做個辨音小測驗，看看是不是聽懂更多了呢？請聽光碟播放，寫出正確的字。

MP3-124

1. chase / trace

2. treats / cheats

3. cheese / trees

4. chips / trips

解答

1. The phone company was unable to (trace) the call.

2. How well a business does depends on how it (treats) customers.

3. The price of (trees) has risen steadily over the past year.

4. No refunds are available on any of our bargain (chips)

句子聽讀力　重音：主詞、動詞

教學說明：

在英文中，單字有音節以及重音的問題。當我們把範圍從字拉大到句子時，就會發現在句中也會有被強調或被略過的字。在一般情況下，一個句子的重音會放在主要的主詞和動詞上。

- The man stares at his daughter.
- Carl drives to work.
- The tiger escaped from his cage.
- The building collapsed in the earthquake.

某些特定詞性的字在句子中通常不會是重音處。

- 代 名 詞：I met her yesterday.
- be 動詞：Paul was right.
- 助 動 詞：Cats can swim.
- 介 系 詞：Go to hell!
- 冠　　詞：Can you close the window?
- 連 接 詞：Bob and Carrie went fishing.

否定的助動詞則通常會是句子的重音處。

- I can't hear you.
- Don't be late.
- It hasn't rained in months.
- You shouldn't skip class.

以上所說的只是一般規則，因為說話者在各種不同的狀況下，會故意強調某些字，即使那些字在一般情況下不會是重音。如以下對話為例：

A: You didn't print out the agenda?
B: No. I thought you did.

A: The restaurant is on Grand Avenue?
B: No. It's on Grant Avenue.

A: Let's meet on Thursday at 5:00.
B: Tuesday at 5:00?
A: No, Thursday at 5:00.

聽力小測驗：
請聽光碟播放的句子，並以底線畫出句子中強調的重音字。

MP3-126

1. Tom isn't dumb, you're dumb.

2. Most birds can fly.

3. We haven't finished our report.

4. The typhoon destroyed the town.

5. She gave me a ride in her car.

解答

1. **Tom** isn't dumb, **you're** dumb.
2. Most **birds** can **fly**.
3. We **haven't finished** our report.
4. The **typhoon destroyed** the town.
5. She **gave** me a ride in her car.

多益聽力實戰

MP3-127

請看圖片並聽光碟朗讀圖 1 ～ 4 的四段敘述，選出與圖片最相符的敘述。

1. _____

2. _____

3. _____

4. _____

PART 02 應答問題
QUESTION-RESPONSE

MP3-128

請聽光碟朗讀，並選出最適合的答案填在空格中。

1. _____ **2.** _____ **3.** _____ **4.** _____ **5.** _____

PART 03 簡短對話
CONVERSATION

請聽光碟朗讀從選項 A、B、C、D 中選出正確的答案。

____ **1.** **What does the woman show the man how to do?**
A. Use a printer to print out documents
B. Send documents in an e-mail
C. Use a fax machine to send documents
D. Use a copier to copy the documents

____ **2.** **What does the woman tell the man to do after the documents are in the tray?**
A. Dial the number on the keypad
B. Press the SEND button
C. Wait for the tone
D. Put the cover sheet on top

____ **3.** **What will the man probably do next?**
A. Place the documents in the tray
B. Press the SEND button
C. Place the cover sheet on top of the documents
D. Begin to follow the woman's instructions

PART 04 簡短獨白
SHORT TALK

請聽光碟朗讀,並根據內容回答以下題目。

____ **1.** **Who would be interested in this ad?**
A. Homeowners
B. Appliance owners
C. Motorcycle owners
D. Car owners

____ **2.** **What is the special price being offered?**
A. $20
B. 10% off
C. $27
D. $30

____ **3.** **How long will the offer last?**
A. One week, starting today
B. Three months
C. Until the end of this week
D. Until the end of today

PART 01 照片描述 PHOTOGRAPHS

1. D　A. The person is shopping at a store.
這個人正在店裡購物。
B. The man is showing his ID card.
男士正在出示他的身分證。
C. The man is charging his computer.
男士正在替電腦充電。
D. The person is charging a product online.
這個人正在線上用信用卡買東西。

2. C　A. The people are working at a production facility.
人們正在製造場工作。
B. The men are training for a competition.
男士們正在為比賽訓練。
C. The people are using the gym facilities.
人們正在使用健身房設施。
D. The workers are assembling exercise equipment.
工人們正在組裝運動器材。

3. A　A. The man is working at the console.
男士正在控制台前工作。
B. The man is typing a document on his computer.
男士正在用他的電腦打文件。
C. The man is playing video games.
男士正在玩電玩遊戲。
D. The man is entering his ATM password.
男士正在輸入他的提款機密碼。

4. B　A. The man is oiling the bicycle chain.
男士正在幫單車鏈條上油。
B. The man is adjusting the gears.
男士正在調整齒輪。
C. The man is preparing his cycling gear.
男士正在準備他騎單車的裝備。
D. The man is fixing the scooter.
男士正在修理機車。

PART 02 應答問題 QUESTION-RESPONSE

1. C Q: How do you ensure the safety of factory workers?
你如何確保工廠員工安全？
A. Yes. The factory is very safe.
是的。工廠非常安全。
B. Of course. All of our workers are insured.
當然。所有員工都有投保。
C. We follow strict safety guidelines.
我們遵循嚴格的安全指導方針。

2. B Q: What does the warranty cover?
保固包含什麼？
A. It's a two-year warranty.
這是兩年的保固。
B. Parts and labor.
零件及原廠送修服務。
C. It costs an extra $50.
要另外支付五十美元。

3. B Q: Do you take your car in for regular maintenance?
你的車有定期送去保養嗎？
A. Yeah. It seems like I'm always getting it fixed.
有啊。我老是在修它。
B. Yes. That's why it runs so well.
有的。所以車子狀況才這麼好。
C. No. My car hasn't broken down yet.
沒有。我的車還沒拋錨過。

4. A Q: Kevin works as a crane operator.
凱文為一名起重機駕駛。
A. Oh. I didn't know he worked in construction.
喔。我不知道他任職於建築業。
B. He always was interested in animals.
他一向對動物很有興趣。
C. It's hard to imagine him working on a farm.
真難想像他在農場工作。

5. C Q: What is this forklift used for?
這個堆高機是做什麼用的？
A. It's a type of exercise machine.
這是一種運動機。
B. That's a salad fork.
那是一支沙拉叉。
C. To stack cargo in the warehouse.
用來疊放倉庫貨物。

PART 03 簡短對話 CONVERSATION

M: Hey, Pam. Can you show me how to use this thing?
嗨，潘。可以教我怎麼用這玩意嗎？

W: Sure. Are these the documents you want to send?
可以啊。這些是你想傳的文件嗎？

M: Yes. And here's the cover sheet.
是的。這是封面頁。

W: OK. First, you put the documents face up in the tray, and then the cover sheet on top.
好的。首先，將文件正面朝上放到托盤上，然後將封面頁放在最上頭。

M: All right. What next?
好了。下一步是什麼？

W: Now, just dial the number on the keypad like you would a regular phone number and wait for the tone.
現在，就像撥一般電話一樣，在鍵盤上撥號，然後等聲音響。

M: OK. What's that sound?
好的。那是什麼聲音？

W: That means it's connected. Now you just press the SEND button.
那表示有接通。現在你只要按下「傳送」鍵就行了。

1. **C**　Q: 女人教男人做什麼？
　　　　A. 用印表機把文件印出來
　　　　B. 用電子郵件傳送文件
　　　　C. 用傳真機傳送文件
　　　　D. 用影印機影印文件

2. **D**　Q: 女人告訴男人文件放到托盤後要做什麼？
　　　　A. 在鍵盤上撥號
　　　　B. 按下「傳送」鍵
　　　　C. 等聲音響
　　　　D. 將封面頁放在最上頭

3. **B**　Q: 男人接下來應該會做什麼？
　　　　A. 將文件放到托盤上
　　　　B. 按下「傳送」鍵
　　　　C. 將封面頁放在文件上頭
　　　　D. 開始遵照女士的指示

PART 04 簡短獨白 SHORT TALK

Quick Lube is happy to announce a special limited offer. Come in this week, and you'll receive a $10 discount on our complete lube service, which normally costs $30. This service includes up to five quarts of quality oil and a new oil filter. But that's not all. We also clean exterior windows, vacuum interior floors, and check and replenish your transmission fluid, wiper fluid and battery water. We're so confident in the quality of our service that we offer a three-month satisfaction guarantee. Remember, oil changes are the single most important maintenance procedure, so don't put it off any longer. Our offer expires this Sunday, so come on down to one of our convenient locations today!

快可潤滑油很開心公布限時特惠活動。只要在這個星期蒞臨,將享全套潤滑油服務折扣十元的優惠,平常價格為三十元。此項服務包含至多五夸脫高品質機油和一個全新濾油器。但好康還不只這樣,我們還會清潔外部車窗、用吸塵器清理車內地板,以及檢查並裝滿變速箱油、雨刷清潔液和電瓶液。我們對我們的服務品質相當有信心,所以提供三個月滿意保證。記住,換機油是保養過程中最重要的部分,可千萬別再拖了。此項優惠只到這個星期日,今天就到離你最近的店消費吧!

1. **D** Q: 誰會對這則廣告有興趣?
A. 擁有房子的人
B. 擁有家電的人
C. 擁有摩托車的人
D. 擁有汽車的人

2. **A** Q: 店家提供的特惠價是多少?
A. 二十元
B. 打九折
C. 二十七元
D. 三十元

3. **C** Q: 特惠活動時間為多久?
A. 一星期,從今天開始
B. 三個月
C. 到這星期為止
D. 到今天為止

CHAPTER **14**
生產品管篇

教學重點

- ⊙ 生產品管重點單字
- ⊙ 易混淆字：defective / detective
- ⊙ [l]、[r] 的發音
- ⊙ 字尾加 s 與動詞過去式加 ed

多益實戰

- ⊙ Part 1 照片描述
- ⊙ Part 2 應答問題
- ⊙ Part 3 簡短對話
- ⊙ Part 4 獨白對話

主題字彙與發音

聽聽看這些單字的正確發音，並比較英美腔調的不同。

---

quality (n.) 品質
[`kwɑləti]

material (n.) 材料
[mə`tiriəl]

defect (n.) 瑕疵
[`dɪfɛkt]

yield rate (n.) 良率
[iild ret]

inspector (n.) 檢驗員
[ɪn`spɛktɚ]

capacity (n.) 產能
[kə`pæsəti]

conform (v.) 符合規格
[kən`fɔrm]

process (n.) 程序，流程
[`prɑsɛs]

verify (v.) 驗證
[`vɛrəfaɪ]

efficiency (n.) 效率
[ɪ`fɪʃənsi]

enhance (v.) 加強
[ɪn`hɛns]

requirement (n.) 要求
[rɪ`kwaɪrmənt]

assembly (n.) 組裝
[ə`sɛmbəlli]

replacement (n.) 替換
[rɪ`plesmənt]

uniform (n.) 一致
[`junə͵fɔrm]

repair (v.) 修理
[rɪ`pɛr]

criteria (n.) 標準
[kraɪ`tɪrɪə]

repel (v.) 防護
[rɪ`pɛl]

control (v.) 控制
[kən`trol]

procedure (n.) 程序
[prə`sidʒɚ]

主題易混淆字

聽力上也常會遇到的一個問題,就是有些字的發音非常相近,
在聽的時候,如果沒有整合前後文內容,很容易就聽錯。
以下我們整理了幾組容易弄錯的單字,請聽光碟朗讀,選出句中出現的字。

字音

1. brand / blend

2. quality / quantity

3. criterion / criteria

4. defective / detective

5. rebel / repel

字義

6. defects 不足 / 瑕疵

7. assembly 組裝 / 集會

8. cut 縮短 / 減少

9. uniform 一致 / 制服

10. guarantee 保證書 / 保證

解答

1. The coffee produced by that company is a **blend** of several different beans.（混合）
2. The factory produces a large **quantity** of products each month.（數量）
3. Products are required to meet strict quality **criteria**.（品管標準,單數 criterion）
4. The quality control staff makes use of several **detective** devices.（偵測）
5. Quality inspectors test the lenses to make sure they **repel** moisture and dust.（防護）
6. Products with **defects** are either repaired or replaced.（瑕疵）
7. Quality tests are performed at each stage of the **assembly** process.（組裝）
8. The strike at the factory resulted in a **cut** in production.（減少）
9. All parts are measured and tested to ensure **uniform** quality.（一致）
10. We **guarantee** that our products are manufactured to the highest standards.（保證）

單字聽讀力 ｜ 聽懂 [l]、[r] 的發音

MP3-133

教學說明：

主題單字中，「quality」、「conform」，你知道如何正確發音嗎？[l] 發音時，要把舌尖抵在上排牙齒後方，振動聲帶，空氣自然從舌頭兩旁送出。這個發音常看到的拼寫可能是 l 或 ll。

現在就讓我們來聽聽正確的發音，並且跟著大聲念出來吧。

| [l] | light | towel | little | clown | valley |
| | tall | English | yellow | learn | help |

發 [r] 的時候，必須要捲舌，並振動聲帶。舌尖若捲得不夠後方，聲音就會變得很像 [l] 而造成混淆。這個發音常看到的拼寫可能是 r、rr 或 wr。

| [r] | right | tower | litter | crown | very |
| | sorry | writer | cream | store | |

辨音測驗：

MP3-134

經過了剛才的發音練習，現在讓我們做個辨音小測驗，看看是不是聽懂更多了呢？請聽光碟播放，圈出正確的單字。

1. collect / correct

2. right / light

3. wrist / list

4. feel / fear

5. peeper / paople

解答

1. Can you (correct) my paper for me?
2. It's hard to find the (right) outfit.
3. If you like the watch, you should put it on your (list).
4. What do you (fear) about getting older?
5. You should report the (peeper) to the police.

MP3-135

教學說明：

● **字尾加 s 的唸法**

在一般時候，遇到名詞複數、動詞第三人稱單數，或是所有格時，字尾只要多加一個子音 [s]（前接無聲子音）或 [z]（前接有聲子音或母音）即可，不會增加音節數。但是當字尾是下列發音時，進行上面三種變化就要多加一個音節 [ɪz]。

字尾發音	例字
[s]	face [fes] → faces [ˋfesɪz] class → classes fax → faxes
[ʃ]	brush [brʌʃ] → brushes [ˋbrʌʃɪz] wish → wishes radish → radishes
[z]	rose [roz] → roses [ˋrozɪz] buzz → buzzes advise → advises
[tʃ]	watch [wɑtʃ] → watches [ˋwɑtʃɪz] hunch → hunches church → churches
[dʒ]	badge [bædʒ] → badges [ˋbædʒɪz] college → colleges manage → manages

● **動詞過去式加 ed 的唸法**

通常一般動詞形成過去式，字尾只要多加一個子音 [t]（前接無聲子音）或 [d]（前接有聲子音或母音）。但是當字尾是下列發音時，進行時態變化就要多加一個音節 [ɪd]。

字尾發音	例字
[t]	rest [rɛst] → rested [ˋrɛstɪd] complete → completed illustrate → illustrated
[d]	need [nid] → needed [ˋnidɪd] provide → provided reward → rewarded

聽力小測驗：

請聽光碟朗讀下列句子，並判別套色字的發音為下列何者。

[s]　[z]　[ɪz]　[t]　[d]　[ɪd]

1. Slow drivers often get passed by other cars.

2. Crows landed on the tree's branches.

3. The crooks pawned the stolen bicycles.

4. The sheriffs showed their badges to the suspects.

5. The apprentices who skipped classes were scolded and punished.

解 答

1. Slow drivers often get passed by other cars.
　　　　[z]　　　　　　[t]　　　　[z]

2. Crows landed on the tree's branches.
　　[z]　[ɪd]　　　　[z]　[ɪz]

3. The crooks pawned the stolen bicycles.
　　　　[s]　[d]　　　　　[z]

4. The sheriffs showed their badges to the suspects.
　　　　[s]　[d]　　　[ɪz]　　　　[s]

5. The apprentices who skipped classes were scolded and punished.
　　　　[ɪz]　　　[t]　[ɪz]　　　　[ɪd]　　　[t]

PART 01 PHOTOGRAPHS 照片描述

請看圖片並聽光碟朗讀圖 1 ～ 4 的四段敘述，選出與圖片最相符的敘述。

1. _____

2. _____

3. _____

© Diliiy / Shutterstock.com

4. _____

PART 02 QUESTION-RESPONSE 應答問題

請聽光碟朗讀，並選出最適合的答案填在空格中。

1. _____   2. _____   3. _____   4. _____   5. _____

PART 03 簡短對話
CONVERSATION

MP3-139

請聽光碟朗讀從選項 A、B、C、D 中選出正確的答案。

_____ **1.** What is the main topic of the discussion?
A. Bicycling
B. Production
C. Lay-offs
D. Quality control

_____ **2.** Why does the woman think the bicycles should be manufactured overseas?
A. It will let the company lay off workers.
B. It will help the company improve quality.
C. It will help the company save money.
D. It will allow the company to raise prices.

_____ **3.** What is the man most concerned about?
A. The quality of their products
B. The cost of their bicycles
C. Shipping costs
D. Employee job security

PART 04 簡短獨白
SHORT TALK

MP3-140

請聽光碟朗讀，並根據內容回答以下題目。

_____ **1.** Who would be listening to this talk?
A. Quality inspectors
B. Factory employees
C. Customers
D. Retail employees

_____ **2.** What should you do if you're not satisfied with your Techlux appliance?
A. Return it for a refund
B. Return it to the store for exchange
C. Send it back to the manufacturer
D. Send it back to the factory

_____ **3.** When are Techlux appliances inspected?
A. When they are returned by customers
B. Before they are sold to customers
C. When they arrive at the retail outlet
D. Before they leave the factory

PART 01 照片描述 PHOTOGRAPHS

1. **B**   A. The podium is set up for the assembly.
這講台是為集會而設置的。
B. The assembly line is automated.
這條裝配線是自動化的。
C. The equipment is set up at the construction site.
這些設備設置在工地裡。
D. The microscope is set up at the lab.
這台顯微鏡設置在實驗室裡。

2. **D**   A. The reporter is interviewing the workers.
記者正在訪問工人。
B. The workers are on their lunch break.
工人正在吃午餐休息。
C. The mechanics are repairing the machine.
技師正在修理機器。
D. The inspector is observing the workers.
視察員正在視察工人。

3. **A**   A. The man is demonstrating that the cell phone can repel water.
那位男士在示範手機可以防水。
B. The man is rebelling by throwing someone's phone in the water.
那位男士把某個人的手機丟到水裡以示抗議。
C. The man accidentally dropped his cell phone in the water.
那位男士不小心把他的手機掉進水裡。
D. The man is washing his cell phone in the washing machine.
那位男士正在用洗滌機清洗手機。

4. **C**   A. The artist is putting his signature on his work.
藝術家正在他的作品上簽名。
B. The man is inspecting the parts for quantity.
那位男士正在檢查零件的數量。
C. The inspector is checking the parts for quality.
檢查員正在檢查零件的品質。
D. The technician is drilling holes in the parts.
技師正在零件上鑽洞。

PART 02 應答問題 QUESTION-RESPONSE

1. **B** Q: Can you recommend a good, inexpensive camera?
可以推薦我一台好用又平價的相機嗎？

    A. Yes, it's quite cheap.
對啊，這很便宜。

    B. This one is good value for the money.
這一台很超值。

    C. Actually, I'm just browsing, thanks.
其實我只是逛逛而已，謝謝。

2. **A** Q: Is this product manufactured locally?
這項產品是本地製造的嗎？

    A. No, it's made overseas.
不，它是在海外生產的。

    B. Yes, it's imported to this country.
對，它是進口到國內來的。

    C. We have a local production facility.
我們在本地有工廠。

3. **C** Q: Is the production line in continuous operation?
目前生產線的運作是不中斷的嗎？

    A. Yes, we produce products from eight a.m. to twelve a.m.
對，我們從早上八點到凌晨十二點都在生產產品。

    B. Yes, we plan to have it run 24 hours a day.
對，我們之後打算讓它二十四小時運作。

    C. No, we only have two shifts.
不，我們只有兩班輪流。

4. **A** Q: What does the number on the quality control stamp indicate?
品管章上面的數字是什麼意思？

    A. It shows who inspected the product.
顯示誰檢查過這個產品。

    B. It's the postage amount.
這是郵資。

    C. Yes, you call that number if the product is defective.
對，如果產品有瑕疵就打那個電話號碼。

5. **B** Q: We must strive to improve quality control procedures.
我們必須努力改進品管流程。

    A. Yes. Product quality is much better now.
對，產品的品質現在好多了。

    B. Yes. The current level of defects is unacceptable.
對，目前的不良率令人無法接受。

    C. I don't think that's a good way to improve quality.
我不覺得那是提高品質的好方法。

PART 03 簡短對話 CONVERSATION

M: Why do you think we should move production of our bicycles overseas? Aren't you worried that we'd be forced to lay off a lot of employees?

為什麼妳認為我們應該要將腳踏車生產移往海外？妳不會擔心我們會被迫裁撤很多員工嗎？

W: Well, it would be much cheaper, and if we don't cut costs, we'll have to lay people off anyway.

這個嘛，成本會降低很多，而且如果我們不降低成本，我們無論如何都得裁員。

M: I guess you have a point. But if we let someone else manufacture our bicycles for us, how can we maintain control over quality?

妳說的也有道理。但如果我們讓別人為我們製造腳踏車，我們如何能控管品質？

1. **B**   Q: 這段談話的主題是什麼？
      A. 腳踏車運動
      B. 產品製造
      C. 裁員
      D. 品管

2. **C**   Q: 為什麼那位女士認為腳踏車應該移往海外製造？
      A. 能讓公司裁員。
      B. 能讓公司改善品質。
      C. 能幫公司省錢。
      D. 能讓公司提高售價。

3. **A**   Q: 那位男士最擔心什麼？
      A. 他們產品的品質
      B. 他們腳踏車的成本
      C. 貨運成本
      D. 員工的工作保障

PART 04 簡短獨白 SHORT TALK

We guarantee that strict quality control is maintained for all of the appliances manufactured by our company. Defective appliances are either destroyed or repaired before they leave our production facility. This means that when Techlux appliances arrive at retail outlets, they have been thoroughly inspected to ensure that they are free from defects. We are therefore confident that you will be satisfied with your Techlux appliance, and that it will provide you with many years of carefree use. Nevertheless, if you're not fully satisfied with your purchase, simply take it back to the place of purchase within 30 days for replacement.

我們保證,本公司製造的所有家電都經過嚴格的品管。有瑕疵的家電在出廠前均已被銷毀或修復,亦即泰克朗克斯的家電送到零售據點時,已經通過徹底的檢查,以確保沒有瑕疵。因此,我們深信各位一定會滿意所購買的泰克朗克斯產品,讓各位安心使用多年。儘管如此,如果你們對購買的產品並不完全滿意,只要在三十天內送回原先購買的地方替換即可。

1. C Q: 聽這段話的人會是誰?
A. 品管員
B. 工廠員工
C. 顧客
D. 零售店雇員

2. B Q: 如果你對泰克朗克斯家電不滿意的話,你該怎麼做?
A. 退貨退款
B. 退回店家換貨
C. 寄回製造商
D. 寄回工廠

3. D Q: 泰克朗克斯家電在何時接受檢查?
A. 被顧客退回時
B. 賣給顧客前
C. 送達零售據點時
D. 出廠前

CHAPTER 15
市場行銷篇

教學重點

- ⊙ 市場行銷重點單字
- ⊙ 易混淆字：prospective / perspective
- ⊙ [dr]、[dʒ] 的發音
- ⊙ 縮寫字的發音

多益實戰

- ⊙ Part 1 照片描述
- ⊙ Part 2 應答問題
- ⊙ Part 3 簡短對話
- ⊙ Part 4 獨白對話

主題字彙與發音

聽聽看這些單字的正確發音，並比較英美腔調的不同。

marketing (n.) 行銷
[`mɑrkɪtɪŋ]

recession (n.) 衰退，不景氣
[rɪ`sɛʃən]

campaign (n.)（社會）運動，活動
[kæm`pen]

expansion (n.) 擴展，擴大
[ɪk`spænʃən]

prospect (n.) 前景，前途
[`prɑspɛkt]

advertisement (n./ v.)
廣告；登廣告
[ædvɚ`taɪzmənt]

trend (n.) 局勢，潮流
[trɛnd]

retail (n./a./v.) 零售
[`ritelɚ]

channel (n.) 通路；途徑
[`tʃænəl]

niche (a./n.) 分眾的，利基
[nɪtʃ]

inflation (n.) 通貨膨脹
[ɪn`fleʃən]

raise (v.) 提高
[rez]

adopt (v.) 採用
[ə`dɑpt]

share (n.) 市佔率
[ʃɛr]

competition (n.) 競爭
[ˌkɑmpə`tɪʃən]

strategy (n.) 策略
[`strætədʒi]

consume (v.) 消耗，耗盡
[kən`sum]

convince (v.) 說服，使確信
[kən`vɪns]

profit (n.) 獲利
[`prɑfɪt]

evaluation (n.) 評估，估算
[ɪˌvæljʊ`eʃən]

主題易混淆字

MP3-142

聽力上也常會遇到的一個問題,就是有些字的發音非常相近,
在聽的時候,如果沒有整合前後文內容,很容易就聽錯。
以下我們整理了幾組容易弄錯的單字,請聽光碟朗讀,選出句中出現的字。

字音

1. sell / sale

2. affected / effected

3. prospective / perspective

4. rise / raise

5. adapted / adopted

字義

6. share 市佔率 / 股份

7. display 顯示 / 陳列擺設

8. copy 影本 / 文案

9. promotion 升職 / 促銷

10. prospects 潛在客戶 / 前景展望

解答

1. These items will be on **sale** until next Friday.（特價銷售）
2. The recession has **affected** the restaurant chain's expansion plans.（影響）
3. The company is looking for new ways to attract **prospective** clients.（潛在的）
4. If we want to keep making a profit, we need to **raise** prices.（提高）
5. Sales have risen 15% since the store **adopted** a new marketing plan.（採用）
6. The firm's market **share** has fallen over the past year.（市佔率）
7. The clothing store changes its window **display** each season.（陳列擺設）
8. Jim Peters in Marketing is responsible for ad **copy**.（文案）
9. The sales manager hopes to get a **promotion** this year.（升職）
10. The company is optimistic about its **prospects** for the coming year.（前景展望）

單字聽讀力 | 聽懂 [dr]、[dʒ] 的發音

MP3-143

教學說明：

[dr] 由 [d] 和 [r] 兩個子音組成，須連在一起快速發出，後方通常會跟著一個母音，常見的拼字即為 dr。[dʒ] 的發音是從嘴巴送出氣體，同時會振動聲帶。拼寫方式可能是 j、g、ge 或 dge。

現在就讓我們來聽聽正確的發音，並且跟著大聲念出來吧。

[dr]	drip	draw	drool	address	withdraw
[dʒ]	gyp	jaw	jewel	edge	page

辨音測驗：

MP3-144

經過了剛才的發音練習，現在讓我們做個辨音小測驗，看看是不是聽懂更多了呢？請聽光碟播放的句子，並圈出正確的單字。

1. drunk / junk

2. drain / Jane

3. drugs / jugs

4. drudge / judge

解答

1. Someone is coming to pick up the (junk).
2. I think something is wrong with our (drain).
3. That company manufactures (drugs).
4. Andrew doesn't want to work as a (judge) anymore.

句子聽讀力 | 縮寫字的發音

教學說明：
來聽聽「代名詞和助動詞的縮寫」（I'm/She's/He's/They're...）在句中的發音會是什麼狀況。

代名詞＋助動詞的縮寫：
在一般情況下，句中的代名詞通常不是重音所在。例如：

- They read my book.
- He loves his job.
- Have you seen his paintings?
- We know his brother.

代名詞（I/you/she/he...）和助動詞（am/is/are/will/would...）縮寫以後，在句中就成了一個音節單位，而且由於代名詞的關係，這個音節不是重音所在，在聽的時候容易被忽略而沒抓到相關重點。例如：

- I'll ask him.
- He's my best friend.
- I don't think they're coming.
- We'll be there at seven.

雖然代名詞及其縮寫形式在句中通常不是重音所在，但說話者也可以視情況加重這些字，表示強調或對比。例如以下對話：

A: I'm gonna win.
B: No, I'm gonna win.

A: I think you're dumb.
B: I'm not dumb. You're dumb!

A: He's the best student in the class.
B: No, she's the best student in the class.

A: Why don't you take out the trash?
B: Mom asked you to take out the trash, not me.

聽力小測驗：
請聽光碟播放的句子，套色字（代名詞）若是重音請圈出。

MP3-146

1. A: I think I'm the smartest one in our family.

   B: No way. I'm the smartest.

2. A: Aren't you good at math?

   B: No, you're the one who's good at math.

   A: I suppose you're right.

3. A: Is this pen mine?

   B: No, it's mine. That one is yours.

4. A: Is that your brother over there?

   B: You mean that guy? The one in the leather jacket?

   A: Not that guy, the one standing next to him.

解答

1. A: I think I'm the smartest one in our family.

   B: No way. (I'm) the smartest.

2. A: Aren't you good at math?

   B: No, (you're) the one who's good at math.

   A: I suppose you're right.

3. A: Is this pen mine?

   B: No, it's (mine). (That) one is yours.

4. A: Is that your brother over there?

   B: You mean (that) guy? The one in the leather jacket?

   A: Not (that) guy, the one standing next to him.

多益聽力實戰

PART 01 PHOTOGRAPHS 照片描述

MP3-147

請看圖片並聽光碟朗讀圖 1 ～ 4 的四段敘述，選出與圖片最相符的敘述。

1. _____

2. _____

3. _____

4. _____

PART 02 QUESTION-RESPONSE 應答問題

MP3-148

請聽光碟朗讀，並選出最適合的答案填在空格中。

1. _____   **2.** _____   **3.** _____   **4.** _____   **5.** _____

PART 03 簡短對話
CONVERSATION

請聽光碟朗讀從選項 A、B、C、D 中選出正確的答案。

____ **1.** **How many stores does Gino's plan to have in five years?**
   A. 3
   B. 5
   C. 6
   D. 8

____ **2.** **What is the objective of the marketing plan?**
   A. To switch to all-fresh ingredients
   B. To become the biggest chain in the county
   C. To advertise using direct mail and radio ads
   D. To remodel Gino's existing restaurants

____ **3.** **When will evaluation of the plan begin?**
   A. At the start of next year
   B. In two months' time
   C. At the end of this year
   D. In two years' time

PART 04 簡短獨白
SHORT TALK

請聽光碟朗讀，並根據內容回答以下題目。

____ **1.** **Who is probably listening to this talk?**
   A. Automobile buyers
   B. Sales personnel
   C. Customers
   D. Competitors

____ **2.** **Where will the listeners be this afternoon?**
   A. On the freeway
   B. In a showroom
   C. At home
   D. In a seminar

____ **3.** **What will be discussed in detail?**
   A. Which cars have more features
   B. What the key to making a sale is
   C. What makes their cars better
   D. How to be more convincing

PART 01 照片描述 PHOTOGRAPHS

1. **B**   A. The bookstore is having a big sale today.
今天書店大特價。
   B. There are many books for sale at the book fair.
書展上買得到很多書。
   C. These sales clearks are selling books.
這些店員在賣書。
   D. The public library is quite crowded today.
今天公共圖書館人很多。

2. **A**   A. The salesman is showing the car to a prospective buyer.
業務員把車展示給想買的顧客。
   B. The man is getting his automobile repaired at the garage.
這男人把車子帶到車行維修。
   C. The driver is getting his tank filled at the gas station.
駕駛在加油站加油。
   D. The attendant is parking the man's car in the parking lot.
泊車員正在把那位先生的車停到停車場。

3. **C**   A. Fashions for the new season are on display.
新一季的流行服飾正在展示。
   B. The women are shopping for clothes at the sale.
這些婦女正在特賣會購買衣物。
   C. A sale is being advertised in the window display.
櫥窗裡秀出特賣會的廣告。
   D. The men's fashion store is having a sale.
男服飾店正在舉行特賣。

4. **C**   A. The company is raising prices.
公司要提高售價。
   B. The company is losing market share.
公司的市佔率正在流失。
   C. The company's sales are rising.
公司的營業額正在提昇。
   D. The firm's suppliers are raising their prices.
公司的供應商正在提高售價。

PART 02 應答問題 QUESTION-RESPONSE

1. B Q: Have you finished writing the ad copy yet?
你的廣告文案寫完了嗎？
A. No. The copier isn't working.
沒有。影印機壞了。
B. Yes. Would you like to read it?
是的。你要讀一下嗎？
C. I can make copies if you like.
如果你要，我可以影印幾份。

2. C Q: Are you developing any new sales prospects?
你有在開發新的客戶嗎？
A. No. We're satisfied with our current sales strategy.
沒有。我們對目前的銷售策略很滿意。
B. Yes. Sales prospects are good.
對的。銷售前景很看好。
C. Yes. I'm in contact with several potential clients.
有的。我正與幾個可能的客戶聯絡。

3. A Q: Can't we raise money by selling more shares?
我們不能釋出更多股份來募集資金嗎？
A. Yes. That's one way to fund our expansion.
可以。這是我們募資擴展生意的方法之一。
B. Yes. A higher share of the market means higher profits.
可以。較高市佔率代表較高獲利。
C. No. We're losing market share to the competition.
不能。我們的市佔率正一步步被競爭對手搶走。

4. B Q: Have you seen the new sales projections?
你有看到新的銷量預估嗎？
A. Which sales project are you talking about?
你在講哪一個銷售計畫？
B. Yes. They seem too optimistic to me.
有的。在我看來似乎太樂觀了。
C. No. The projector is broken.
沒有。投影機壞掉了。

5. A Q: Was the promotion at your store successful?
你店裡的促銷活動順利嗎？
A. Yes. Sales increased by nearly 30%.
是的。業績成長了將近百分之三十。
B. Yes. I was promoted to a management position.
是的。我升到了主管的職位。
C. Yes. The grand opening is next week.
是的。下星期舉行開幕儀式。

PART 03 簡短對話 CONVERSATION

M: Could you tell me a little bit about your new marketing plan?
可以稍微跟我談一談你新的行銷計畫嗎？

W: Sure. Gino's pizza is one of the most popular pizza chains in Springfield, but our goal is to become the largest chain in the entire county within five years.
好的。季諾比薩店是春田市最受歡迎的比薩連鎖店之一，但我們的目標是在五年內成為郡內最大的比薩連鎖店。

M: I see. And how do you plan to achieve that?
了解。那你打算要怎麼達到目標？

W: We're going to remodel our existing three stores, switch to using all-fresh ingredients to create word of mouth, and expand by opening one new store per year.
我們要翻修我們現有的三個店面，改成全面採用新鮮食材，讓我們的店能被口耳相傳，並以每年一間新店面的速度來擴充。

M: OK. What about advertising?
嗯。那廣告宣傳呢？

W: Our advertising efforts will focus on direct mail and radio ads to keep costs low.
我們重點會放在傳單和電台廣告上來降低宣傳成本。

M: Great idea. And when are you going to launch the plan?
好主意。那你什麼時候要開始進行這個計畫？

W: The plan will be implemented in two months, and the first evaluation will be held early next year.
這計畫兩個月內會開始施行，明年初做第一次實施情況評估。

1. **D** Q: 照季諾的計畫五年內會有幾家店？
   A. 3   C. 6
   B. 5   D. 8

2. **B** Q: 行銷計畫的目標為何？
   A. 改成全面採用新鮮食材   C. 用廣告信和電台廣告宣傳
   B. 成為郡內最大的連鎖店   D. 翻修季諾現有的餐廳

3. **A** Q: 什麼時候會開始評估實施情況？
   A. 明年初   C. 今年底
   B. 兩個月內   D. 兩年內

PART 04 簡短獨白 SHORT TALK

What is the key to making a sale? We need to understand what customers need and determine which cars are best suited to their needs. In addition, we need to convince them that our cars are better than those of our competitors. But how do we do that? What features do our cars have that our competitors' cars don't? We'll be discussing this in detail in the seminar later this afternoon. But that will just be the beginning. After work, I want you to keep thinking about how to get potential buyers interested in our cars, whether you're driving on the freeway or at home having dinner with your family. That way, when you're talking to customers in the showroom, you'll be more confident and convincing.

達成交易的關鍵是什麼？我們必須理解顧客的需求，並決定哪一輛車最符合他們的需要。另外，我們必須說服他們，我們的汽車比同行的要好。但這要怎麼做呢？我們的車有什麼功能是我們的競爭者沒有的？我們會在下午的講習中詳細討論這點。但這只是個起頭。我要你們在下班後持續思考，怎麼樣才能吸引潛在顧客對我們的汽車感興趣，無論是在公路上開車，或是在家與家人吃晚餐的時候。如此一來，你在展售中心與顧客說話時，就會更有自信也更具說服力。

1. **B** Q: 聽這段演說的人可能是誰？
A. 買車的人
B. 業務人員
C. 顧客
D. 競爭對手

2. **D** Q: 聽眾下午會在哪裡？
A. 高速公路上
B. 展售中心
C. 家裡
D. 講座會中

3. **C** Q: 什麼事情會被詳細討論？
A. 哪些車的功能較多
B. 達成交易的關鍵點
C. 他們的車比較好的地方
D. 如何更具說服力

CHAPTER 16
求職面試篇

教學重點

⊙ 求職面試重點單字
⊙ 易混淆字：perfection / profession
⊙ [h]、[f] 的發音
⊙ 助動詞的重音

多益實戰

⊙ Part 1 照片描述
⊙ Part 2 應答問題
⊙ Part 3 簡短對話
⊙ Part 4 獨白對話

主題字彙與發音

聽聽看這些單字的正確發音，並比較英美腔調的不同。

recruit (v.) 招募
[rɪ`krut]

apply (v.) 應徵，應試
[ə`plaɪ]

interview (n.) 面談
[`ɪntɚvju]

hire (v.) 雇用
[haɪr]

fire (v.) 解雇
[faɪr]

candidate (n.) 面試者；候選人
[`kændədet]

accomplishment (n.) 成就
[ə`kamplɪʃmənt]

reject (v.) 拒絕，回絕
[rɪ`dʒɛkt]

personnel (n.) 人事
[ˌpɝsə`nɛl]

experienced (a.) 有經驗的
[ɪk`spɪrɪənst]

résumé (n.) 履歷
[`rɛzəme]

income (n.) 收入
[`ɪnˌkʌm]

bonus (n.) 獎金；紅利
[`bonəs]

offer (n.) 工作機會
[`ɔfɚ]

recommendation (n.) 推薦
[ˌrɛkəmən`deʃən]

career (n.) 生涯
[kə`rir]

diploma (n.) 學歷
[dɪ`plomə]

application (n.) 應試
[æplə`keʃən]

competent (a.) 能勝任的，稱職的
[`kampətənt]

expectation (n.) 期望；預期
[ˌɛkspɛk`teʃən]

主題易混淆字

聽力上也常會遇到的一個問題，就是有些字的發音非常相近，
在聽的時候，如果沒有整合前後文內容，很容易就聽錯。
以下我們整理了幾組容易弄錯的單字，請聽光碟朗讀，選出句中出現的字。

字音

1. personnel / personal

2. competent / confident

3. celery / salary

4. perfection / profession

5. hire / fire

6. formal / former

字義

7. interview 面談 / 採訪

8. classified 機密的 / 分類的

9. communication 溝通 / 通訊

10. benefits 好處 / 福利

解答

1. Our **personnel** manager will make the final decision about your application.（人事）
2. We're looking to hire experienced, **confident** sales reps.（有自信的）
3. Margaret is looking for a better **salary** package.（薪資）
4. At our firm, we demand **perfection** from our employees.（盡善盡美）
5. It is illegal to **hire** employees based on their race or sex.（雇用）
6. Make sure to list all your **former** jobs on your résumé.（先前的）
7. I had an **interview** for a job as a reporter.（面試）
8. I found out about the position from your **classified** ad.（分類的）
9. Members of our engineering team must possess strong **communication** skills.（溝通）
10. Our company offers excellent **benefits**.（福利）

單字聽讀力 | 聽懂 [h]、[f] 的發音

MP3-153

教學說明：

主題單字中，「hire」、「fire」，你知道如何正確發音嗎？[h] 是無聲子音，發音時雙唇微開，自然將氣從喉間送出。常見的拼字是 h，有時候 wh 也發這個音。[f] 也是一個無聲子音，和 [h] 音相似。和 [h] 不同的地方是發音的嘴型，發 [f] 時上排牙齒輕咬下唇，發音時自然將氣送出。常見的拼字有 f、ff、ph 和 gh。

現在就讓我們來聽聽正確的發音，並且跟著大聲念出來吧。

[h]　horse　hire　ahead　behave　who
[f]　force　fire　taffy　photo　laugh

辨音測驗：

MP3-154

經過了剛才的發音練習，現在讓我們做個辨音小測驗，看看是不是聽懂更多了呢？請聽光碟播放的句子，並圈出句中出現的單字。

1. hold / fold

2. hired / fired

3. hair / fair

4. hear / fear

5. heat / feet

解答

1. Please do not cut, (fold) or staple this form.

2. How many employees were (hired) last year?

3. Male employees are expected to keep their (hair) short.

4. You need to speak louder so everyone can (hear) you.

5. Exposure to (heat) may damage your laptop.

句子聽讀力 | 助動詞的重音

MP3-155

教學說明：

助動詞是英文句子的重要元素，在否定句和疑問句中一定有助動詞，而且還有為數不少的情態助動詞，因此掌握其重音對於聽力理解很重要。

在一般情況下，疑問句中的助動詞通常不讀重音。例如：

- What do you think?
- Why did he leave?
- Where has she been?
- Who does he like?

在一般情況下，否定句中的助動詞和 not 縮寫時，為了強調否定意涵，通常要讀重音。例如：

- He won't say.
- She doesn't know.
- I can't help you.
- We haven't eaten yet.
- They wouldn't come.

如果助動詞在句尾（通常是簡答句），通常讀重音；或者是用來表示強調或對比時也會讀重音。例如：

- Yes, I do.（簡答句，助動詞在句尾）
- OK, I will.
- Sure, I can.
- He said he didn't go, but he did go.（用助動詞強調對比）
- She doesn't think I can swim, but I can swim.

聽力小測驗：

MP3-156

請聽光碟播放的句子，套色字助動詞若是重音請畫圈（○），非重音請畫叉（×）。

1. _____ What did you see?

2. _____ No way, I won't tell you that!

3. ____ Do I like steak? Yes, I do.

4. ____ How have you been lately?

5. ____ When does the movie start?

6. ____ If you can't come tomorrow, when can you come?

7. ____ I haven't had time to read the article.

解答

1. ✕   **2.** ◯   **3.** ◯   **4.** ✕

5. ✕   **6.** ◯   **7.** ◯

PART 01 PHOTOGRAPHS 照片描述

請看圖片並聽光碟朗讀圖 1 ～ 4 的四段敘述，選出與圖片最相符的敘述。

1. _____

2. _____

3. _____

4. _____

PART 02 QUESTION-RESPONSE 應答問題

請聽光碟朗讀，並選出最適合的答案填在空格中。

1. _____ **2.** _____ **3.** _____ **4.** _____ **5.** _____

PART 03 簡短對話
CONVERSATION

MP3-159

請聽光碟朗讀從選項 A、B、C、D 中選出正確的答案。

_____ **1.** **Why does the man call the woman?**
A. To offer her a job
B. To ask her out on a date
C. To tell her when to start work
D. To set up an interview

_____ **2.** **How did the man and woman meet?**
A. At work
B. At a job interview
C. At a conference
D. At a trade show

_____ **3.** **When will the man and woman meet next?**
A. Tuesday at 2:30
B. Thursday at 10:30
C. Tuesday at 10:30
D. Thursday at 2:30

PART 04 簡短獨白
SHORT TALK

MP3-160

請聽光碟朗讀,並根據內容回答以下題目。

_____ **1.** **What are job applicants required to provide?**
A. Their past salaries
B. Samples of their work
C. Recommendation letters
D. A copy of their diploma

_____ **2.** **What must applicants include in their résumés?**
A. Their grade point average
B. Their long-term career goals
C. Their career attainments
D. Their university major

_____ **3.** **Who should apply for the positions being offered?**
A. Designers
B. Engineers
C. Managers
D. Scientists

PART 01 照片描述 PHOTOGRAPHS

1. D　A. The woman is decorating her apartment.
　　　那位女士在布置她的公寓。
　　B. The mover is helping someone move.
　　　搬家工人在幫人搬家。
　　C. The woman has probably just been hired.
　　　那位女士大概剛被錄用。
　　D. The woman has probably just been fired.
　　　那位女士大概剛被解雇。

2. B　A. The reporter is interviewing the woman.
　　　記者在訪問那位女士。
　　B. The man is wearing formal clothes to his job interview.
　　　那位男士穿著正式服裝參加工作面試。
　　C. The interviewer is asking the man about his former job.
　　　面試官在問那位男士以前做過的工作。
　　D. The interviewer is wearing a formal suit.
　　　面試官穿著正式西裝。

3. C　A. The woman is examining classified documents.
　　　那位女士在檢查機密文件。
　　B. The woman is enjoying the Sunday paper.
　　　那位女士在享受讀星期天日報的樂趣。
　　C. The woman is looking for a job in the classified ads.
　　　那位女士在分類廣告中找工作。
　　D. The secretary is reading a magazine on her break.
　　　祕書正利用休息時間看雜誌。

4. B　A. The interviewer is reading the man's résumé.
　　　面試官在讀那位男士的履歷。
　　B. The man is filling out a job application.
　　　那位男士在填寫工作申請表格。
　　C. The couple is writing their grocery list.
　　　那對夫妻在寫他們的購物清單。
　　D. The waiter is taking the customer's order.
　　　服務生正為顧客點餐。

PART 02 應答問題 QUESTION-RESPONSE

1. **B** Q: What are your salary expectations?
你期望的待遇是多少？
A. Yes, I expect to receive a salary.
是的，我期待拿到薪水。
B. It depends on what the position involves.
要看這份工作要做些什麼。
C. This is exactly the salary I was expecting.
這正是我期待的薪資待遇。

2. **C** Q: Are you willing to work overtime?
你願意加班嗎？
A. I always work overtime.
我總是加班。
B. I'm looking for a full-time position.
我要找份全職工作
C. Yes, if necessary.
可以的，如果有必要的話。

3. **A** Q: Where do you see yourself in 10 years?
你期望十年後的生涯發展是什麼樣子？
A. I hope to be in a management position.
我希望做到管理職。
B. I'll still be living in the same place.
我仍然會住在同樣的地方。
C. I've accomplished a lot in that time.
我那段時間完成了很多事情。

4. **A** Q: What benefits does your company offer?
你們公司提供什麼福利？
A. We provide medical and dental insurance.
我們提供一般醫療保險和牙齒保險。
B. Our company is very profitable.
我們公司很賺錢。
C. We offer high salaries to our employees.
我們提供高薪給員工。

5. **C** Q: Would you be willing to relocate?
你會願意調到其他地方工作嗎？
A. Sure, I don't mind commuting.
可以，我不介意通勤。
B. Actually, I live pretty close to the office.
其實，我住得離公司很近。
C. Yes, but not overseas.
可以，但不要到海外。

PART 03 簡短對話 CONVERSATION

M: Hello, Sandra Libby?
　　妳好，是珊卓拉麗比嗎？

W: Yes, this is Sandra.
　　對，我是珊卓拉。

M: Hi, this is Bob Miller at Gordon & Miller.
　　嗨，我是高登米勒事務所的鮑伯米勒。

W: Hi, Mr. Miller. How are you?
　　嗨，米勒先生。你好嗎？

M: I'm fine. I'm just calling to tell you that you're one of three candidates we're considering for the position, and we'd like you to come in for another interview on Tuesday at 10:30.
　　很好。我是打來告訴妳，妳是我們這個職缺考慮中的三位人選之一，我們想請妳來參加另一次面試，在星期二十點半。

M: That's great news! I'll be there.
　　太好了！我會去。

1. **D** 　Q: 為什麼那位先生要打給那位女士？
　　　A. 要給她一份工作
　　　B. 要和她約會
　　　C. 要告訴她什麼時候開始上班
　　　D. 要敲定一場面試

2. **B** 　Q: 那位先生和那位女士是怎麼認識的？
　　　A. 在工作上
　　　B. 在工作面試中
　　　C. 在會議中
　　　D. 在商展中

3. **C** 　Q: 那位先生和那位女士是怎麼認識的？
　　　A. 星期二下午兩點半
　　　B. 星期四上午十點半
　　　C. 星期二上午十點半
　　　D. 星期四下午兩點半

PART 04 簡短獨白 SHORT TALK

All job applicants should submit a cover letter, résumé, salary requirements and portfolio samples. In your cover letter, be sure to talk about your long-term professional goals. Your résumé should list all relevant work experience, starting with your most recent job, as well as specific achievements in your career and highest academic degree attained. We are currently hiring for entry-level positions in our graphic design department, and offer competitive salaries with a full benefits package. For prompt consideration, please submit your application materials through our corporate website by November 30th.

所有應徵者都必須繳交一份求職信、履歷、期望待遇和作品集。在求職信中,務必要列出你的長期生涯目標。你的履歷要列出所有相關工作經驗,從最近一份工作開始列,還要寫出工作生涯中的具體成就以及最高學歷。我們的平面設計部門目前有基層職務的空缺,會提供優渥的薪水和全套福利。為便於即時回覆,請在十一月三十日前透過本公司網站繳交你的應徵資料。

1. B Q: 應徵者必須提供什麼?
A. 以前的薪資
B. 工作成果樣品
C. 推薦信
D. 文憑的影本

2. C Q: 應徵者的履歷要包含什麼資料?
A. 學科平均成績
B. 長期事業目標
C. 工作成就
D. 大學主修科目

3. A Q: 誰應該應徵這家公司提供的職缺?
A. 設計師
B. 工程師
C. 經理
D. 科學家

教學重點

- ⊙ 薪資升遷重點單字
- ⊙ 易混淆字：access / assess
- ⊙ 英美口音比較 [æ] [ɑ]
- ⊙ 英美腔比較：字尾不同的發音

多益實戰

- ⊙ Part 1 照片描述
- ⊙ Part 2 應答問題
- ⊙ Part 3 簡短對話
- ⊙ Part 4 獨白對話

主題字彙與發音

聽聽看這些單字的正確發音，並比較英美腔調的不同。

salary (n.) 薪資
[ˋsæləri]

position (n.) 職位
[pəˋzɪʃən]

promotion (n.) 升遷
[prəˋmoʃən]

demotion (n.) 降職
[dɪˋmoʃən]

review (n.) 考績
[rɪˋvju]

health insurance (n.) 健保
[hɛθ ɪnˋʃurəns]

assess (v.) 評估
[əˋsɛs]

bottleneck (n.) 瓶頸
[ˋbatəlˌnɛk]

compensation (n.) 薪酬
[ˌkɑmpənˋseʃən]

improve (v.) 改善
[ɪmˋpruv]

commission (n.) 佣金
[kəˋmɪʃən]

assurance (n.) 保證
[əˋʃurəns]

asset (n.) 寶貴人才
[ˋæsɛt]

resign (v.) 辭職
[rɪˋzaɪn]

benefit (n.) 公司福利
[ˋbɛnəfɪt]

suggestion (n.) 建議
[səˋdʒstʃən]

retirement (n.) 退休
[rɪˋtaɪrmənt]

frustrated (a.) 挫折的，失意的
[ˋfrʌstretɪd]

performance (n.) 表現
[pɝˋfɔrməns]

afford (v.) 有能力負擔……
[əˋford]

主題易混淆字

聽力上也常會遇到的一個問題，就是有些字的發音非常相近，
在聽的時候，如果沒有整合前後文內容，很容易就聽錯。
以下我們整理了幾組容易弄錯的單字，請聽光碟朗讀，選出句中出現的字。

字音

1. rise / raise

2. salary / celery

3. promotion / demotion

4. review / preview

5. access / assess

字義

6. compensation 薪酬 / 賠償

7. commission 委員會 / 佣金

8. asset 財產 / 寶貴人才

9. tips 小費 / 建議

10. benefits 公司福利 / 好處

解答

1. The boss promised he would give me a **raise**.（加薪）
2. Are you satisfied with your **salary**?（薪水）
3. I'm going to quit if I don't get the **promotion**.（升遷）
4. The results of your **review** will determine whether you receive a bonus.（考績）
5. The test is used to **assess** employees' management potential.（評估）
6. Employees at that company receive excellent **compensation**.（薪資待遇）
7. Most salespeople work on **commission**.（佣金）
8. The marketing manager is a real **asset** to the organization.（寶貴人才）
9. I can give you some **tips** if you like.（建議）
10. The position offers excellent pay and **benefits**.（福利）

單字聽讀力 | 英美口音比較 [æ]、[ɑ]

MP3-163

教學說明：

在一般的情況下，美式口音中的 [æ] 在英式口音也唸相同的音。一般來說若 [æ] 後面的子音為 [f] [θ] [s] [nt] [ns] [ntʃ] [nd] [mpl]，則在英式口音中常唸成 [ɑ]，但仍有例外。

現在就讓我們來聽聽正確的發音，並且跟著大聲念出來吧。

[æ]	rat	flag	back	catch	sang
美腔唸 [æ] 英腔唸 [ɑ]	can't	path	laugh	branch	sample

例：Please put your hat on the rack.

例：When should we pla<u>nt</u> the gra<u>ss</u>?

辨音測驗：

MP3-164

經過了剛才的發音練習，現在讓我們做個辨音小測驗，看看是不是聽懂更多了呢？請聽光碟播放的句子，並寫出句中出現的單字。

1. Can I _____ you a question?

2. I don't understand your _____.

3. It's time to give the dog a _____.

4. Would you like a _____ of wine?

5. I only ate _____ of the sandwich.

解答

1. ask

2. example

3. bath

4. glass

5. half

句子聽讀力 | 英美腔比較：字尾不同的發音

教學說明：

● **以 -ate 和 -atory 結尾的單字**

大多數以 -ate 結尾的兩音節單字，美式發音中重音置前；英式發音重音在後。

兩音節：-ate donate　pulsate　migrate　rotate　translate

如果 -ate 結尾的單字為三個音節以上，則英美重音相同。

多音節：-ate demonstrate　calculate　accelerate

如果將單字拉長，變成以 - atory 結尾的形容詞，英美式的重音都會不固定，請聽以下生字：

重音不同 → circulatory　inflammatory　discriminatory

重音相同 → regulatory　celebratory　participatory

● **以 -ary -ery –ory 結尾的單字**

單字的重音不在這些字根的前面一個音節時，美式發音中，字根大多會唸成兩個音節，且母音的唸法各有不同；但在英式發音中常只發一個音節 [ri]，或是唸成 [əri]。

cemetery　military　category　hereditary

聽力小測驗：

請聽光碟播放的句子，並寫出空格中的單字。

1. Michael _____ some of his old clothes to charity.

2. I set my phone to _____ during the movie.

3. The manager _____ a letter to his secretary.

4. People like him really _____ me.

5. Our office is _____ in the downtown area.

解答

1. donated
2. vibrate
3. dictated
4. frustrate
5. located

多益聽力實戰

PART 01 PHOTOGRAPHS 照片描述

MP3-167

請看圖片並聽光碟朗讀圖 1 ～ 4 的四段敘述，選出與圖片最相符的敘述。

1. _____

2. _____

3. _____

4. _____

PART 02 QUESTION-RESPONSE 應答問題

MP3-168

請聽光碟朗讀，並選出最適合的答案填在空格中。

1. _____　　**2.** _____　　**3.** _____　　**4.** _____　　**5.** _____

請聽光碟朗讀從選項 A、B、C、D 中選出正確的答案。

____ **1.** **Why is the man depressed?**
A. Because there's no room for advancement at his company
B. Because he doesn't like his job
C. Because he doesn't make enough money
D. Because he makes less money than his co-workers

____ **2.** **How often are raises given at his company?**
A. Once a year
B. Twice a year
C. Once every two years
D. Every six months

____ **3.** **What does the woman suggest?**
A. That the man ask his company for a raise
B. That the man ask his boss for a promotion
C. That the man ask his company for better benefits
D. That the man find a job at another company

PART 04 簡短獨白
SHORT TALK

請聽光碟朗讀，並根據內容回答以下題目。

____ **1.** **Who is the audience for this talk?**
A. Executives
B. Students
C. Employees
D. Customers

____ **2.** **What size are annual raises?**
A. 2%
B. 3%
C. 5%
D. 10%

____ **3.** **What benefit is not provided to all full-time employees?**
A. Bonuses
B. Retirement plan
C. Paid vacation
D. Health Insurance

解答與解析

PART 01 照片描述 PHOTOGRAPHS

1. B A. There's a paycheck on the table.
桌上有一張薪資支票。
B. Someone has left the waiter a tip.
有人留小費給服務生。
C. Someone has received a bonus.
有人得到獎金。
D. Today is payday at the restaurant.
今天是餐廳的發薪日。

2. C A. The standing man is firing the other man.
站著的男人把另一個男人炒魷魚。
B. The man in front of the desk is handing in a report.
站在桌前的男人正在交報告。
C. The man in front of the desk is being demoted.
站在桌前的男人被貶職了。
D. The man in front of the desk is being promoted.
站在桌前的男人升官了。

3. A A. The woman is conducting a performance review.
那位女人正在考核績效。
B. The man is conducting a performance review.
那位男人正在考核績效。
C. The woman is conducting a performance preview.
那位女人正在預檢績效。（編註：主管針對部屬來年的目標提出指導，有別於事後檢討的 performance review）
D. The students are reviewing for an exam.
學生們正在做考前複習。

4. D A. The students got high scores on the exam.
學生們考試得了高分。
B. The woman is satisfied with her benefits.
那位女人對她的福利很滿意。
C. The woman is angry she didn't get a promotion.
那位女人很氣她沒有獲得升遷。
D. The woman is excited about her raise.
那位女人很興奮她加薪了。

PART 02　應答問題 QUESTION-RESPONSE

1. **A**　Q: Are you paid on a commission basis?
　　　　你賺的是佣金嗎？
　　　　A. No. I'm paid by the hour.
　　　　　不。我賺的是時薪。
　　　　B. Yes. You'll receive a 5% commission.
　　　　　對。你可以抽成百分之五。
　　　　C. Yes. The committee pays my salary.
　　　　　對。我的薪水是委員會付的。

2. **B**　Q: Caroline is an asset to the department.
　　　　卡蘿琳是這部門的寶貴人才。
　　　　A. I didn't realize she was so wealthy.
　　　　　我不知道她這麼富有。
　　　　B. Yes. She's a valuable employee.
　　　　　對。她是很珍貴的員工。
　　　　C. I didn't know she owned the department.
　　　　　我不知道這部門是她的。

3. **B**　Q: Are there any benefits to working the night shift?
　　　　值夜班有什麼好處嗎？
　　　　A. Medical and dental insurance.
　　　　　醫療和牙醫保險。
　　　　B. I don't have to drive in rush-hour traffic.
　　　　　我不必在交通尖鋒時間開車。
　　　　C. No. I like working at night.
　　　　　不。我喜歡在晚上工作。

4. **C**　Q: Why are you getting demoted?
　　　　你為什麼被貶職？
　　　　A. Because I'm the top salesman in my department.
　　　　　因為我是部門裡的頂尖業務員。
　　　　B. Because the company can't afford to give me a raise.
　　　　　因為公司沒錢替我加薪。
　　　　C. My supervisor isn't satisfied with my performance.
　　　　　我的主管不滿意我的表現。

5. **C**　Q: When was the last time you got a raise?
　　　　你上次加薪是什麼時候？
　　　　A. Yes. I got a raise in January.
　　　　　對。我一月時有加薪。
　　　　B. We can't afford to give you a raise.
　　　　　我們沒錢替你加薪。
　　　　C. It's been nearly two years.
　　　　　將近兩年前了

PART 03 簡短對話 CONVERSATION

W: You look depressed, honey. What's wrong?
老公，你看起來很沮喪耶。怎麼了？

M: It's the end of the month again, and we can't afford to pay our bills.
又到月底了，我們沒錢繳帳單。

W: Didn't you get a raise six months ago?
你六個月前不是加薪了嗎？

M: It was really small—and it's a long time till my next annual raise.
只有加一點一而且離我下次的年度加薪還要好久。

W: Why not switch companies?
為什麼不換家公司上班？

M: In this economy? I'm lucky to have a job at all. Actually, there's a management opening in my department. My boss encouraged me to apply for it, and it offers better pay and benefits.
在經濟這麼差的時候？我有工作已經很幸運了。其實我們部門有一個管理職缺，我的老闆鼓勵我應徵，薪水跟福利都比較好。

1. `C` Q: 為什麼那位男人心情不好？
A. 因為他在公司裡沒有發展空間
B. 因為他不喜歡他的工作
C. 因為他賺的錢不夠多
D. 因為他賺的錢比同事少

2. `A` Q: 他的公司多久調薪一次？
A. 一年一次
B. 一年兩次
C. 兩年一次
D. 六個月一次

3. `D` Q: 那位女人給了什麼建議？
A. 要那位男人要求公司加薪
B. 要那位男人要求老闆升他的官
C. 要那位男人向公司要求更好的福利
D. 要那位男人找別家公司的工作

PART 04　簡短獨白 SHORT TALK

Next on the agenda today is compensation and benefits. Starting salaries for each position are determined by the personnel department, and annual raises are calculated at 2% above the average inflation rate, which is set at 3%. In addition, Christmas bonuses are given to outstanding employees when company profit goals are met. Unfortunately, due to the recession, there have been no bonuses for the last two years. However, we're confident that the situation will improve this year. Now, on to benefits. You all start with a week of paid vacation, and receive an additional day for each year of service. And everyone with two years of service is eligible for the retirement plan. We also provide health insurance for all full-time employees. If you have any questions, please contact the personnel department.

今天接下來的議程,是薪資待遇及福利。每個職位的起薪由人事部門決定,年度調薪是根據平均通貨膨脹率加 2%,通貨膨脹率設在 3%。另外,耶誕節獎金會頒給傑出員工,只要公司的獲利目標有達成。很不幸地,因為景氣衰退,前兩年都沒有獎金。儘管如此,我們有信心今年的情況會改善。現在來談談福利。你們一開始都有一個星期的給薪假,每工作一年就多一天。工作兩年以上的員工,就有資格加入退休金計畫。我們也提供健康保險給所有全職員工。如果你們有什麼問題,請與人事部門聯絡。

1. C　Q: 這段話講給誰聽?
　　　A. 高階主管
　　　B. 學生
　　　C. 員工
　　　D. 客戶

2. C　Q: 每年調薪幅度多少?
　　　A. 2%
　　　B. 3%
　　　C. 5%
　　　D. 10%

3. B　Q: 哪一項福利不是所有全職員工都有?
　　　A. 獎金
　　　B. 退休金計畫
　　　C. 給薪假
　　　D. 健康保險

CHAPTER 18
居家生活篇

教學重點

⊙ 居家生活重點單字
⊙ 易混淆字：ladder / latter
⊙ [aʊ] 和 [ɔɪ] 的發音
⊙ 連音技巧：「and」、「of」的發音

多益實戰

⊙ Part 1 照片描述
⊙ Part 2 應答問題
⊙ Part 3 簡短對話
⊙ Part 4 獨白對話

主題字彙與發音

聽聽看這些單字的正確發音，並比較英美腔調的不同。

chair (n.) 椅子
[tʃɛr]

couch (n.) 沙發
[kaʊtʃ]

mattress (n.) 床墊
[`mætrɪs]

wardrobe (n.) 衣櫃
[`wɔrd‚rob]

pillow (n.) 枕頭
[`pɪlo]

lamp (n.) 檯燈
[læmp]

quilt (n.) 棉被
[kwɪlt]

curtain (n.) 窗簾
[`kɝtən]

sheet (n.) 床單
[ʃit]

table (n.) 桌子
[`tebəl]

sink (n.) 水槽
[sɪnk]

stove (n.)（瓦斯）爐
[stov]

pot (n.) 湯鍋
[pɑt]

cupboard (n.) 櫥櫃
[`kʌbəd]

bowl (n.) 碗
[bol]

plate (n.) 盤子
[plet]

faucet (n.) 水龍頭
[`fɔsɪt]

counter (n.) 流理台
[`kaʊntə]

refrigerator (n.) 冰箱
[rɪ`frɪdʒə‚retə]

glass (n.) 玻璃杯
[glæs]

主題易混淆字

MP3-172

聽力上也常會遇到的一個問題，就是有些字的發音非常相近，
在聽的時候，如果沒有整合前後文內容，很容易就聽錯。
以下我們整理了幾組容易弄錯的單字，請聽光碟朗讀，選出句中出現的字。

字音

1. lamp / ramp

2. couch / coach

3. ladder / latter

4. oven / often

5. removal / remover

字義

6. shade 窗簾 / 蔭涼處

7. wardrobe 衣櫃 /（整套）衣服

8. vacuum 真空 / 吸塵器

9. frame （相、畫）框 / 架子

10. iron 鐵質 / 熨斗

解答

1. There's a **ramp** for wheelchairs.（斜坡道）
2. The dog isn't allowed to sit on the **couch**.（沙發）
3. I need a **ladder** to change the light bulb.（梯子）
4. Do you use the kitchen **often**?（經常）
5. The stain **remover** is in the cupboard.（去漬劑）
6. If it gets too sunny, just sit in the **shade**.（陰涼處）
7. I added a few new shirts to my **wardrobe**.（整套衣服）
8. Did you empty the dust out of the **vacuum**?（吸塵器）
9. The house has a wooden **frame**.（房屋骨架）
10. You should take **iron** before meals.（鐵質）

單字聽讀力 | 聽懂 [aʊ] 和 [ɔɪ] 的發音

MP3-173

教學說明：

主題單字中，「couch」、「counter」，你知道如何正確發音嗎？講話時，[aʊ] 和 [ɔɪ] 是容易混淆的發音。如果不知道怎麼念對，就容易聽不懂。

現在就讓我們來聽聽正確的發音，並且跟著大聲念出來吧。

| [ɔɪ] | coin | noise | choice | employ | destroy |
| [aʊ] | now | town | ground | south | count |

辨音測驗：

MP3-174

經過了剛才的發音練習，現在讓我們做個辨音小測驗，看看是不是聽懂更多了呢？聽光碟朗讀並選出下列短文中 4 個含有 [ɔɪ]、4 個含有 [aʊ] 的單字。

I used to live downtown, but it was too noisy. It did have its good points, though. It was easy to get around, and there were lots of choices when it came to eating out. But it was just too loud, and I ended up moving to the suburbs. I enjoy living there much more.

[ɔɪ]：

[aʊ]：

解答

| [ɔɪ] | noisy | points | choices | enjoy | |
| [aʊ] | down | town | around | out | loud |

句子聽讀力 | 連音技巧：「and」、「of」的發音

教學說明：

在句子中的 and，通常都會被唸成 [ən] 或甚至只有 [n]，而不是 [ænd]。

比較：now and then

now and then
　　　 ╳

pen and ink

pen and ink
　　　 ╳

在句子中的 of 通常會被唸成 [əv]，而不是 [ɔf] 或 [ɑf]。

比較：I can't think of anything.

I can't think of anything.

Mom bought a bag of apples.

Mom bought a bag of apples

聽力小測驗：

綜合之前所學連音技巧，將需連音的地方標記。標記後，可做跟讀，練習句子連音技巧。

Jane: Alice told our boss I'm not a good worker.

Stuart: Why would she do that? You're a great worker.

Jane: Maybe she's out of her mind. No, I think she's jealous.

Stuart: So she told our boss that, did she? That's strange.

Jane: I'm so tired of her talking about me behind my back.

Stuart: Now that you mention it, some of us went out last Friday for a drink after work...

Jane: I was gonna go, but I was too busy that day.

Stuart: Anyway, Alice was there, and she said you were quitting. Is that true?

Jane: No! I've had enough. I don't know what to think of her anymore.

解 答

Jane: Alice told our boss I'm not a good worker.

Stuart: Why would she do that? You're a great worker.

Jane: Maybe she's out of her mind. No, I think she's jealous.
[sɑʊ tə vɚ]

Stuart: So she told our boss that, did she? That's strange.

Jane: I'm so tired of her talking about me behind my back.
[də vɚ]

Stuart: Now that you mention it, some of us went out last Friday for a
[tʃ]   [mə vʌs]

drink after work...

Jane: I was gonna go, but I was too busy that day.

Stuart: Anyway, Alice was there, and she said you were quitting. Is that true?
[ən]   [dʒ]

Jane: No! I've had enough. I don't know what to think of her anymore.
[kə vɚ]

多益聽力實戰

請看圖片並聽光碟朗讀圖 1 ～ 4 的四段敘述,選出與圖片最相符的敘述。

1. _____

2. _____

3. _____

4. _____

PART 02 QUESTION-RESPONSE 應答問題

請聽光碟朗讀,並選出最適合的答案填在空格中。

1. _____ **2.** _____ **3.** _____ **4.** _____ **5.** _____

PART 03 簡短對話
CONVERSATION

請聽光碟朗讀從選項 A、B、C、D 中選出正確的答案。

____ **1.** What kind of business does the man work for?
A. A manufacturing company
B. A repair company
C. A construction company
D. A real estate agency

____ **2.** According to the man, what does the woman need to do first?
A. Schedule the project
B. Get a permit
C. Have her roof replaced
D. Get an estimate

____ **3.** When did the woman think the project would begin?
A. Next month
B. Later in the week
C. The day after the estimate was made
D. Next week

PART 04 簡短獨白
SHORT TALK

請聽光碟朗讀，並根據內容回答以下題目。

____ **1.** What is the main thing being advertised?
A. Free refreshments
B. Real estate
C. Home furniture
D. Office furniture

____ **2.** When will the sale take place?
A. This weekend
B. Until August 31st
C. Next Saturday and Sunday
D. This Saturday

____ **3.** What does the speaker suggest that listeners do?
A. Hire a designer to help them choose furniture
B. Visit Bargain Basement Furniture
C. Browse the Bargain Basement Furniture website
D. Print out coupons for additional discounts

PART 01 照片描述 PHOTOGRAPHS

1. **B**　A. There are no shelves on the walls.
牆上沒有任何的架子。
B. There are two chairs in the room.
房裡有兩張椅子。
C. The room is quite messy.
房間滿髒亂的。
D. There is a couch in the living room.
客廳裡有一張沙發。

2. **C**　A. There are two onions on the counter.
流理台上有兩顆洋蔥。
B. The counter is empty.
流理台上是空的。
C. There is a plate under the bowl.
有個盤子在碗底下。
D. The meal is ready to eat.
這頓餐已經準備好可以吃了。

3. **D**　A. Nobody is sitting on the coaches.
沒有人坐在車廂上。
B. There is a big chair by the window.
窗戶旁邊有個大椅子。
C. There is a ramp in the room.
房間裡有個斜坡。
D. There are pillows on the couches.
沙發上有抱枕。

4. **B**　A. The appliance is made of iron.
這個器具是用鐵做的。
B. There's an iron on the ironing board.
熨燙板上有個熨斗。
C. There are clothes hanging in the wardrobe.
衣櫥裡有衣服掛著。
D. There's a small basket on the table.
桌上有個小籃子。

PART 02 應答問題 QUESTION-RESPONSE

1. **C** Q: What did you do with the leftovers?
你怎麼處理剩菜？

A. There weren't any left over.
並沒有剩下任何東西。

B. They were the only ones left.
這些是唯一剩下的。

C. I put them in the freezer.
我把剩菜放到冰庫裡了。

3. **B** Q: Do you have free delivery?
你們有免費外送嗎？

A. Thanks, that would be great.
謝謝，那真是太好了。

B. Yes, if you order a large pizza.
有，點一份大批薩即可。

C. No, do you?
沒有，你有嗎？

3. **B** Q: Can you remove the stain from this shirt?
你們能把襯衫上這個污點清除嗎？

A. No thanks.
不了，謝謝。

B. Well, we'll try our best.
我們會盡力而為。

C. Yes, we can clean the shorts.
可以，我們可以把短褲洗乾淨。

4. **A** Q: When can you come install my cable?
你何時可以來幫我安裝有線電視？

A. Between three and five this afternoon.
今天下午三點到五點之間。

B. Last night at seven.
昨晚七點。

C. But I didn't order cable.
可是我沒有訂購有線電視。

5. **C** Q: Do you provide boxes for us to put our things in?
貴公司會提供我們紙箱裝東西嗎？

A. Yes, we can move your boxes for you.
有，我們可以幫你們搬箱子。

B. That's OK, we don't need any boxes.
沒關係，我們不需要箱子。

C. Yes, but we charge extra for that.
有，但是要另外收費。

PART 03 簡短對話 CONVERSATION

M: Rick's Roofing Construction. How can I help you today, ma'am?
瑞克屋頂工程公司，有什麼能為妳服務的，小姐？

W: Hi, my name is Teresa Parks. One of your employees came by yesterday and gave me an estimate for having my roof replaced. I'd like to go ahead with the project, and I was just wondering what the next step is.
嗨，我叫泰瑞莎派克。你們一位員工昨天過來幫我開一份更換屋頂的估價單，我想要進行這個工程案，不知道接下來我該怎麼做？

M: Ah, yes, Ms. Parks—I have your file here. Well, first you'll need to apply to the city for a building permit. Then just give us a call and we can schedule the project for some time next month.
啊，是的，派克小姐，我手邊有妳的資料。首先妳需要向市政府申請一份施工許可證，然後再打電話來約下個月的施工時間就可以了。

W: Oh, I thought you'd be able to start next week—at least that's what the man who made the estimate said.
喔，我以為你們下星期就能動工——至少作估價的那個先生是這麼說的。

1. **C** Q: 這個男士是從事什麼工作的？
   A. 製造公司
   B. 維修公司
   C. 建築工程公司
   D. 房屋仲介公司

2. **B** Q: 根據電話上的男士所說，這位女士首先該做什麼？
   A. 約施工時間
   B. 申請許可證
   C. 換新她的屋頂
   D. 拿到估價單

3. **D** Q: 女士以為案子什麼時候可以動工？
   A. 下個月
   B. 這個星期晚點的時間
   C. 開估價單的隔天
   D. 下星期

PART 04 簡短獨白 SHORT TALK

Would you like to brighten up your house with new furniture? Now's the time! Bargain Basement Furniture is having a two-day half-off sale next weekend. That's right—half off of our already low prices! And if you show up at opening time on Saturday, you'll receive a coupon for an additional 20% off, which is valid until August 31st. You can also enjoy free refreshments while browsing our great selection of living room, bedroom, kitchen and bathroom items. We'll also have a designer on site to help you choose the best pieces for your home. So what are you waiting for? Come on down to Bargain Basement Furniture and take advantage of our low low sale prices!

你想要用新的家具讓房子看起來更明亮嗎？就趁現在！地下廉價家具商場將在下週末有兩天的半價特賣。沒錯——就是我們已經超低價再半價！如果你在星期六開門時來，還可再獲得一張八折優惠券，八月三十一日前都可使用。你還能在瀏覽我們精選的客廳、臥室、廚房及浴室產品時，享用免費小點心。現場還會有設計師幫你選擇最適合你家的家具。你還等什麼？現在就來地下廉價家具商場，用超低的價格佔便宜吧！

1. C Q: 這則廣告的主要訴求是什麼？
A. 免費小點心
B. 房地產
C. 居家家具
D. 辦公室家具

2. C Q: 特賣會何時舉行？
A. 這個週末
B. 到八月三十一日
C. 下星期六及星期日
D. 這星期六

3. B Q: 說話者建議聽者做什麼？
A. 雇用設計師幫他們選家具
B. 參觀地下廉價家具商場
C. 瀏覽地下廉價家具商場的網站
D. 印出額外折扣的優惠券

CHAPTER 19
租屋維修篇

教學重點

⊙ 租屋維修重點單字
⊙ 易混淆字：faucet / facet
⊙ [ɜ]、[ɔr] 的發音
⊙ 母音 [ə] 的弱化

多益實戰

⊙ Part 1 照片描述
⊙ Part 2 應答問題
⊙ Part 3 簡短對話
⊙ Part 4 獨白對話

主題字彙與發音

MP3-181

聽聽看這些單字的正確發音，並比較英美腔調的不同。

maintenance (n.) 維修，保養
[`mentənəs]

hardware store (phr.) 五金行
[`hard͵wɛr stor]

suite (n.) 套房
[swit]

garage (n.) 車庫
[gə`raʒ]

utility (n.) 水電
[ju`tɪlətɪ]

tenant (n.) 房客
[`tɛnənt]

bedroom (n.) 臥室
[`bɛd͵rʊm]

repairman (n.) 維修工人
[rɪ`pɛrmən]

fix (v.) 修理
[fɪks]

furniture (n.) 傢具
[`fɜnɪtʃə]

apartment (n.) 公寓
[ə`partmənt]

studio (n.) 套房
[`stjudɪ͵o]

furnished (a.) 附家具的
[`fɜnɪʃt]

plumber (n.) 水管工人
[`plʌmə]

flush (v.) 沖馬桶
[flʌʃ]

landlord (n.) 房東
[`lænd͵lord]

faucet (n.) 水龍頭
[`fɔsɪt]

rent (n.) 房租租金
[rɛnt]

property (n.) 房屋物件
[`prapəti]

主題易混淆字

聽力上也常會遇到的一個問題，就是有些字的發音非常相近，
在聽的時候，如果沒有整合前後文內容，很容易就聽錯。
以下我們整理了幾組容易弄錯的單字，請聽光碟朗讀，選出句中出現的字。

字音

1. apartment / department

2. furnished / finished

3. bedroom / bathroom

4. faucet / facet

字義

5. garage 車庫 / 停車場 / 修車廠

6. toilet 廁所 / 馬桶

7. utility 公共事業 / 效用

8. studio 工作室 / 套房

9. hardware 硬體 / 五金

10. property 物件 / 財產

解答

1. Which floor is your **department** on?（部門）
2. Did you ask if the unit was **furnished**?（有附家具的）
3. How many **bathrooms** does the house have?（浴室）
4. Which **facet** are you having problems with?（方面）
5. I took the bus to work because my car was at the **garage**.（修車廠）
6. Did you remember to flush the **toilet**?（馬桶）
7. We weren't impressed by the **utility** of the service.（功效）
8. Do you think I should rent the **studio** or the one-bedroom?（套房）
9. I bought my tools at the **hardware** store down the street.（五金）
10. The real estate agent has a new **property** to show us.（物件）

單字聽讀力 聽懂 [ɝ]、[ɔr] 的發音

MP3-183

教學說明：

[ɝ] 是一個母音，發音時要捲舌，和國字「兒」相似，常見的拼字有 ir、er、ur、or、ear。

[ɔr] 是母音 [ɔ] 後面接捲舌子音 [r]，容易與 [ɝ] 混淆，要仔細跟讀揣摩發音時的口形差異。此發音常見的拼字是 or、ar、oar、oor、aur。

現在就讓我們來聽聽正確的發音，並且跟著大聲念出來吧。

| [ɝ] | heard | word | nurse | circle | perfect |
| [ɔr] | hoard | ward | Norse | door | aura |

辨音測驗：

MP3-184

經過了剛才的發音練習，現在讓我們做個辨音小測驗，看看是不是聽懂更多了呢？請聽光碟播放的句子，並圈出句中出現的單字。

1. bird / board

2. shirts / shorts

3. herd / hoard

4. fur / four

解答

1. Do you see that ⬭board⬭ over there?

2. Could you wash these ⬭shorts⬭ for me?

3. There's a ⬭herd⬭ of sheep in the field.

4. The woman has ⬭fur⬭ coats in her closet.

句子聽讀力 │ 母音 [ə] 的弱化

MP3-185

教學說明：

母音 [ə] 配上子音，有時候會變得很弱，弱到幾乎只剩下子音單獨發音，好像少了一個音節一樣，易造成聽音時混淆。

母音 [ə] 在字中的省略情況。

- general
- professional
- veteran
- national
- diagonal

在字尾的母音 [ə] 後面若接子音 [l] 或 [n]，[ə] 的音會很不明顯。所以有些書上會把 [əl] 標示成 [l̩]，[ən] 標示成 [n̩]，代表子音加強及 [ə] 的弱化。

- Please press the button.
- Two is an even number.
- This channel has too many commercials.
- There's a table in the kitchen.
- Rotten food tastes awful.

上述的情況在單字加上 -ing 之後，母音會弱化得更明顯，由 le 結尾的動詞，甚至會省略 e 再加 -ing，拼寫時容易寫錯。

- The girl is buttoning her shirt.
- What's happening?
- Are you traveling with your family?
- The man is sharpening the knife.
- Is something troubling you?
- The grapes are ripening on the vine.

聽力小測驗：
請聽音辨別拼字，把底線下方的字母重新排列，拼出正確的單字。

MP3-186

1. I had _____ and eggs for breakfast.
　　　　n b c o a

2. The restaurant serves French _____ cooking.
　　　　　　　　　e i r a g n l o

3. My sweater is _____.
　　　　　　i n e a u g v n l r

4. Who is _____ your taxes?
　　　　i d l a n n h g

5. Exercising will _____ your heart.
　　　　　　n h t e t s r n g e

解答

1. I had **bacon** and eggs for breakfast.
2. The restaurant serves French **regional** cooking.
3. My sweater is **unraveling**.
4. Who is **handling** your taxes?
5. Exercising will **strengthen** your heart.

多益聽力實戰

PART 01
PHOTOGRAPHS 照片描述

請看圖片並聽光碟朗讀圖 1 ～ 4 的四段敘述，選出與圖片最相符的敘述。

1. _____

2. _____

© Webitect / Shutterstock.com

3. _____

4. _____

PART 02
QUESTION-RESPONSE 應答問題

請聽光碟朗讀，並選出最適合的答案填在空格中。

1. _____   **2.** _____   **3.** _____   **4.** _____   **5.** _____

PART 03 簡短對話
CONVERSATION

MP3-189

請聽光碟朗讀從選項 A、B、C、D 中選出正確的答案。

_____ **1. What needs to be fixed?**
   A. A sink
   B. A water pipe
   C. A bathroom
   D. A toilet

_____ **2. Who are the man and woman having the conversation?**
   A. Landlords
   B. Tenants
   C. Plumbers
   D. Runners

_____ **3. How will the man and woman handle the problem?**
   A. They will call a plumber.
   B. They will fix it themselves.
   C. They will call the landlord.
   D. They will pay the water bill.

PART 04 簡短獨白
SHORT TALK

MP3-190

請聽光碟朗讀，並根據內容回答以下題目。

_____ **1. Who is the speaker?**
   A. A tour guide
   B. The owner of the house
   C. A landlord
   D. The current tenant

_____ **2. When will the new tenant be able to move in?**
   A. May 5th
   B. May 30th
   C. June 1st
   D. June 5th

_____ **3. How much will the new tenant have to pay at that time?**
   A. $1,000
   B. $2,000
   C. $3,000
   D. $4,000

PART 01 照片描述 PHOTOGRAPHS

1. **B**　A. There are towels in the shower.
淋浴間裡有毛巾。

B. The lid of the toilet is down.
馬桶的蓋子是蓋著的。

C. The walls of the toilet are painted white.
廁所的牆壁被漆成白色。

D. The toilet is occupied.
廁所裡有人。

2. **D**　A. The waiter is showing the couple to their table.
服務生正幫那對夫婦帶位。

B. The landlord is kicking out the tenants.
房東正把房客趕走。

C. The couple has come to see the apartment.
那對夫婦來看公寓。

D. The agent is showing the couple a property.
仲介正展示房屋物件給那對夫婦看。

3. **C**　A. The repairman is fixing the facet.
修理工人正在修理方面。

B. The man is turning on the water.
那個男人正打開水。

C. The person is repairing the faucet.
那個人正在修理水龍頭。

D. The sink is ready to use.
洗臉台可以用了。

4. **A**　A. The bedroom is furnished.
臥室裡有家具。

B. There's a couch in the living room.
客廳裡有沙發。

C. The curtains are open.
窗簾是拉開的。

D. The apartment is for rent.
公寓正在招租。

PART 02 應答問題 QUESTION-RESPONSE

1. B Q: Can utility bills be paid online?
水電瓦斯帳單可以在網上繳嗎？
A. It's very convenient, isn't it?
很方便，不是嗎？
B. No. You have to pay by check.
不行。你必須用支票付款。
C. I paid the bill last week.
我上個星期付了帳單。

2. C Q: How many bedrooms does the apartment have?
公寓裡有幾間臥房？
A. The apartment has three bathrooms.
公寓裡有三間衛浴。
B. Yes. It has many bedrooms.
對。有很多間臥房。
C. Two, one with an attached bathroom.
兩間，一間有附衛浴。

3. A Q: Does the apartment building have a garage?
公寓大廈裡有車庫嗎？
A. Yes. There's one in the basement.
有。地下室有一個車庫。
B. No, but there's a repair shop nearby.
沒有，但附近有一間修車店。
C. The house has a two-car garage.
房子有一間可放兩輛車的車庫。

4. C Q: When is rent due?
什麼時候要繳房租？
A. It's 800 dollars a month.
一個月八百元。
B. That would be fine.
沒關係。
C. On the first of the month.
每個月的第一天。

5. B Q: Does the place come furnished?
屋子裡有家具嗎？
A. Yes. The place is finished.
有，屋子完工了。
B. No. That's why the rent is so cheap.
沒有。所以房租才這麼便宜。
C. All of our furniture is on sale.
我們所有的家具都在特賣。

PART 03 簡短對話 CONVERSATION

M: How long has it been running for?

水流了多久？

W: Uh, let's see…since yesterday, I think. I remember flushing, and then the water just kept running. It hasn't stopped since then.

嗯，我想想……大概是從昨天開始。我記得沖了水後，水就一直流。從那時候就沒停過了。

M: I guess we'd better call the landlord. He won't be happy if the water bill goes through the roof—especially since he's paying it.

我想我們最好打給房東。如果水費暴漲，他一定會不高興——尤其水費是他付的。

W: Actually, he gave us the number of the plumber he usually uses. He said we could just send him the bill and he would reimburse us.

其實，他給過我們他熟的水電工的電話。他說我們只要將帳單寄給他，他會退錢給我們。

1. **D**　Q: 什麼東西需要修理？
　　A. 洗臉盆
　　B. 水管
　　C. 廁所
　　D. 馬桶

2. **B**　Q: 對話中的男女是什麼身份？
　　A. 房東
　　B. 房客
　　C. 水電工
　　D. 跑步者

3. **A**　Q: 那對男女會如何處理這個問題？
　　A. 他們會打給水電工。
　　B. 他們會自己修理。
　　C. 他們會打給房東。
　　D. 他們會付水費。

PART 04 簡短獨白 SHORT TALK

First, I'd like to welcome you all and thank you for coming today. I hope you didn't have any trouble finding the place. The current tenant will be leaving on May 30th, and we'll be having people come in to clean the carpets and paint, so the unit will be ready to move in on the 5th of the following month. The rent is a thousand dollars a month, and the cost to move in is first and last month's rent plus a security deposit equal to one month's rent. All utilities are included in the rent, so it's a pretty good deal. We also have another unit for rent on the same floor that's similar to this one. Now, unless anyone has any questions, I'll take you on a tour of the place.

首先，我要歡迎各位，謝謝你們今天過來。我希望這地方不會太難找。目前的房客將會在五月三十日遷出，然後我們會請人來清潔地毯和粉刷牆壁，所以房子可以在隔月的五號入住。房租一個月一千元，要先付頭尾兩個月的租金還有等同於一個月房租的保證金。所有水電瓦斯費用都包含在租金內，所以很划算。我們同一層樓也有另一間類似的房子要出租。如果各位沒有問題的話，我就帶你們參觀一下。

1. **C** Q: 說話的人是誰？
   A. 一位導遊
   B. 獨棟房屋的屋主
   C. 房東
   D. 目前的房客

2. **D** Q: 新房客何時能遷入？
   A. 五月五日
   B. 五月三十日
   C. 六月一日
   D. 六月五日

3. **C** Q: 新房客入住時要付多少錢？
   A. 一千元
   B. 兩千元
   C. 三千元
   D. 四千元

CHAPTER 20
運動健身篇

教學重點

⊙ 運動健身重點單字
⊙ 易混淆字：metal / medal
⊙ 子音 [ts]、[tʃ] 的發音
⊙ be 動詞的輕重音

多益實戰

⊙ Part 1 照片描述
⊙ Part 2 應答問題
⊙ Part 3 簡短對話
⊙ Part 4 獨白對話

主題字彙與發音

聽聽看這些單字的正確發音，並比較英美腔調的不同。

exercise (n.) 運動，鍛鍊
[`ɛksɚˌsaɪz]

health (n.) 健康
[hɛlθ]

shape (n.) 外形
[ʃep]

pool (n.) 游泳池
[pul]

weight (n.) 重量，體重
[wet]

player (n.) 運動員
[`pleɚ]

compete (v.) 對抗，比賽
[kəm`pit]

train (v.) 訓練，培養
[tren]

fitness (n.) 健康
[`fɪtnɪs]

physical (a.) 身體的，肉體的
[`fɪzɪkəl]

strength (n.) 力，力量
[strɛŋθ]

gym (n.) 健身房
[dʒɪm]

court (n.) 球場
[kort]

coach (n.) 教練
[kotʃ]

athlete (n.) 運動員
[`æθlit]

racquet (n.) 球拍
[`rækɪt]

goal (n.) 得分
[gol]

treadmill (n.) 跑步機
[`trɛdˌmɪl]

dumbbell (n.) 啞鈴
[`dʌmˌbɛl]

muscle (n.) 肌肉
[`mʌsəl]

aerobics (n.) 有氧運動
[ˌeə`robɪks]

主題易混淆字

聽力上也常會遇到的一個問題，就是有些字的發音非常相近，
在聽的時候，如果沒有整合前後文內容，很容易就聽錯。
以下我們整理了幾組容易弄錯的單字，請聽光碟朗讀，選出句中出現的字。

字音

1. play / pray

2. balls / bowls

3. sore / score

4. metal / medal

字義

5. club 俱樂部 / 高爾夫球桿

6. exercise 練習 / 運動

7. pool 游泳池 / 撞球

8. court 法庭 / 球場

9. shape 體形 / 體能

10. weight 體重 / 舉重（器材）

解答

1. It's common for sports teams to **pray** before games.（禱告）
2. What brand of **balls** do you prefer?（球）
3. Do you ever get **sore** playing basketball?（痠痛）
4. The gymnast won three gold **medals** at the Olympics.（獎牌）
5. What brand of golf **clubs** would you recommend?（球杆）
6. The teacher assigned an **exercise** at the end of class.（練習）
7. We used to play **pool** every day after school.（撞球）
8. The player is scheduled to appear in **court** on Monday.（法庭）
9. I'm too out of **shape** to play sports.（體能）
10. Be careful to lower the **weight** slowly.（槓鈴，舉重器材）

單字聽讀力 | 聽懂子音 [ts]、[tʃ] 的發音

MP3-193

教學說明：

[ts] 由 [t] 和 [s] 兩個子音組成，會連在一起快速發出，這個音通常在「名詞的複數型」、「動詞的第三人稱單數」、「主詞和 is、has 的縮寫」會聽得到，常見的拼字為 ts、t's、tz。

現在就讓我們來聽聽正確的發音，並且跟著大聲念出來吧。

[ts] arts　eats　what's　pizza　spritz

[tʃ] 的發音是從唇齒間發出氣音，它的拼寫可能是 ch、tch，少數情況下 t 也發 [tʃ]，如 future。

[tʃ] arch　each　watch　cheap　catcher

辨音測驗：

MP3-194

經過了剛才的發音練習，現在讓我們做個辨音小測驗，看看是不是聽懂更多了呢？請聽光碟播放的句子，並圈出句中出現的單字。

1. mats / match

2. Ritz / rich

3. Scots / Scotch

4. bats / batch

5. coach / coats

解答

1. My job as a corporate recruiter is to (match) employee skills and experience to the specific positions.

2. We'll be staying at the (Ritz) hotel during the conference.

3. The (Scotch) company was founded over 100 years ago.

4. We should return the defective (batch) to the manufacturer.

5. When we travel on business, we usually fly in (coach).

句子聽讀力 | be 動詞的輕重音

教學說明：
be 動詞在句中各個位置的輕重音會有些不同。be 動詞在句中或句首時，通常不會是重音所在。在一般對話中，這些 be 動詞的母音都會呈現弱化現象。例如：

am [æm] → [əm]
are [ɑr] → [ər]
were [wɚ] → [wə]（尤其是在英式發音）
was [wʌz] → [wəz]

句中： It was hard.
Prices are rising.
The movie was excellent.
Where were you yesterday?

句首： Am I right?
Are you going to the dance?
Were they wearing suits?
Was Dan at the party?

即使如此，有時候說話者還是會隨著說話的情境選擇加重 be 動詞。例如以下對話。

A: I don't think you're telling the truth.
B: I am telling the truth!

A: Martha said you weren't at the meeting.
B: But I was at the meeting.

A: I heard the speakers were boring.
B: They were boring.

be 動詞如果是否定形式，則通常會是句子的重音。
Aren't you glad we have a day off?
Wasn't your father a lawyer?
Isn't she beautiful?
Weren't you supposed to call me?

聽力小測驗：
請聽光碟播放的對話，套色字若是重音，請將該字圈出。

MP3-196

A: Were you home at around 8:00 last night?

B: Yeah, I was home.

A: But I called and nobody answered. I don't think you were home yet.

B: No, I was home at that time. I was probably in the shower. Weren't you supposed to call me at 8:30?

A: No, you told me to call at 8:00. Are you sure you were there?

B: Am I sure? Yes, I'm sure!

解答

A: Were you home at around 8:00 last night?

B: Yeah, I was home.

A: But I called and nobody answered. I don't think you were home yet.

B: No, I was home at that time. I was probably in the shower. Weren't you supposed to call me at 8:30?

A: No, you told me to call at 8:00. Are you sure you were there?

B: Am I sure? Yes, I'm sure!

多益聽力實戰

PART 01 照片描述
PHOTOGRAPHS

MP3-197

請看圖片並聽光碟朗讀圖 1 ～ 4 的四段敘述，選出與圖片最相符的敘述。

1. _____

2. _____

© Webitect / Shutterstock.com

3. _____

4. _____

PART 02 應答問題
QUESTION-RESPONSE

MP3-198

請聽光碟朗讀，並選出最適合的答案填在空格中。

1. _____　　**2. _____**　　**3. _____**　　**4. _____**　　**5. _____**

PART 03 簡短對話
CONVERSATION

請聽光碟朗讀從選項 A、B、C、D 中選出正確的答案。

_____ **1.** **Where does this conversation probably take place?**
A. At a tennis court
B. At school
C. At home
D. At the gym

_____ **2.** **Why doesn't the man want to play tennis?**
A. Because he has a knee injury
B. Because he isn't in good condition
C. Because he doesn't like tennis
D. Because he can't borrow a racquet

_____ **3.** **What will the man do on Saturday?**
A. Stay at home and rest
B. Practice tennis by himself
C. Go work out at the gym
D. Play tennis with the woman

PART 04 簡短獨白
SHORT TALK

請聽光碟朗讀，並根據內容回答以下題目。

_____ **1.** **Who is probably making this speech?**
A. A business manager
B. A school teacher
C. A football coach
D. A basketball fan

_____ **2.** **When does the speech take place?**
A. At the beginning of a game
B. During practice
C. After the first half
D. In the middle of the day

_____ **3.** **What is the main purpose of the speaker?**
A. To teach
B. To motivate
C. To praise
D. To criticize

PART 01 照片描述 PHOTOGRAPHS

1. **C**   A. The mother and daughter are playing pool.
媽媽和女兒在打撞球。
B. The girl is teaching the woman how to swim.
那位女孩在教那位女人游泳。
C. The girl is learning how to swim in the pool.
那位女孩在游泳池裡學游泳。
D. The people are swimming in the lake.
人們在湖裡游泳。

2. **A**   A. The woman has just received a medal.
那位女人剛得到了一面獎牌。
B. The woman is happy about her metal.
那位女人對她的金屬很滿意。
C. The athlete is preparing to compete.
那位運動員正準備開始比賽。
D. The woman is shaking hands with the athlete.
那位女人在和運動員握手。

3. **B**   A. The weights are too heavy for the woman.
這槓鈴對那位女人來説太重了。
B. The man is lifting weights at the gym.
那位男人在健身房裡舉重。
C. The man and woman are trying to lose weight.
那位男人和那位女人正試著減重。
D. The man is helping the woman lift weights.
那位男人在幫助那位女人舉重。

4. **D**   A. The team is training for a competition.
隊伍在為比賽受訓。
B. The students are raising their hands in class.
學生們在課堂中舉手。
C. The dancers are performing for the audience.
舞者們在為觀眾表演。
D. The people are exercising at the gym.
人們在健身房裡運動。

PART 02 應答問題 QUESTION-RESPONSE

1. **B** Q: Why are you in such good shape?
你的體能怎麼那麼好？

A. Thank you for noticing.
謝謝你注意到。

B. Because I work out every day.
因為我每天都運動。

C. You look great!
你的狀況看起來真好。

2. **C** Q: Could you explain the rules of the game to me?
你可以為我解釋比賽規則嗎？

A. I wish you would.
我真希望你能。

B. Yeah. I don't know how to play.
可以。我不知道比賽怎麼進行。

C. Sure. They're pretty simple.
好啊。規則很簡單。

3. **A** Q: Do you like to exercise?
你喜歡運動嗎？

A. No. I'm kind of lazy.
不。我有點懶。

B. Yes. I did the exercises.
對。我有做練習。

C. The exercise was lots of fun.
那個練習很有趣。

4. **C** Q: How often do you go to the gym?
你多久上一次健身房？

A. Yes. I do.
對。我有。

B. I didn't know you worked out.
我不知道你有運動。

C. Every other day.
每兩天一次。

5. **B** Q: Do you know the score?
你知道比數嗎？

A. My legs are really sore.
我的腿很痠。

B. It's 43 to 27.
四十三比二十七。

C. Could you tell me what it is?
你可以告訴我這是什麼嗎？

PART 03 簡短對話 CONVERSATION

W: Hey, Tim. How would you like to come play tennis with us this Saturday? My partner hurt his knee, so I need a new one.

嗨，提姆。這個星期六要不要來跟我們打網球？我的球友傷到膝蓋，所以我需要一位新夥伴。

M: No thanks, Sis. I'm completely out of shape. And I don't have a racquet.

不，謝了，姊。我的體能完全不行了。而且我沒有球拍。

W: Oh, come on. I can lend you one. Weren't you on the tennis team in college?

噢，來嘛。我可以借你一支。你大學時不是參加過網球隊嗎？

M: Yeah, but that was a long time ago. I see you're not gonna let me say no though, so I guess I'll see you on the court. I better get off the couch now and go practice.

對啊，但那是很久以前了。可是我看妳是不會讓我拒絕的，那就球場上見吧。我最好現在就離開沙發去練習。

1. **C**　Q: 這段對話有可能在哪裡聽到？
　　　　A. 在網球場上
　　　　B. 在學校
　　　　C. 在家裡
　　　　D. 在健身房

2. **B**　Q: 為什麼那位男人不想打網球？
　　　　A. 因為他膝蓋受傷
　　　　B. 因為他的身體狀況不好
　　　　C. 因為他不喜歡網球
　　　　D. 因為他借不到球拍

3. **D**　Q: 那位男人在星期六會做什麼？
　　　　A. 待在家裡休息
　　　　B. 自己練習打網球
　　　　C. 在健身房運動
　　　　D. 跟那位女人打網球

PART 04 簡短獨白 SHORT TALK

All right, boys. We may be down by twenty points, but this isn't over yet. We can still win this thing. The other team is playing hard, so we need to play harder in the second half! We really need to score, but we also need to keep the other guys from scoring. You all know what you need to do, so the important thing is to stay focused. Just remember the plays you learned during practice. If we work as a team, we still have a chance of winning. Now get out on the field and play ball!

聽好，孩子們。我們落後二十分，但比賽還沒結束，我們還是能贏。對方打得很賣力，所以我們下半場要打得更賣力！我們很需要得分，但也很需要阻止對方得分。該怎麼做，你們都知道了，所以重點是要保持專注。記得練習時學到的打法就對了。如果我們好好團隊合作，依舊有機會獲勝。現在上場去比賽吧！

1. **C** Q: 這段話大概是誰講的？
   A. 公司經理
   B. 學校老師
   C. 足球教練
   D. 籃球迷

2. **C** Q: 這段話會在什麼時候聽到？
   A. 比賽一開始
   B. 練習的時候
   C. 上半場結束後
   D. 一天的中午

3. **B** Q: 說話者的主要用意是什麼？
   A. 教導人
   B. 激勵人
   C. 讚美人
   D. 批評人

CHAPTER 21
醫療保健篇

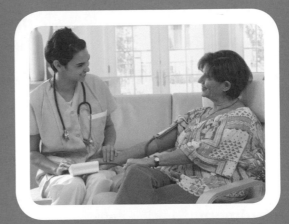

教學重點

⊙ 醫療保健重點單字
⊙ 易混淆字：patients / patience
⊙ 子音 [ʃ]、[ʒ]、[tʃ]、[dʒ]
⊙ 字尾常見的發音問題

多益實戰

⊙ Part 1 照片描述
⊙ Part 2 應答問題
⊙ Part 3 簡短對話
⊙ Part 4 獨白對話

主題字彙與發音

MP3-201

聽聽看這些單字的正確發音，並比較英美腔調的不同。

hospital (n.) 醫院
[`hɑspɪtəl]

physician (n.) 醫師，內科醫生
[fɪ`zɪʃən]

x-ray (n.) X 光
[`ɛks`re]

examination (n.) 檢查
[ɪg͵zæmə`neʃən]

medical (a.)
醫學的，醫術的，醫療的
[`mɛdɪkəl]

treatment (n.) 治療，治療法
[`tritmənt]

health care (phr.)
保健，保健事業
[hɛlθ kɛr]

cavity (n.) 蛀牙
[`kævəti]

flu shot (phr.) 流感疫苗
[flu ʃat]

blood pressure (phr.) 血壓
[blʌd`prɛʃɚ]

disease (n.) 疾病
[dɪ`ziz]

diagnose (v.) 診斷
[daɪəg`noz]

prevent (v.) 預防
[prɪ`vɛnt]

dentist (n.) 牙醫
[`dɛntɪst]

chest (n.) 胸腔
[tʃɛst]

surgery (n.) 手術
[`sɜdʒəri]

appointment (n.) 約診
[ə`pɔɪntmənt]

patient (n.) 病患
[`peʃənt]

clinic (n.) 診所
[`klɪnɪk]

allergic (a.) 過敏的
[ə`lɜdʒɪk]

主題易混淆字

聽力上也常會遇到的一個問題,就是有些字的發音非常相近,
在聽的時候,如果沒有整合前後文內容,很容易就聽錯。
以下我們整理了幾組容易弄錯的單字,請聽光碟朗讀,選出句中出現的字。

字音

1. hard / heart

2. filling / feeling

3. patients / patience

4. test / taste

5. breath / breathe

6. cold / code

字義

7. rate 費用 / 速率

8. cavity（牙的）蛀洞 /
   （身體的）腔

9. scale 刻度 / 體重計

10. operate 動手術 / 操作

解答

1. My doctor thinks I may have **heart** disease.（心臟）
2. Do you have any **feeling** in your mouth?（感覺）
3. John was impressed by his doctor's skill and **patience**.（耐心）
4. Your **test** results will be ready on Friday.（化驗）
5. The doctor asked me to **breathe** deeply while he listened to my chest.（呼吸）
6. You ought to see a doctor about your **cold**.（感冒）
7. Should I be worried about my heart **rate**?（速率）
8. The dentist examined the patient's oral **cavity**.（腔）
9. The nurse used a **scale** to measure my weight.（體重計）
10. If your condition gets any worse, we may have to **operate**.（動手術）

單字聽讀力 | 聽懂子音 [ʃ]、[ʒ]、[tʃ]、[dʒ]

MP3-203

教學說明：

[ʃ] 的發音是從門齒間送出氣體，不會振動聲帶。常看到的拼寫可能是 sh、c、ch、ci、s、ss 或 ti。[ʒ] 和 [ʃ] 的發音嘴形很相似，但 [ʒ] 發音時會從喉嚨振動聲帶發出。[ʒ] 的拼字變化不多，通常是 si 或 s。

[ʃ]　sure　　fresh　　action　　machine　　ocean

[ʒ]　vision　usually　seizure　　measure　　garage

[dʒ] 和 [tʃ] 的嘴形相似，但 [dʒ] 要從喉嚨振動聲帶發出，它的拼寫可能是 j、g、ge 或 dge。

[tʃ] 的發音也是從門齒間送出氣體，它的拼寫可能是 ch、t 或 tch。

[tʃ]　kitchen　future　　catcher　　question　　which

[dʒ]　jacket　general　page　　fridge　　large

辨音測驗：

MP3-204

經過了剛才的發音練習，現在讓我們做個辨音小測驗，看看是不是聽懂更多了呢？請聽光碟播放，圈出跟題目發音相同的字。

1. shop / job
2. chips / jeeps
3. catch / cash
4. porridge / porch
5. conversion / convention

解答

1. A new (shop) just opened up at the mall.
2. How much do those (jeeps) cost?
3. Did you (cash) the check that I gave you?
4. The (porridge) is too hot.
5. Are you going to the (convention) next week?

句子聽讀力 │ 字尾常見的發音問題

教學說明：

● **字尾有三個子音時該怎麼辦？**

在英文中常會因為不同的動詞變化，或是名詞的單複數而讓一個字的結尾有多達三個子音。在發這些字的時候，常會有省略或是弱化其中某個音的狀況，才能夠發得更自然。

1. conducts → conduc**ts** [kən`dʌks]：conducts 字尾本來是由 [k] [t] [s] 三個音形成，但實際發音時會把 [t] 弱化。

2. clients → clien**ts** [`klaɪns]：clients 字尾本來是由 [n] [t] [s] 形成，但實際發音時會把 [t] 弱化。

3. diamonds → diamon**ds** [`daɪəməns]：diamonds 字尾本來是由 [n] [d] [s] 形成，但實際發音時會把 [d] 弱化。

4. accents → accen**ts** [`æksɛns]：accents 字尾本來是由 [n] [t] [s] 形成，但實際發音時會把 [t] 弱化。

5. risked → ris**ked** [rɪst]：risked 字尾本來是由 [s] [k] [t] 形成，但實際發音時會把 [k] 弱化。

● **別忽略字尾最後的子音**

我們在發音時，很容易不小心忽略掉字尾最後的子音，特別是經過時態變化的字。這樣的忽略容易造成困擾，應該儘量避免。

◆ jump →不可省略字尾 [p]

◆ laughed →不可省略字尾 [t]

◆ against →不可省略字尾 [t]

● **別在子音後擅自添加母音**

另外一個常見的發音問題，就是我們常會不自覺地在子音後擅自加上母音。

◆ dogs [dɔgz] 不可唸成 [dɔgəz]

◆ last [læst] 不可唸成 [læstə]

◆ L.A. [`ɛl `e] 不可唸成 [`ɛlə `e]

聽力小測驗：
請聽光碟的句子，判斷句中套色字是否有發音弱化現象。請在弱化的字母下畫底線。

MP3-206

1. All of the products have arrived on time.

2. The lady bothered other audience members when she coughed.

3. The can of almonds got stale because I left it open.

4. My parents asked me to wash my hands.

5. We wrapped lots of presents on Christmas Eve.

解答

1. All of the produc_ts have arrived on time.
2. The lady bothered other audience members when she coughed.
3. The can of almon_ds got stale because I left it open.
4. My paren_ts as_ked me to wash my han_ds.
5. We wrapped lots of presen_ts on Christmas Eve.

多益聽力實戰

請看圖片並聽光碟朗讀圖 1～4 的四段敘述，選出與圖片最相符的敘述。

1. _____

2. _____

3. _____

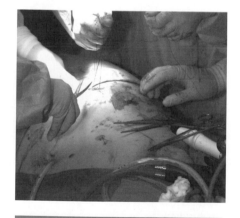

4. _____

PART 02 QUESTION-RESPONSE 應答問題

請聽光碟朗讀，並選出最適合的答案填在空格中。

1. _____ **2.** _____ **3.** _____ **4.** _____ **5.** _____

PART 03 簡短對話
CONVERSATION

MP3-209

請聽光碟朗讀從選項 A、B、C、D 中選出正確的答案。

____ **1.** Why does the woman call the man?
A. To reschedule his appointment
B. To set up a teeth cleaning appointment
C. To remind him about his appointment
D. To review his work schedule

____ **2.** What will the man do on Monday?
A. Have his teeth cleaned
B. Go to a convention
C. Attend an important meeting
D. Get a cavity filled

____ **3.** When will the man get his teeth cleaned?
A. Tuesday at 10:00 a.m.
B. Monday at 2:00 p.m.
C. Friday at 10:00 a.m.
D. Thursday at 1:00 p.m.

PART 04 簡短獨白
SHORT TALK

MP3-210

請聽光碟朗讀,並根據內容回答以下題目。

____ **1.** Where is the flu shot event being held?
A. In the hospital parking lot
B. In the main lobby
C. In the second floor lobby
D. In the cafeteria

____ **2.** How many doses of the shot were available last year?
A. 2,000
B. 3,000
C. 4,000
D. 6,000

____ **3.** Who should NOT get the flu shot?
A. The elderly
B. Young children
C. People who have had the flu
D. Pregnant women

PART 01　照片描述 PHOTOGRAPHS

1. **B**　A. The dentists are looking at the patient's cavities.
    牙醫正在看病人的蛀牙。
    B. The doctor is holding an x-ray of a patient's chest cavity.
    醫生正拿著一張病人胸腔的 X 光片。
    C. The doctors can see the patient's bones on the screen.
    醫生可以在螢幕上看到病人的骨頭。
    D. The doctor is explaining the x-ray to his patient.
    醫生正在向病人解釋 X 光片。

2. **D**　A. The nurse is taking a blood sample from the patient.
    護士正在抽取病人的血液樣本。
    B. The woman is donating blood at the clinic.
    這位女士正在診所捐血。
    C. The nurse is giving the patient a flu shot.
    護士正在給病人注射流感疫苗。
    D. The nurse is measuring the woman's blood pressure.
    護士正在測量這位女士的血壓。

3. **C**　A. The surgeons may have to operate on the patient.
    外科醫生可能必須要替病人動手術。
    B. The doctors are examining the patient.
    醫生正在為病人做檢查。
    C. The surgeons are operating on the patient.
    外科醫生正在替病人動手術。
    D. The doctors are operating the medical equipment.
    醫生正在操作醫療儀器。

4. **B**　A. The patient is having a dental x-ray taken.
    病人正在照牙齒的 X 光片。
    B. The woman is getting a cavity filled.
    這位女士正在補牙。
    C. The woman is having her braces adjusted.
    這位女士正在調整她的牙套。
    D. The woman is happy she doesn't have any cavities.
    這位女士很得意她沒有任何的蛀牙。

PART 02 應答問題 QUESTION-RESPONSE

1. **C** Q: How often should I floss my teeth?
我應該多久用牙線清潔一次牙齒？

A. Yes. Flossing is very important.
是的。用牙線清潔牙齒很重要。

B. You should always floss your teeth.
你必須一直用牙線清潔牙齒。

C. At least once a day.
至少一天一次。

2. **A** Q: Does it hurt when I press here?
我按這裡的時候會痛嗎？

A. A little bit.
有一點。

B. I'm not sure. Let me try.
我不確定。我來試試看。

C. I never press there.
我從不按那裡。

3. **B** Q: I'm calling to confirm your doctor's appointment on Thursday at 2:00 p.m.
我打電話來和你確認星期四下午兩點和醫師的預約。

A. Actually, 2:30 would be better for me.
其實，兩點半我會比較方便。

B. Thank you. I'll be there.
謝謝。我會到。

C. I'm sorry. The doctor isn't available.
抱歉，醫生沒有空。

4. **C** Q: Would you like me to prescribe you a painkiller?
要我開個止痛藥給你嗎？

A. Yes, a prescription is necessary for those.
是的，那需要處方箋。

B. How bad does it hurt?
這有多痛？

C. Actually, the pain isn't too bad.
其實，沒有那麼痛。

5. **A** Q: Do you know if you're allergic to any medications?
你知道你是否對任何藥物過敏嗎？

A. Not that I know of.
據我所知沒有。

B. Yes. I've taken those before.
是的。我已經吃過那種（藥）了。

C. I didn't know you were allergic to drugs.
我不知道你對藥物過敏。

PART 03 簡短對話 CONVERSATION

W: Hi, I'm calling to remind you that you have an appointment to get your teeth cleaned next Monday at 2:00 p.m.

嗨，我打電話來提醒你，下星期一下午兩點你有預約洗牙。

M: Oh, no! I completely forgot, and I can't make it then. Can I reschedule my appointment?

糟糕！我完全忘記了，我沒辦法去。我可以重新預約嗎？

W: Certainly. We have 10:00 a.m. openings on Tuesday and Friday, and a 1:00 p.m. opening on Thursday.

當然可以。我們星期二和星期五早上十點、星期四下午一點這幾個時段都能約。

M: Let's see. I'll be at a convention on Monday and Tuesday, and I have an important meeting Friday morning, so I'll come in Thursday afternoon then.

讓我瞧瞧。我星期一和星期二要參加研討會，星期五早上有個重要的會議，所以我星期四下午可以去。

1. [C] Q: 為什麼這位女人會打電話給男人？
   A. 要重新安排他的預約
   B. 要敲定一個洗牙的預約
   C. 要提醒他有個預約
   D. 要檢視他的工作行程

2. [B] Q: 這男人星期一會做什麼？
   A. 洗牙
   B. 去一個研討會
   C. 參加一個重要的會議
   D. 補牙

3. [D] Q: 這位男人什麼時候會去洗牙？
   A. 星期二的早上十點
   B. 星期一的下午兩點
   C. 星期五的早上十點
   D. 星期四的下午一點

PART 04 簡短獨白 SHORT TALK

Can I have your attention please? This is a special announcement from the Good Hope Hospital administration. As flu season approaches, we're pleased to announce our annual flu shot event. The event will take place from October 25h to the 29th, and the location has been changed from the parking lot to our second floor lobby. To get there, take the elevator in the main lobby to the second floor, pass the cafeteria and turn right. The hospital has 6,000 doses available, double the amount of last year's event. 2,000 doses are reserved for children. The shot is recommended for almost everyone over three years of age. Exceptions include people allergic to eggs, people who currently have the flu, and expecting mothers. Don't miss this chance to beat the flu!

請注意，這是來自好望醫院行政處的特別公告。因應流感季節即將來臨，我們很樂於告訴大家本醫院一年一度的流感疫苗注射活動。這個活動會從十月二十五日持續到二十九日，地點也從停車場換到了二樓的大廳。要抵達二樓大廳，你可以搭乘中央大廳的電梯到二樓，經過自助餐廳，然後右轉。醫院備有六千劑疫苗，是去年活動的兩倍。其中有兩千劑疫苗預留給兒童。三歲以上幾乎每個人都建議來接種疫苗。對雞蛋過敏、目前患有流感者，以及孕婦皆不在建議接種人士範圍內。別錯過這次打敗流感的機會！

1. **C** Q: 流感疫苗注射在哪裡舉辦？
   A. 在醫院的停車場
   B. 在中央大廳
   C. 在二樓大廳
   D. 在自助餐廳

2. **B** Q: 去年備有的流感疫苗有幾劑？
   A. 兩千
   B. 三千
   C. 四千
   D. 六千

3. **D** Q: 誰不該接種流感疫苗？
   A. 年長者
   B. 幼童
   C. 曾得過流感的人
   D. 孕婦

CHAPTER 22
表演篇

教學重點

⊙ 表演重點單字
⊙ 易混淆字：previews / reviews
⊙ [θ]、[ð]、[t] 的發音
⊙ 重音的變化

多益實戰

⊙ Part 1 照片描述
⊙ Part 2 應答問題
⊙ Part 3 簡短對話
⊙ Part 4 獨白對話

主題字彙與發音

聽聽看這些單字的正確發音，並比較英美腔調的不同。

play (n.) 戲劇，劇本
[ple]

conduct (v.) 指揮
[kən`dʌkt]

drama (n.) 戲劇，劇本
[`dramə]

preview (n.) 預告
[`pri͵vju]

show (n.) 表演，演出節目，秀
[ʃo]

performance (n.) 表演
[pɚ`fɔrməns]

actress/actor (n.) 男演員，女演員
[`æktrɪs] / [`æktɚ]

instrument (n.) 樂器
[`ɪnstrəmənt]

director (n.) 導演
[də`rɛktɚ]

symphony (n.) 交響樂
[`sɪmfənɪ]

review (n.) 影評，書評
[rɪ`vju]

concert (n.) 音樂會，演唱會
[`kansɚt]

musician (n.) 音樂家
[mju`zɪʃən]

box office (n.) 票房
[baks `ɔfɪs]

pianist (n.) 鋼琴師
[pɪ`ænɪst]

theater (n.) 劇院
[`θiətɚ]

script (n.) 劇本
[skrɪpt]

costume (n.) 戲服
[`kastjum]

orchestra (n.) 交響樂團
[`ɔrkɪstrə]

rehearsal (n.) 排練
[rɪ`hɜsəl]

主題易混淆字

聽力上也常會遇到的一個問題，就是有些字的發音非常相近，
在聽的時候，如果沒有整合前後文內容，很容易就聽錯。
以下我們整理了幾組容易弄錯的單字，請聽光碟朗讀，選出句中出現的字。

字音

1. previews / reviews

2. play / pray

3. actress / actors

4. seats / sheets

5. contacted / conducted

6. arena / area

字義

7. stage 舞台 / 階段

8. performance 表現 / 表演

9. instrument 樂器 / 儀器

10. film 底片 / 電影

解答

1. I hear the movie got good **reviews**.（評價）
2. There's a Christmas **play** at our church each year.（戲劇）
3. I didn't recognize any of the **actors** in the movie.（演員）
4. We asked the usher if we could change our **seats**.（位子）
5. He has **conducted** the orchestra for many years.（指揮）
6. My favorite band is playing at the local **arena** this Saturday.（體育館）
7. All the actors on the **stage** bowed.（舞台）
8. The next **performance** starts at 8:30.（表演）
9. The performers all played their **instruments** so well.（樂器）
10. Do you know a good place to get **film** developed?（底片）

單字聽讀力 | 聽懂 [θ]、[ð]、[t] 的發音

MP3-213

教學說明：

[θ] 是一個無聲子音，發音時要將舌頭吐出，讓空氣從兩旁自然送出。但牙齒只要自然地和舌頭輕觸即可，千萬不要刻意地咬住舌頭，把它做得太「到位」，這樣反而聽起來會很不自然。這個發音常看到的拼寫是 th。

[θ]　thumb　month　birthday　thirsty　north

[ð] 的發音位置和 [θ] 相似，不同的地方就是 [ð] 是一個有聲子音，發音時必須振動聲帶。這個發音常看到的拼寫也是 th。

[ð]　this　father　breathe　weather　those

英文中 th 拼字雖然很容易發成 [ð] 或 [θ]，但千萬不要看到 th 就急著把舌頭吐出來。很多時候 th 也會發成 [t]。

[t]　Thailand　Thomas　thyme　Thames

辨音測驗：

MP3-214

經過了剛才的發音練習，現在讓我們做個辨音小測驗，看看是不是聽懂更多了呢？請聽光碟播放的句子，並判別底線處的發音為何。

1. Mrs. Thatcher thanked her Thai neighbor for the wreath.

2. This path leads south to the lighthouse.

3. My other brother is brushing his teeth in the bathroom.

4. Why are you wearing that thick sweater in this weather?

5. Martha's father turned thirty-three on Thursday.

解答

1. Mrs. **Th**atcher thanked her **Th**ai neighbor for **th**e wreath.
　　　[θ]　　　　　　　　　[t]　　　　　　　　　[ð]
2. This pa**th** leads sou**th** to the lighthouse.
　　　　[θ]　　　　　[θ]
3. My o**th**er brother is brushing his tee**th** in the ba**th**room.
　　　[ð]　　　　　　　　　　　[θ]　　　　　[θ]
4. Why are you wearing that **th**ick sweater in this wea**th**er?
　　　　　　　　　[θ]　　　　　　　　　　　[ð]
5. Mar**th**a's father turned **th**irty-three on **Th**ursday.
　　　[θ]　　　　　　[θ]　　　　　[θ]

句子聽讀力　重音的變化

教學說明：

mark（記號）這個字前面加上了 re 變成 remark（評論），這時候重音究竟是放在 re 還是 mark 呢？在英文中有許多二音節的字（如 remark），其實都是從一個單音節的字（如 mark）衍生出來的。當它們形成為二音節的字時，重音通常會放在字根所在的音節：[rɪˋmɑrk]。

一音節字根	二音節衍生字
move [muv]	remove [rɪˋmuv]
art [ɑrt]	artist [ˋɑrtɪst]
like [laɪk]	dislike [dɪsˋlaɪk]
come [kʌm]	become [bɪˋkʌm]
fame [fem]	famous [ˋfeməs]
take [tek]	mistake [mɪsˋtek]

在英文中有些字的名詞與動詞同形但發音不同，這個時候，名詞的重音會在第一音節，動詞則會在第二音節。

例如：record [ˋrɛkəd] (n.) 紀錄；唱片 ／ [rɪˋkɔrd] (v.) 記錄；錄音

名詞（重音在第一音節）	動詞（重音在第二音節）
contrast [ˋkɑn͵træst]	contrast [kənˋtræst]
object [ˋɑbdʒɪkt]	object [əbˋdʒɛkt]
desert [ˋdɛzət]	desert [dɪˋzət]
present [ˋprɛzənt]	present [prɪˋzɛnt]
produce [ˋprodus]	produce [prəˋdus]
rebel [ˋrɛbəl]	rebel [rɪˋbɛl]

不過，還是有許多同時具有名詞與動詞詞性的英文字發音相同：

名詞／動詞重音同音節
answer [ˈænsɚ]
picture [ˈpɪktʃɚ]
travel [ˈtrævəl]
reply [rɪˈplaɪ]
promise [ˈprɑmɪs]
visit [ˈvɪzɪt]

聽力小測驗：
請聽光碟播放的句子，畫出套色字的重音節處。

MP3-216

1. Several convicts escaped from the prison.

2. The rebel army has been fighting against the government for years.

3. The suspect's statement conflicts with the facts.

4. How many presents did you get for Christmas?

5. Local residents object to the proposed construction project.

解答

1. Several **con**victs escaped from the prison.
2. The **re**bel army has been fighting against the government for years.
3. The suspect's statement con**flicts** with the facts.
4. How many **pre**sents did you get for Christmas?
5. Local residents ob**ject** to the proposed construction **proj**ect.

多益聽力實戰

請看圖片並聽光碟朗讀圖 1 ～ 4 的四段敘述，選出與圖片最相符的敘述。

1. _____

2. _____

3. _____

4. _____

PART 02 QUESTION-RESPONSE 應答問題

請聽光碟朗讀，並選出最適合的答案填在空格中。

1. _____   2. _____   3. _____   4. _____   5. _____

PART 03 簡短對話
CONVERSATION

請聽光碟朗讀從選項 A、B、C、D 中選出正確的答案。

_____ **1.** **Why does the man want to see the play?**
A. Because it's getting great reviews
B. Because it's a very popular play
C. Because his friend thinks it's worth seeing
D. Because he has nothing to do on Saturday

_____ **2.** **What does the woman say about her friend Betty?**
A. Betty's taste is different than hers when it comes to plays.
B. Betty has bad taste in plays.
C. Betty doesn't like plays very much.
D. Betty doesn't like plays unless they are different.

_____ **3.** **Why does the man suggest seeing the play on Thursday?**
A. Because tickets are cheaper on weekdays
B. Because tickets are still available on Thursday
C. Because that's the only day they both have free time
D. Because he thinks it will be less crowded

PART 04 簡短獨白
SHORT TALK

請聽光碟朗讀，並根據內容回答以下題目。

_____ **1.** **What kind of performance is being held this afternoon?**
A. A dance
B. A concert
C. A film
D. A play

_____ **2.** **What can guests do during the intermission?**
A. Meet the performers
B. Buy refreshments
C. Turn off their phones
D. Purchase tickets

_____ **3.** **How can guests buy tickets for future shows?**
A. Leave a message
B. Order them by mail
C. Contact the box office
D. Book them online

PART 01　照片描述 PHOTOGRAPHS

1. B　A. The audience is waiting for the movie to start.
觀眾正在等電影開演。
B. A large crowd is gathered for the concert.
大批的觀眾聚集在演唱會場地。
C. Everyone is dressed up for the opera.
每個人都為了看歌劇演出盛裝打扮。
D. People are standing in line to buy concert tickets.
人們正在排隊買演唱會門票。

2. C　A. The actress on the right is wearing a hat.
在右邊的女演員戴著一頂帽子。
B. The actors are rehearsing their lines.
演員們正在練習台詞。
C. The performers are wearing fancy costumes.
表演者穿著花俏別緻的戲服。
D. People are dancing at the disco.
人們正在舞廳跳舞。

3. A　A. The musicians are playing their instruments.
樂師們正在演奏他們的樂器。
B. The conductor is conducting the orchestra.
指揮家正在指揮交響樂團。
C. The researchers are adjusting their instruments.
研究員正在調整他們的儀器。
D. The symphony is playing to a full house.
這場交響樂在滿座的觀眾前演出。

4. D　A. There is no film in the camera.
相機裡沒有底片。
B. The couple is watching a movie.
這對男女正在看電影。
C. The man has an aisle seat.
這個男人坐在走道座位。
D. The film hasn't started yet.
電影還沒有開始。

PART 02 應答問題 QUESTION-RESPONSE

1. **B** Q: Two tickets for the seven o'clock show, please.
請給我兩張七點整表演的票。

A. Yes, we still have tickets for the eight o'clock show.
是的，我們還有八點整表演的票。

B. That'll be 20 dollars.
這樣是二十元。

C. Sorry, the eleven o'clock show is sold out.
抱歉，十一點整的票已經賣完了。

2. **A** Q: Would you like to go to the symphony with me?
你想跟我去聽交響樂嗎？

A. Thanks for asking, but I don't like classical music.
謝謝你邀請我，但我不喜歡古典樂。

B. Maybe. What actors are in it?
或許吧。演員有誰？

C. Yes, we went to the symphony last week.
是的，我們上星期有去聽交響樂。

3. **C** Q: Can you help us find our seats?
你可以幫我們找到座位嗎？

A. Yes. Where did you last see them?
可以，你最後一次看到它們是在哪裡？

B. Our seats are in the middle of Aisle 2.
我們的座位是在第二走道的中間。

C. Sure. Could I see your tickets?
好的，我可以看看你們的票嗎？

4. **C** Q: Sorry, madam. There's no smoking in the theater.
小姐，抱歉。劇院裡不能抽菸。

A. OK. I'll be sure not to smoke.
好的，我不會抽菸的。

B. Yes. Thank you for not smoking.
是的。謝謝你不抽菸。

C. I'm sorry. I'll put it out right away.
抱歉，我立刻把菸熄掉。

5. **B** Q: We should change seats, shouldn't we?
我們應該換座位吧，不是嗎？

A. Sorry, there are no seats available.
抱歉，沒空位了。

B. Yeah. I can barely see the stage from here.
是啊，這裡幾乎看不到舞台。

C. I don't think so. These seats are terrible.
我不這麼想。這些座位很糟糕。

PART 03 簡短對話 CONVERSATION

M: If you're free this Saturday, would you like to see the new play at the Bay Street Theater? The reviews aren't great, but a friend recommended it.

如果妳這個星期六有空的話，想不想一起去灣街戲院看那齣舞台劇？評論不是很好，但有個朋友推薦它。

W: My friend Betty's seen it too, and she didn't like it. But her taste in plays is much different than mine. I'd actually like to see it, but it'll be packed on the weekend.

我朋友貝蒂也去看了，但她不喜歡這齣戲。不過她對舞台劇的品味和我大不相同。我其實很想看，但週末人一定會很多。

M: In that case, why don't we go on Thursday? Tickets are also cheaper during the week.

這樣的話，那我們何不星期四去？週間的票也會比較便宜。

1. **C**　Q: 為什麼這位男士想要去看舞台劇？
　　A. 因為這齣舞台劇評價很高
　　B. 因為這是個很受歡迎的舞台劇
　　C. 因為他的朋友覺得這齣舞台劇很值得看
　　D. 因為他星期六沒事做

2. **A**　Q: 關於她的朋友貝蒂，這個女人說了什麼？
　　A. 說到舞台劇，貝蒂的品味和她的不同。
　　B. 貝蒂對於舞台劇的品味很差。
　　C. 貝蒂不是很喜歡舞台劇。
　　D. 貝蒂不喜歡舞台劇，除非它們風格很不一樣。

3. **D**　Q: 為什麼這位男士建議星期四去看這齣舞台劇？
　　A. 因為在非週末期間票會比較便宜
　　B. 因為禮拜四的票還有剩
　　C. 因為只有那天他們倆都有空
　　D. 因為他覺得那時候人會比較少

PART 04 簡短獨白 SHORT TALK

Ladies and gentlemen, welcome to Olive Tree Theater for this afternoon's performance of The Secret Garden by the Olive Tree Theater Troupe. The performance will begin in five minutes. There will be two acts, with a 20 minute intermission in between. During the intermission, there will be snacks on sale in the lobby. We now ask you to please turn off all cell phones and other electronic devices, and remind you that no photography is permitted during the performance. After the show, you can buy tickets at our box office for all of the performances this season. Our box office is also open Monday to Friday, 11:00 a.m. to 4:00 p.m. You can either buy tickets in person, or call our box office at 366-6688. We'd like to thank you for coming, and hope you enjoy the show.

先生、女士，歡迎來到橄欖樹劇院觀賞今天下午由橄欖樹劇團演出的《祕密花園》。表演將在五分鐘後開始。本齣戲有兩幕，中間有二十分鐘的中場休息時間。在中場休息時間大廳將會販售點心。現在請您關掉所有的手機和其他電子裝置。提醒您，在演出期間禁止攝影拍照。演出結束後，你可以在我們的售票處購買我們這一季所有演出的票。我們的售票處在星期一到星期五的早上十一點到下午四點也有營業。您可以親自到現場購買，或是來電 366-6688 到我們的售票處。感謝您的蒞臨，祝您看戲愉快。

1. **D** Q: 今天下午舉辦了什麼種類的演出？
A. 舞蹈
B. 音樂會
C. 電影
D. 舞台劇

2. **B** Q: 來賓在中場休息時可以做什麼？
A. 和表演者見面
B. 買茶點
C. 關掉手機
D. 買票

3. **C** Q: 來賓要怎麼買到之後演出的票？
A. 留下訊息
B. 以郵件訂購
C. 和購票處聯絡
D. 在網路上訂票

CHAPTER 23
大眾媒體篇

教學重點

- ⊙ 大眾媒體重點單字
- ⊙ 易混淆字：media / medium
- ⊙ 英美口音比較 [ɑ] [ɒ]
- ⊙ R 發音在英腔中的種種情況

多益實戰

- ⊙ Part 1 照片描述
- ⊙ Part 2 應答問題
- ⊙ Part 3 簡短對話
- ⊙ Part 4 獨白對話

主題字彙與發音

聽聽看這些單字的正確發音，並比較英美腔調的不同。

mass media (phr.) 大眾傳播媒體
[mæs `midɪə]

microphone (n.) 擴音器，麥克風
[`maɪkrə,fon]

camera (n.) 照相機
[`kæmərə]

gossip (n.) 閒話，聊天，流言蜚語
[`gɑsəp]

scandal (n.) 醜聞，醜事
[`skændəl]

exclusive (a.) 排外的，除外的
[ɪk`sklusɪv]

coverage (n.) 新聞報導
[`kʌvərɪdʒ]

low profile (phr.) 低姿態，低調
[lo `profaɪl]

demonstration (n.)
示威，示威運動
[,dɛmən`streʃən]

strike (v./n.) 罷工
[straɪk]

crowd (n.) 群眾
[kraʊd]

media (n.) 媒體
[`midɪə]

broadcast (n./v.) 廣播
[`brɔd,kæst]

press conference (n.) 記者會
[prɛs `kɑnfərəns]

comment (n./v.) 評論
[`kɑmɛnt]

channel (n.) 頻道
[`tʃænəl]

cable (n.) 有線電視
[`kebəl]

issue (v.) 出刊，發行
[`ɪʃjʊ]

package (n.) 方案
[`pækɪdʒ]

photographer (n.) 攝影記者
[fə`tɑgrəfɚ]

主題易混淆字

聽力上也常會遇到的一個問題，就是有些字的發音非常相近，
在聽的時候，如果沒有整合前後文內容，很容易就聽錯。
以下我們整理了幾組容易弄錯的單字，請聽光碟朗讀，選出句中出現的字。

字音

1. media / medium

2. life / live

3. microphone / megaphone

4. desk / disk

字義

5. radio 收音機 / 無線電 / 廣播

6. station 車站 / 電台（頻道）

7. network 網路 / 無線電視廣播網

8. reception 接待會，宴會 / 收訊

9. channel 管道 /（電視）頻道

10. press 新聞媒體 / 印刷機

解答

1. Social **media** are very popular with young people.（媒體）
2. The show is recorded in front of a **live** audience.（現場）
3. The speaker talked to the crowd through a **megaphone**.（大聲公）
4. Thomas works as a news **desk** editor.（新聞台）
5. Who is your favorite **radio** DJ?（廣播）
6. That **station** plays mostly classical music.（頻道）
7. Now that I have cable, I hardly ever watch **network** TV.（無線）
8. You should put the TV in this room because the **reception** is better.（收訊）
9. There are lots of good shows on that **channel**.（頻道）
10. Freedom of the **press** is under attack in many countries.（新聞媒體）

單字聽讀力 | 英美口音比較 [ɑ]、[ɒ]

教學說明：

美式口音中 [ɑ] 的音常出現在 o 或是 a 的拼字上，與中文「啊」發音類似，在英式口音中，國際音標寫成 [ɒ]。差別在唸 [ɒ] 時，口腔內會圓一點，舌頭也會比較緊，比較像中文的「喔」。

[ɑ] 和 [ɒ]　clock　watch　shop　job　hot

拼字為 ar 時，美式口音讀作 [ɑr]，但英式口音不會發 [ɒr]，而唸 [ɑ]。

[ɑr] 和 [ɑ]　mark　yard　start　park　large

綜合以上情況，在美國人唸 o 短音時，會與英國人唸有 ar 的字聽起來很像，例如 hot 和 heart。

例如： Who used up all the hot water?

The old man has a weak heart.

辨音測驗：

經過了剛才的發音練習，現在讓我們做個辨音小測驗，看看是不是聽懂更多了呢？請聽光碟播放的句子，並圈出句中出現的單字。

1. part / pot

2. heart / hot

3. shark / shock

4. large / lodge

解答

1. There's a⟨pot⟩of stew on the stove.

2. The patient had a⟨heart⟩attack on the way to the hospital.

3. The swimmer was attacked by a⟨shark⟩.

4. Do you have this jacket in a⟨large⟩?

句子聽讀力 | R 發音在英腔中的種種情況

教學說明：

R 在字首或與其他子音合念時，英美腔都會把 R 念出來。

- 字首：red　right　roast
- 與其他子音合念：treat　pray　criminal

R 的音在句中或句尾時，英式口音會省略 [r]，在 [er] [ɪr] [ɚ] [ʊr] 四組音上，
R 的聲音減弱，改讀作 [eə] [ɪə] [ə] [ʊə]。

- 句中與字尾：girl　more　air　ear　major　tour

字尾的 R 遇上了後面的字為母音開頭，配合連音有可能會唸出 R 的音，視
各地區口音而定。

car: car engine

four: four apples

corner: corner office

聽力小測驗：

請聽光碟播放的句子，判斷問答是否相符。相符請打圈（○），
不相符請打叉（×）。

1. _____

2. _____

3. _____

4. _____

解答

1. ✗ A: Do you work downtown?

　　　 B: Sometimes I walk, sometimes I take the bus.

2. ○ A: Did you major in law?

　　　 B: No, but I took several law classes.

3. ○ A: Driving here is really dangerous.

　　　 B: Yeah. I would never drive here.

4. ✗ A: Do you have a quarter?

　　　 B: Yes. Everybody in sales has a quota.

多益聽力實戰

PART 01 PHOTOGRAPHS 照片描述

MP3-227

請看圖片並聽光碟朗讀圖 1 ～ 4 的四段敘述，選出與圖片最相符的敘述。

1. _____

2. _____

© Lars Plougmann / flickr.com

3. _____

4. _____

PART 02 QUESTION-RESPONSE 應答問題

MP3-228

請聽光碟朗讀，並選出最適合的答案填在空格中。

1. _____ **2.** _____ **3.** _____ **4.** _____ **5.** _____

PART 03 CONVERSATION 簡短對話

請聽光碟朗讀從選項 A、B、C、D 中選出正確的答案。

_____ **1.** **What does the man want to do?**
A. Return a package to the post office
B. Stop receiving cable TV service
C. Cancel his satellite radio service
D. Switch to the basic package

_____ **2.** **What does the woman suggest the man do?**
A. Upgrade to the premium package
B. Switch to a less expensive package
C. Return the package for a refund
D. Look up his information

_____ **3.** **According to the man, why can't he afford the service?**
A. Because it's not worth the cost
B. Because there are too many channels
C. Because the premium package is more expensive than the basic package
D. Because he doesn't have a job

PART 04 SHORT TALK 簡短獨白

請聽光碟朗讀，並根據內容回答以下題目。

_____ **1.** **Who is probably the speaker?**
A. A writer
B. The owner
C. A publisher
D. A reporter

_____ **2.** **Who is the audience?**
A. A newspaper staff
B. Magazine employees
C. Internet workers
D. Fashion models

_____ **3.** **What will start next week?**
A. A newspaper
B. A fashion magazine
C. A television show
D. A fashion website

解答與解析

PART 01 照片描述 PHOTOGRAPHS

1. **D**   A. The man is singing for the crowd.
　　　　那位男人在為群眾獻唱。
　　B. The man is talking into a megaphone.
　　　　那位男人對著大聲公講話。
　　C. The crew is filming a movie.
　　　　工作人員在拍電影。
　　D. The reporter is holding a microphone.
　　　　記者拿著麥克風。

2. **C**   A. The talk show host is interviewing her guest.
　　　　脫口秀主持人在訪問來賓。
　　B. The husband and wife are sitting in their living room.
　　　　丈夫和妻子坐在客廳。
　　C. The man and woman are presenting the news.
　　　　那位男人和女人在報新聞。
　　D. The woman is speaking at the conference.
　　　　那位女人在會議中發言。

3. **B**   A. The man is driving to the station.
　　　　那位男人開車要去車站。
　　B. The driver is changing stations.
　　　　駕駛在切換電台頻道。
　　C. The man is turning on the TV.
　　　　那位男人打開電視。
　　D. The driver is starting the car.
　　　　駕駛在發動汽車。

4. **B**   A. The woman is listening to her stereo.
　　　　那位女人在聽她的音響。
　　B. The DJ is talking on the radio.
　　　　DJ 在廣播電台上講話。
　　C. The operator is connecting a call.
　　　　接線生接通一通電話。
　　D. The girl is adjusting the radio.
　　　　那位女生在調整收音機。

PART 02 應答問題 QUESTION-RESPONSE

1. **A**
Q: Is this a live broadcast?
這是現場直播嗎？
A. No. It was recorded earlier.
不是，是之前就錄好的。
B. Yes. It's about his life.
是的，是關於他的生活。
C. Yes. It was recorded yesterday.
是的，是昨天錄的。

2. **C**
Q: How is the TV reception here?
這裡的電視收訊如何？
A. Great. The food was excellent.
很好。食物很棒。
B. Not bad. I saw it on TV.
還不賴。我在電視上看到它。
C. Bad. That's why I have cable.
很差，所以我才裝有線電視。

3. **A**
Q: Are you sending someone to the press conference?
你會派人去記者會嗎？
A. Yes. One of our reporters is going.
會。我們有一個記者要去。
B. No. I don't have a press.
沒有。我沒有印刷機。
C. I'm not sure who's holding the conference.
我不確定這個會議是誰辦的。

4. **B**
Q: What station are you playing?
你在聽哪一個廣播頻道？
A. The bus station.
公車站。
B. 91.5 FM.
91.5 FM。
C. Yes. I changed the station.
對。我換了頻道。

5. **C**
Q: My lawyer told me not to talk to the media.
我的律師叫我別對媒體發言。
A. Sorry, no comment.
抱歉，無可奉告。
B. Don't worry, I'm not a medium.
別擔心，我不是個靈媒。
C. Sounds like good advice.
聽起來是好建議。

PART 03 簡短對話 CONVERSATION

M: Hi. My name is Donald Richards, and I'm calling to cancel my service.
嗨。我的名字是唐納德理查茲，我打來是要取消我的電視服務。

W: Sure. One moment while I look up your information. May I ask why you've decided to cancel?
沒問題。請稍候一下，讓我查詢您的資料。可以請教您為什麼要取消服務嗎？

M: Well, it's kind of expensive, and I never watch most of the channels. I guess it's just not worth the cost.
嗯，收費有點貴，而且大部分頻道我都沒看，我覺得有點不划算。

W: I see here that you've subscribed to our premium package. Would you consider switching to basic cable? It's much cheaper, and includes fewer channels.
我這裡看到你選了我們的尊榮方案，你有考慮換到基本方案嗎？比較便宜，頻道也比較少。

M: I did consider it, but I can't even afford the basic package right now. I'm out of work at the moment, so I'm afraid I'll have to just cancel my service.
我考慮過了，但我現在連基本方案都付不起。我目前沒有工作，所以恐怕只能取消這個服務。

1. **B**   Q: 這位男人想要做什麼？
     A. 把包裹還給郵局
     B. 停止有線電視服務
     C. 取消衛星電台服務
     D. 轉換到基本方案

2. **B**   Q: 那位女人建議那位男人做什麼？
     A. 升級到尊榮方案
     B. 轉換到比較便宜的方案
     C. 把包裹拿回去退款
     D. 查他的資料

3. **D**   Q: 根據那位男人的說法，為什麼他付不起使用服務的費用？
     A. 因為不划算
     B. 因為頻道太多
     C. 因為尊榮方案比基本方案貴
     D. 因為他沒有工作

PART 04 簡短獨白 SHORT TALK

I'm sad to say that next month's issue of our magazine will be the last. We've been losing money for several years, and the owner has been unable to find a buyer. So many newspapers and magazines have been put out of business by the Internet, and now it's finally our turn. I've really enjoyed being your supervisor, and I'd like to thank all of you—writers, editors, reporters, photographers—for your valuable contributions over the years. As you may know, a small staff will be kept on to run our fashion site, which will go online next week. Anyway, we still have one last issue to put out, so it's time to get to work. Let's make our last issue the best one yet!

我很難過地宣布，下個月出刊的這一期雜誌將會是最後一期。我們已經虧損好幾年，老闆又一直找不到買家。很多報紙和雜誌已經因網路影響而關門大吉，現在終於輪到我們了。當你們的主管很快樂，我想要感謝所有人這些年的寶貴貢獻，包括作者、編輯、記者、攝影師。你們或許已經知道了，有少數員工會繼續留下來經營我們的時尚網站，下星期就會上線。不管怎樣，我們還有最後一期要出版，現在該去工作了。讓我們把最後一期的雜誌做到最好！

1. **C** Q: 說話者有可能是誰？
   A. 作者
   B. 老闆
   C. 發行人
   D. 記者

2. **B** Q: 聽眾是誰？
   A. 一名報社員工
   B. 雜誌社的雇員
   C. 網路工作者
   D. 時裝模特兒

3. **D** Q: 下星期會開始推出什麼？
   A. 一份報紙
   B. 一本時尚雜誌
   C. 一個電視節目
   D. 一個時尚網站

教學重點

⊙ 合約保固重點單字
⊙ 易混淆字：discuss / disgust
⊙ 子音 [v] 和 [w] 的跟讀
⊙ 子音 [p]、[t]、[k] 的送氣程度

多益實戰

⊙ Part 1 照片描述
⊙ Part 2 應答問題
⊙ Part 3 簡短對話
⊙ Part 4 獨白對話

主題字彙與發音

聽聽看這些單字的正確發音，並比較英美腔調的不同。

strict (a.) 嚴格的
[strɪkt]

lawyer (n.) 律師
[`lɔjɚ]

withdraw (v.) 收回，取回，提取
[wɪð`drɔ]

support service (n.) 支援服務
[sə`port sɜvɪs]

permit (v.) 許可，准許
[pɚ`mɪt]

promise (n.) 承諾，諾言
[`pramɪs]

rescission (n.) 廢止，取消，撤回，解約
[rɪ`sɪʒən]

annual (a.) 一年的，一年一次的
[`ænjʊəl]

penalty (n.) 處罰，刑罰
[`pɛnəlti]

punishment (n.) 處罰，懲罰
[`pʌnɪʃmənt]

party (n.) 當事人，某方
[`parti]

term (n.) 期限
[tɝm]

valid (a.) 有效的
[`vælɪd]

expiration (n.) 到期
[ˌɛkspə`reʃən]

contract (n.) 合約
[`kantrækt]

sign (v.) 簽約
[saɪn]

warranty (n.) 保證書，保固
[`wɔrənti]

agreement (n.) 協議
[ə`grimənt]

signature (n.) 簽名
[`sɪgnətʃɚ]

reputation (n.) 信譽，名聲
[ˌrɛpjə`teʃən]

主題易混淆字

聽力上也常會遇到的一個問題，就是有些字的發音非常相近，
在聽的時候，如果沒有整合前後文內容，很容易就聽錯。
以下我們整理了幾組容易弄錯的單字，請聽光碟朗讀，選出句中出現的字。

字音

1. contract / contact

2. discuss / disgust

3. copy / coffee

4. signing / sighing

5. owe / own

字義

6. draft 匯票 / 草稿

7. cover 包含 / 覆蓋

8. parties 當事人，某方 / 聚會

9. term 期，期限 / 條款

10. valid 有效的 / 有根據的

解答

1. The **contract** will be signed this Friday.（合約）
2. Did you **discuss** the details of the agreement?（討論）
3. I'll send you a **copy** by mail.（副本）
4. Do you know if the two companies are close to **signing**?（簽約）
5. Once you sign this contract, you'll **own** the house.（擁有）
6. We're writing up the final **draft** right now.（草稿）
7. What exactly does the warranty **cover**?（包含）
8. The two **parties** met to go over the contract.（當事人）
9. What is the **term** of the contract?（期限）
10. Is the warranty still **valid**?（有效）

單字聽讀力 | 子音 [v]、[w] 的跟讀

MP3-233

教學說明:

[v] 和 [w] 這兩個子音的發音不難,但發 [v] 這個有聲子音時,上門齒要緊扣下唇,如果沒做到這點,變成嘟唇,就會唸成 [w] 的音,尤其是在字首,特別容易讓人混淆。

現在就讓我們來聽聽正確的發音,並且跟著大聲念出來吧。

[v]	vest	every	travel	of	Stephen
[w]	west	away	white	one	square

辨音測驗:

MP3-234

經過了剛才的發音練習,現在讓我們做個辨音小測驗,看看是不是聽懂更多了呢?請聽光碟播放的句子,並圈出句中出現的單字。

1. wet / vet

2. wail / veil

3. wary / very

4. Walt / vault

5. worse / verse

解答

1. Try to keep the dog from getting ⟨wet⟩

2. The bride's ⟨veil⟩ attracted a lot of attention.

3. Children should be ⟨wary⟩ of strangers.

4. Is there a ⟨Walt⟩ at your bank?

5. Which poem do you think is ⟨worse⟩?

句子聽讀力 | 子音 [p]、[t]、[k] 的送氣程度

MP3-235

教學說明：

為了不讓初學者混淆，多數老師一開始教英文發音時，會避免談到子音 p、t、k 送氣強弱的不同。以下是這三個子音在不同情況下的發音方式。

在字首或字中的重音位置，p、t、k 在發音時一般都會有強烈的爆破氣音。

- Peel those potatoes for me, please.
- I keep my pay in a checking account.
- Tom is returning to school in September.
- This apple pie is pretty tasty!

p、t、k 在字母 s 之後發音時，爆破氣音不明顯，如果照著發音把字拼寫出來，很可能會把 st、sp、sk 寫成 sd、sb、sg。

- Stan won first prize in the speech contest.
- Steak is more expensive than Spam.
- Professor Scott from Stanford is speaking at the meeting.
- Oscar moved from Austin to Spokane.

以 p、t、k 結束的音節，如果後面的字為子音開頭，常會發很輕的氣音甚至省略，與後面母音開頭的字連音時，也跟 b、d、g 為結尾的字不太好區分。

- His apartment is on the top floor.
- Mark fell asleep at work.
- We walked up the ramp into the boat.
- Philip took off his hat and put it on the rack.

聽力小測驗：

請聽光碟播放的句子，並把氣音明顯的地方劃出來。

MP3-236

1. The car ran the stop sign and hit a truck.

2. The presentation was a total disaster.

3. Does Patrick approve of capital punishment?

4. The president was attacked by a lunatic.

5. How can I get to the accounting department?

6. We went camping on our vacation to Alaska.

7. What happened to you last October?

解答

1. The car ran the stop sign and hit a truck.
2. The presentation was a total disaster.
3. Does Patrick approve of capital punishment?
4. The president was attacked by a lunatic.
5. How can I get to the accounting department?
6. We went camping on our vacation to Alaska.
7. What happened to you last October?

PART 01 照片描述
PHOTOGRAPHS

請看圖片並聽光碟朗讀圖 1 ～ 4 的四段敘述，選出與圖片最相符的敘述。

1. _____

2. _____

3. _____

4. _____

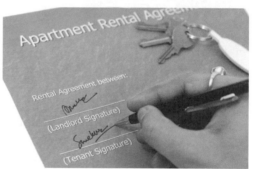

PART 02 應答問題
QUESTION-RESPONSE

請聽光碟朗讀，並選出最適合的答案填在空格中。

1. _____   **2.** _____   **3.** _____   **4.** _____   **5.** _____

PART 03 簡短對話
CONVERSATION

請聽光碟朗讀從選項 A、B、C、D 中選出正確的答案。

_____ **1.** **What are the speakers discussing?**
A. A bank account
B. An employment contract
C. A rental agreement
D. A repair job

_____ **2.** **How much will the woman pay if she moves in?**
A. 1,800 dollars
B. 1,200 dollars
C. 600 dollars
D. A 600 dollar deposit

_____ **3.** **What is the purpose of the deposit?**
A. To cover the rent
B. To pay for possible damage
C. To generate interest
D. To ensure that there is no damage

PART 04 簡短獨白
SHORT TALK

請聽光碟朗讀,並根據內容回答以下題目。

_____ **1.** **Who is the speaker?**
A. A factory repairman
B. An Electric Land employee
C. An Electric Land customer
D. A company lawyer

_____ **2.** **Which of the following is required for the warranty to be valid?**
A. The original packaging
B. An application.
C. A receipt
D. Proof of proper use

_____ **3.** **Which of the following is NOT covered by the warranty?**
A. The USB cable
B. The main unit
C. The earphones
D. The battery

PART 01 照片描述 PHOTOGRAPHS

1. **D**   A. Three people are holding copies in their hands.
三人手上拿著副本。
B. The people are all wearing suits and ties.
這些人都穿西裝打領帶。
C. The people are arguing about the contract.
這些人正針對合約爭論。
D. The people are discussing the contract over coffee.
這些人正邊喝咖啡邊討論合約。

2. **B**   A. The man has been offered a position.
有人提供了男士一個職位。
B. Both parties have reached an agreement.
雙方已達成協議。
C. It's easy to meet people at the party.
派對上很容易與人結識。
D. The men are shaking hands at the party.
男士們在派對上握手。

3. **C**   A. The speakers are giving a presentation.
講者們正在演講。
B. The woman is sighing about the contract.
女人正為合約嘆息。
C. The woman is signing the agreement.
女人正在簽署協議。
D. The woman is giving the man her autograph.
女人在給男人她的親筆簽名。

4. **B**   A. The contact has two signatures on it.
聯絡人上有兩處簽名。
B. The tenant is signing the contract.
房客正在合約上簽名。
C. The car keys are on top of the rental agreement.
車鑰匙在房屋租約上方。
D. The landlord is signing the agreement.
房東正在合約上簽名。

PART 02 應答問題 QUESTION-RESPONSE

1. B Q: Do you have any questions to ask before you sign the agreement?
簽約之前你有任何問題要問嗎？
A. Yes. I'd like to sign the agreement.
有，我想要簽約。
B. No. Everything seems pretty clear.
沒有，看起來都滿清楚的。
C. I think I've answered all your questions.
我想我已經回答你所有問題了。

2. B Q: When will the final draft of the contract be ready?
合約完稿何時能準備好？
A. Yes. It will be ready by next Monday.
是的，下週一會準備好。
B. My secretary is typing it up right now.
我的祕書正在打字完稿中。
C. Please have it on my desk this afternoon.
下午請把完稿放我桌上。

3. C Q: What are the terms of the rental agreement?
租約條款為何？
A. Are pets allowed in the apartment?
公寓裡可以養寵物嗎？
B. I'd like to move in immediately.
我想要馬上搬進來。
C. They're listed on the contract here.
條款明列在這份合約上。

4. A Q: You can sign a one-year contract or go with our monthly plan.
你可以簽一年約或是選用我們月租方案。
A. Which would you recommend?
你推薦哪種方式？
B. OK. That sounds like a good idea.
好，聽起來是個好主意。
C. If you choose the one-year contract, you get a free phone.
簽約一年可得到一隻免費手機。

5. B Q: That price includes the installation fee, right?
價錢包含裝機費用，對吧？
A. The installation fee is 50 dollars.
安裝費用是五十元。
B. Yes, if you go with the two-year plan.
對，如果你選用的是兩年約方案。
C. We can send a technician to your house tomorrow.
我們明天就可以派技師去你家。

PART 03 簡短對話 CONVERSATION

W: It says here that in addition to first and last month's rent, I also need to pay a security deposit when I move in. Could you explain that?

這邊有說除了第一和最後一個月的房租以外，當我搬進來時，還需要付保證金。你能解釋一下嗎？

M: Sure. The deposit is equivalent to one month's rent, and it's used to cover any damage that may occur to the rental unit.

當然。保證金相當於一個月租金，用來支付租賃物任何可能的損壞。

W: I see. So the deposit would be 600 dollars. Will it be returned to me if there is no damage?

懂了，所以保證金六百元。如果沒有任何損毀，保證金會退給我嗎？

M: Yes, of course. And we'll even pay you interest on the deposit.

當然會。我們甚至會付你保證金的利息。

1. **C** Q: 談話者在討論什麼？
   A. 銀行戶頭
   B. 雇用合約
   C. 租賃合約
   D. 維修工作

2. **A** Q: 女士若搬進屋裡，需要付多少錢？
   A. 一千八百元
   B. 一千兩百元
   C. 六百元
   D. 一筆六百元保證金

3. **B** Q: 保證金的目的為何？
   A. 支付租金
   B. 支付可能的損害
   C. 生利息
   D. 確保不會有損害

PART 04 簡短獨白 SHORT TALK

This MP3 player comes with a one-year warranty on parts and service. To be valid, the warranty card must be presented, along with proof of purchase. It only applies to the purchaser, and isn't transferable to any other users. During the 12-month warranty period, Electric Land will repair or replace any defective parts in the main unit. The warranty period for the battery charger, earphones and USB cable, is two months. Electric Land is not responsible for any data stored in the player. All data will be deleted during repairs, so you should make a backup copy before bringing your player for repair. You can have repairs done at any Electric Land location in the country. Also, the warranty does not cover damage caused by normal wear and tear, improper use, or exposure to heat or moisture.

這台 MP3 播放機附有一年內零件及服務保固。須出示保證卡及購買證明才可生效。保固僅適用於購買者，不可轉讓給其他使用者。在十二個月保固期內，電器天地將會維修或更換主機上任何故障零件。充電器、耳機及 USB 傳輸線的保固期為兩個月。電器天地不為任何播放機裡所儲存的資料負責。所有資料將於維修時全部刪除，因此播放機送修前應將資料備份。你可於國內任一電器天地定點辦理維修。還有，保固不包含因一般磨損、不當使用、暴露於高溫或潮濕之下所造成的損害。

1. **B**　Q: 説話者為何人？
   A. 工廠修理工
   B. 電器天地的員工
   C. 電器天地的顧客
   D. 公司律師

2. **C**　Q: 保固單在下列哪項需求下才能生效？
   A. 原品包裝
   B. 申請書
   C. 收據
   D. 正常使用的證明

3. **D**　Q: 保固不包含下列哪項？
   A. USB 傳輸線
   B. 主機
   C. 耳機
   D. 電池

CHAPTER 25
金融理財篇

教學重點

⊙ 金融理財重點單字
⊙ 易混淆字：lawn / loan
⊙ 英美口音的比較：[u] 和 [ju]
⊙ 英美腔單字的不同發音

多益實戰

⊙ Part 1 照片描述
⊙ Part 2 應答問題
⊙ Part 3 簡短對話
⊙ Part 4 獨白對話

主題字彙與發音

MP3-241

聽聽看這些單字的正確發音，並比較英美腔調的不同。

check (v./n.) 支票
[tʃɛk]

loan (n.) 貸款
[lon]

exchange (v./n.) 交易，兌換
[ɪksˋtʃendʒ]

deduct (v.) 扣除，減除
[dɪˋdʌkt]

transaction (n.) 交易，買賣
[trænˋzækʃən]

fund (v./n.) 提供資金；資金，基金
[fʌnd]

invest (v.) 投資
[ɪnˋvɛst]

refund (n.) 退款，退費
[ˋriˏfʌnd]

deposit (n.) 押金，定金
[dɪˋpɑzɪt]

joint account (n.) 共同帳戶
[dʒɔɪnt əˋkaʊnt]

balance (n.)（損益）平衡
[ˋbæləns]

audit (v.) 稽核
[ˋɔdɪt]

budget (v.) 預算
[ˋbʌdʒɪt]

debt (n.) 債
[dɛt]

outstanding (a.)
未付清的（帳款）
[ˋaʊtˋstændɪŋ]

portfolio (n.) 投資組合
[portˋfolɪˏo]

return (v.) 報酬，回報
[rɪˋtɝn]

calculation (n.) 計算
[ˏkælkjəˋleʃən]

yield (v.) 產生（收益）
[jild]

down payment (n.) 頭期款
[daʊn ˋpemənt]

mortgage (n.) 抵押
[ˋmɔrgɪdʒ]

dividend (n.) 股息，紅利
[ˋdɪvɪdɛnd]

主題易混淆字

MP3-242

聽力上也常會遇到的一個問題,就是有些字的發音非常相近,
在聽的時候,如果沒有整合前後文內容,很容易就聽錯。
以下我們整理了幾組容易弄錯的單字,請聽光碟朗讀,選出句中出現的字。

字音

1. file / fill

2. joined / joint

3. old / owed

4. date / debt

5. lawn / loan

字義

6. swipe 偷竊 / 刷（卡）

7. exchange 匯兌 / 交易（所）

8. deposit 存款 / 押金

9. budget 預算 / 平價的

10. checks 支票 / （餐廳）帳單

解答

1. When are you going to **file** your tax form?（申報）
2. My husband and I have a **joint** account.（共同的）
3. The **owed** amount must be paid by the end of the month.（拖欠的）
4. Could you please tell me the **date** on your credit card?（日期）
5. We're considering buying a home without a **loan**.（貸款）
6. Somebody **swiped** my credit card, so I cancelled it.（偷竊）
7. Is there a currency **exchange** window at your bank?（匯兌）
8. A **deposit** is required when you rent a car.（押金）
9. We could only afford to stay at a **budget** hotel.（平價的）
10. Most restaurants don't accept **checks** anymore.（支票）

單字聽讀力 | 英美口音的比較：[u] 和 [ju]

MP3-243

教學說明：

[ju] 這個音常出現在 u 或 ew 的拼字上，不過在子音 [t] [d] [n] [l] [s] [t] 之後，
美式口音會省略 [j]，讀作 [u]，此時就與英式口音有所區別。
現在就讓我們來聽聽正確的發音，並且跟著大聲念出來吧。

[ju]	usual	university	music	mute	few
[u] 或 [ju]	student	tune	assume	due	new

辨音測驗：

MP3-244

經過了剛才的發音練習，現在讓我們做個辨音小測驗，看看是不
是聽懂更多了呢？請聽光碟播放的句子，拼出正確的單字，並判
斷單字發 [u] 還是 [ju] 的音。

1. [u] / [ju]   Can I ____ your phone?

2. [u] / [ju]   I think I've heard that ____ somewhere before.

3. [u] / [ju]   Are there ____ beaches in Sweden?

4. [u] / [ju]   The bride wore a ____ dress.

5. [u] / [ju]   You should start each day with a positive ____.

解 答

1. [ju] use
2. [u] tune
3. [u] nude
4. [ju] beautiful
5. [u] attitude

句子聽讀力 | 英美腔單字的不同發音

MP3-245

教學說明：

有些單字在英美兩地發音不同，全無規則可循，若聽到不熟悉的發音，便要從句意中判斷字義。

	美語發音	英語發音
schedule	[ˋskɛdʒul]	[ˋʃɛdʒul]
either	[ˋiðɚ]	[ˋaɪðə]
privacy	[ˋpraɪvəsi]	[ˋprɪvəsi]
zebra	[ˋzibrə]	[ˋzɛbrə]
tomato	[təˋmeto]	[təˋmɑtəʊ]
figure	[ˋfɪgjɚ]	[ˋfɪgə]
because	[bɪˋkʌz]	[bɪˋkɒz]
z	[zi]	[zɛd]

例：The president has a very busy schedule.

例：You can pay by either cash or credit.

聽力小測驗：

請聽光碟中的句子，並拼出正確的單字。

MP3-246

1. Mary works as a sales _____ at a shoe store.

2. The restaurant serves _____, pizza and salads.

3. The swimmer is trying to set a new world _____.

4. What do you do in your _____ time?

5. _____ Shelly nor Tina knows how to swim.

6. Could you put these flowers in the _____ over there?

解答

1. clerk	2. pasta	3. record
4. leisure	5. Neither	6. vase

多 益 聽 力 實 戰

PART 01 PHOTOGRAPHS 照片描述

請看圖片並聽光碟朗讀圖 1 ～ 4 的四段敘述，選出與圖片最相符的敘述。

1. _____

2. _____

3. _____

4. _____

PART 02 QUESTION-RESPONSE 應答問題

請聽光碟朗讀，並選出最適合的答案填在空格中。

1. _____ **2.** _____ **3.** _____ **4.** _____ **5.** _____

請聽光碟朗讀從選項 A、B、C、D 中選出正確的答案。

____ **1.** **Which of the following forms of identification would probably not be acceptable?**
A. A driver's license
B. A passport
C. A student ID
D. A state-issued ID

____ **2.** **How can the man avoid paying the service charge?**
A. Pay a fee of $5 each month
B. Always have at least $300 in his account
C. Deposit $300 dollars into his savings account
D. Make an opening deposit of at least $50

____ **3.** **How often would the man receive interest payments?**
A. Every day
B. 0.05%
C. Twice a month
D. Once a month

請聽光碟朗讀，並根據內容回答以下題目。

____ **1.** **Who is the speaker?**
A. A TV reporter
B. A financial advisor
C. An economics professor
D. A bank teller

____ **2.** **According to the speaker, what is true about the stock market?**
A. It hasn't reached its bottom.
B. It has an average return of 18 percent.
C. Stock prices will soon be higher.
D. Stocks are too risky for most investors.

____ **3.** **What does the speaker advise investors to do?**
A. Invest in egg producers
B. Invest in more than one thing
C. Stay away from risky investments
D. Put all their money in stocks

解答與解析

PART 01 照片描述 PHOTOGRAPHS

1. A A. The sales assistant is swiping a credit card.
店員正在刷卡。
B. The thief is swiping someone's credit card.
小偷正在偷別人的信用卡。
C. The man is buying something from the vending machine.
男人正在用販賣機買東西。
D. The man is getting money from the ATM.
男人正從提款機領錢。

2. C A. The customer is cashing a check.
顧客正在兌現支票。
B. The man is receiving money from the cashier.
男人從出納員那領取錢。
C. The person is withdrawing cash from the ATM.
那個人正在提款機領錢。
D. The teller is counting cash at the bank.
出納員在銀行點算現金。

3. B A. The woman is working at the stock exchange.
女人在證券交易所上班。
B. The woman is checking the exchange rates.
女人正在查看匯率。
C. The woman is writing down her flight information.
女人正在抄她的班機資訊。
D. The woman is looking at the time in different countries.
女人正在看不同國家的時間。

4. D A. The woman is writing a check.
女人正在開支票。
B. The woman is looking at the menu.
女人正在看菜單。
C. The woman is signing her autograph.
女人正在簽名。
D. The woman is paying her check.
女人正在買單。

1. **A** Q: How much interest does the account pay?
這個帳戶利息有多少？

A. That depends on how much you have in the account.
這要看你帳戶裡有多少錢。

B. Many people have interest in the account.
許多人對這個帳戶有興趣。

C. Yes. It pays two percent interest.
是的，有百分之二的利息。

2. **C** Q: Are you sure we can afford to buy a new car?
你確定我們買得起新車？

A. Actually, I bought it on sale.
其實我是趁特價買的。

B. Yes. New cars are very expensive.
對啊。新車非常貴。

C. Well, we'll have to take out a loan.
嗯，我們得要貸款了。

3. **A** Q: Do you have change for a fifty?
我付五十元，你們有零錢可以找嗎？

A. Sorry. Do you have something smaller?
抱歉。你有更小面額的嗎？

B. Sorry. We don't change money here.
抱歉。我們這裡不能換錢。

C. Sorry. We don't accept small change.
抱歉。我們不接受小額零錢。

4. **B** Q: That'll be $49.85.
總共是四十九塊八五。

A. Thanks. Come again soon.
謝謝。歡迎再度光臨。

B. Can I pay by credit card?
我可以用信用卡嗎？

C. Do you have anything cheaper?
你們有比較便宜的東西嗎？

5. **C** Q: Why is it so important to have good credit?
為什麼有良好的信用如此重要？

A. I agree. Good credit is very important.
我同意。良好的信用非常重要。

B. Some credit cards are better than others.
有的信用卡比其他的更好。

C. It makes it easier to get loans.
貸款會比較容易。

PART 03 簡短對話 CONVERSATION

W: To open a savings account, all you need to show us is two pieces of government-issued ID and proof of address.
你只要出示兩份經政府核發的身份證以及有地址證明的證件即能開立存款帳戶。

M: I see. And how much money do I need to deposit?
我知道了。我需要存多少錢？

W: You need to make an opening deposit of at least $50, and as long as you maintain a minimum balance of $300, the $5 monthly service charge will be waived.
開立帳戶至少要存五十元，然後只要每月帳戶結餘達到最低三百元，就可以免繳每月五元的服務費。

M: OK. And how much interest does the account pay?
好的。這帳戶利息有多少？

W: Interest on the account is 0.05%, and is compounded daily and paid monthly.
這帳戶利息為百分之零點零五，以天計息然後按月付。

1. **C**   Q: 以下何種身份證明文件可能不被接受？
   A. 駕照
   B. 護照
   C. 學生證
   D. 由州核發的身份證

2. **B**   Q: 男子要怎麼做才不用繳服務費？
   A. 每月付五元
   B. 帳戶結餘維持在三百元以上
   C. 存三百元到存款帳戶
   D. 開戶至少存五十元

3. **D**   Q: 男子多久可收到一次利息？
   A. 每天
   B. 百分之零點零五
   C. 每個月兩次
   D. 每個月一次

PART 04 簡短獨白 SHORT TALK

Even though the economy is still in a recession, I believe that stocks are still a good investment. While investors have lost a lot of money over the past year, the market has reached its bottom, so now is a good time to buy stocks before they start to rise in the near future. Over the past 100 years, stocks have had an average return of eight percent, which is much higher than bond returns. However, I don't advise my clients to invest only in stocks, but rather to have a diversified portfolio of stocks, bonds, real estate and precious metals. In other words, don't put all your eggs in one basket. The needs of each investor are different, though. So portfolios are designed based on people's age, income, and the degree of risk they are willing to take.

儘管經濟仍處於衰退中，我仍舊認為股票是項不錯的投資。過去一年投資人賠了不少，然而市場已到達最低點，所以在股票即將開始升值前，現在正是買進的大好時機。過去一百年，股票平均獲利為百分之八，比債券獲利高得多。然而，我不建議我的客戶只投資股票，而是要擁有多角化的投資組合，包括股票、債券、房地產和貴金屬。換句話說，別把雞蛋都放在同一個籃子。每個投資人的需求不盡相同，所以投資組合是依每個人的年齡、收入和願意承擔的風險程度所設計。

1. **B**　Q: 説話者是誰？
　　　A. 電視播報員
　　　B. 理財顧問
　　　C. 經濟學教授
　　　D. 銀行出納員

2. **C**　Q: 根據説話者所言，關於股市何者為真？
　　　A. 尚未到達最低點。
　　　B. 平均獲利為百分之十八。
　　　C. 股價很快就會上升。
　　　D. 對大部分投資人而言，股票風險太高。

3. **B**　Q: 説話者建議投資人做什麼？
　　　A. 投資蛋商
　　　B. 投資超過一種標的
　　　C. 避開有風險的投資
　　　D. 將全部的錢都投資股票

NEW TOEIC
新多益 考前 30 天快速上手 系列
適用對象 沒時間準備多益測驗的考生

總是沒時間做完2小時新多益模擬試題？
非得一次練習200題完整試題？
首創每次15分鐘的新多益快速練習法，考前一月衝刺必備！

**New TOEIC 990
快速上手！
新多益聽力全真試題**
作者：EZ TALK編輯部
（1書2MP3）
定價 **490** 元

**New TOEIC 990
快速上手！
新多益閱讀全真試題**
作者：EZ TALK編輯部
（1書2MP3）
定價 **590** 元

新多益第一次就考好系列
適用對象 專為第一次準備新多益測驗的考生

革除「第一次是考心酸的」迷思，升學求職的好機會不等人，一定要一次就考好！
教你學外國人般背單字，捨棄瑣碎文法規則，依循官方公佈的真實國際職場
（global workplace）命題趨勢，直搗考試重點！
獨創分級測驗！收錄近1000題模擬試題＋解析。隨時驗收學習成果，新多益全面取分！

**第一次就考好
New TOEIC 文法**
作者：EZ TALK編輯部
（1書）
定價 **380** 元

**第一次就考好
New TOEIC 單字**
作者：EZ TALK編輯部
（1書1MP3）
定價 **350** 元

新多益990 高分全攻略系列

適用對象 **專為以多益滿分990為目標的考生**

破解多益常考閱讀句型、嚴選必背關鍵字彙、近500題聽力模擬、超過1000題模考，隨書附贈近12小時的多益函授有聲課程！

革除「補習才會得高分」的迷思，涵蓋字彙、聽力、閱讀、5回模擬試題的多益高分攻略，新多益900分絕對過關！

**New TOEIC 990
新多益高分關鍵字彙**
作者：EZ TALK編輯部
（1書2MP3）

定價 **350**元

**New TOEIC 990
新多益閱讀攻略**
作者：李立萍
（2書1MP3）

定價 **690**元

**New TOEIC 990
新多益聽力攻略**
作者：李立萍
（2書2MP3）

定價 **590**元

**New TOEIC 990
新多益 5回全真試題＋詳解**
作者：EZ TALK編輯部
（2書2MP3）

定價 **590**元

新多益隨身口袋書系列

適用對象 **專為通勤族設計的新單字口袋書**

《TIME Express》美籍主編嚴選「新多益」1300高命中率單字！！
隨身帶著啃，多益單字緊咬不放，每考必中！！
補充衍生字、反義字和同義字。讓你學習事半功倍，單字量倍增超過3,000個！

**一口咬定
New TOEIC多益單字**
作者：EZ TALK編輯部
（1書1MP3）

定價 **249**元

**一天一口
營養單字口袋書**
作者：EZ TALK編輯部
（1書1MP3）

定價 **199**元

讀者基本資料

是否為 EZ TALK 訂戶？　　□是　□否

姓名 _____ 性別 □男　□女

生日　民國 _____ 年 _____ 月 _____ 日

■地址　□□□-□□（請務必填寫郵遞區號）

_____

聯絡電話（日）_____

　　　　（夜）_____

　　　　（手機）_____

E-mail _____
　　　　　（請務必填寫 E-mail，讓我們為您提供 VIP 服務）

職業

□學生　□服務業　□傳媒業　□資訊業　□自由業　□軍公教　□出版業

□補教業　□其他

教育程度

□國中以下　□高中　□專科　□大學　□研究所以上

您從何種通路購得本書？

□一般書店　□量販店　□網路書店　□書展　□郵局劃撥

您對本書的建議……

國家圖書館出版品預行編目（CIP）資料

New TOEIC 第一次就考好聽力 從發音開始 / EZ 叢書館
　編輯部作 . -- 初版 . -- 臺北市：日月文化，2012.04
　320 面，17×23 公分（EZ 叢書館）
　ISBN：978-986-248-255-1（平裝附光碟片）
1. 多益測驗　2. 發音
805.1895　　　　　　　　　　　　　　　　101003184

EZ 叢書館

New TOEIC 第一次就考好聽力 從發音開始

作　　　者：EZ 叢書館編輯部
總 編 審：Judd Piggott
副 總 編：葉瑋玲
副 主 編：陳毅心
文字編輯：李明芳、陳彥廷
美術設計：管仕豪、施舜仁
排版設計：健呈電腦排版股份有限公司
錄 音 員：Michael Tennant / Meilee Saccenti / Terri Pebsworth / Clare Lear /
　　　　　Thomas Brink

發 行 人：洪祺祥
法律顧問：建大法律事務所
財務顧問：高威會計師事務所

發　　　行：日月文化出版股份有限公司
出　　　版：EZ 叢書館
地　　　址：台北市大安區信義路三段 151 號 9 樓
電　　　話：(02) 2708-5509
傳　　　真：(02) 2708-6157
網　　　址：www.ezbooks.com.tw
客服信箱：service@heliopoli.com.tw

總 經 銷：聯合發行股份有限公司
電　　　話：(02) 2917-8022
傳　　　真：(02) 2915-7212
印　　　刷：禹利電子分色有限公司
初　　　版：2012 年 4 月
初版二刷：2013 年 3 月
定　　　價：380 元
I S B N：978-986-248-255-1